NEVER till NOW

THE SIBLINGS OF HEIR BOOK ONE

JENNA LOCKWOOD

Contents

Copyright	VI
Dedication	VII
Author's Note	VIII
Trigger Warnings	IX
Playlist	X
Chapter 1	1
Chapter 2	11
Chapter 3	21
Chapter 4	30
Chapter 5	38
Chapter 6	52
Chapter 7	69
Chapter 8	81
Chapter 9	89
Chapter 10	104
Chapter 11	124
Chapter 12	133
Chapter 13	145
Chapter 14	156
Chapter 15	173

Chapter 16	182
Chapter 17	191
Chapter 18	210
Chapter 19	226
Chapter 20	241
Chapter 21	252
Chapter 22	269
Chapter 23	279
Chapter 24	297
Chapter 25	310
Chapter 26	323
Epilogue	330
Acknowledgements	335
Let's Connect!	337
About Jenna Lockwood	338

Copyright 2022 © Jenna LOCKWOOD

ISBN: 9798847574600

All rights reserved. This book or any portion thereof may not be reproduced or used in any manner whatsoever without the express written permission of the copyright owner except for the use of brief quotations in a book review.

In accordance with the Copyright Act of 1976, the scanning, uploading, and electronic sharing of any part of this book without permission of the author is unlawful piracy and theft of the author's intellectual property.

This is a work of fiction. Names, characters, businesses, places, events, and incidents are either the product of the author's imagination or used in a fictitious manner. Any resemblance to actual persons, living or dead, or actual events is purely coincidental.

Dedication

To those who have never felt the immensity of love, you are worthy of it.

Author's Note

Never Till Now contains sexually explicit scenes, as well as mature and graphic content not suitable for all audiences. Reader discretion is advised.

I encourage you to go in blind, but Trigger Warnings can be found on the NEXT page of this book if need be.

Trigger Warnings

Mentions of sexual abuse and divorce.

Playlist

Gorilla – Bruno Mars
Older Than I Am – Lennon Stella
Please Don't Say You Love Me – Gabrielle Aplin
Control – Zoe Wees
Beauty in the Struggle – Bryan Martin
Nobody – Selena Gomez
Wildest Dreams – Taylor Swift (Epic Orchestra Version)
Glass – Thompson Square
What's Left of Me – Nick Lachey
All I Know So Far – P!nk
Daylight – Taylor Swift (Live From Paris)

Chapter 1

Adam

"You are everything I hoped you *wouldn't* be." A manicured hand connects with my cheek as a sting reverberates through my skin.

"You mean only *one of us* stayed true to our agreement?" I pipe back and watch her red lips part, but she's never been one to admit when wrong. "Was I not clear about my terms from the beginning?"

"People change, Adam." In hopes of diverting my attention or causing a scene in my family's hotel lobby, her arms deliberately cross to perk up her ten-thousand-dollar breasts.

"You did, Miranda. It's over. Not that we had much to begin with."

Her brown locks whip around as she turns on her red-sole heels, which I still believe *I* overpaid for.

Like a predator tracking its prey, guests and employees pretend to mind their own business, but their side-eyes sear through me. Miranda struts out of my family's hotel with brisk intention, swaying her hips as if walking to a beat. My father sure as hell isn't going to let me live this one down. Not only does he hate the way I view relationships, but he also despises any type of negative energy our family can bring to our business, Wheaton Hotels. I run a hand through my hair, square my shoulders and narrow my eyes with warning toward the front desk staff. I dare one of them to mention this to my father. I huff, bringing my fingers up to my neck to loosen my tie. It still isn't enough to relieve built-up tension from work and shit with Miranda.

    I shouldn't still be in my work suit at this hour, but a strong drink before I head up to my room is long overdue. Miranda and I didn't get the chance to hook up this week, and I'd rather someone other than my right hand to get me off. Commitment is no use when most women only want my last name for their bank account.

    My eyes dragged across the polished marble floor leading to the baby grand piano my fingers keep itching to play. Very few people know that on off-hours, I can play the keys as good as the damn people we hire. Getting lost in the keys is a way to channel my frustration with how women can't seem to accept the fact that I'm casual. Work is up to my balls and we are in full swing of our busy season. I don't have time for women wanting more. Our Aspen location has been up and running for just over a month, but still has hiccups requiring visits.

    My eyes land on the bar when blonde curls catch my eye. I wouldn't have noticed her at first glance if it weren't for her hair. Her dress blends into the dark-blue diamond-tucked leather booths. Her elbows rest on the black polished bar counter with a drink in hand. I glance at Max, my childhood best friend slash bartender, with questioning eyes that he silently understands. He's been my wingman since I was a kid trying to hit on my babysitter. His nod signifies she's here alone.

Rolling up the sleeves of my white button-up shirt, I expose my muscular forearms. For some reason, women eat this look up. A lonesome woman at a hotel bar during these late hours tends to signify she's probably on the prowl for someone. The tapping of her foot draws my eyes immediately to the floor and thoughts of her long legs wrapped tightly around my face flash through my mind.

Damn, how long has it been since I last got laid?

I walk up to the counter and don't directly look her way. This game is far too easy. The typical *make them hope you look their way or notice them*. Within a minute, Blondie should be smiling when I look over, and then she'll tell me, "*Hey.*" Or something along those lines. As delectable as she is for a one-night stand, I hope she's from out of town and doesn't care to be contacted again. The last thing I need is another clingy female who thinks she can change me. I sit a couple seats over as Max hands me my top-shelf bourbon. I swing my eyes in her direction, but she pays me no attention. Must be one of those women who won't make the first move. I test the waters to rile her up since Miranda is out of the picture.

"Ah, a gorgeous, lonely girl at the bar." I smile her way.

"Ah, a charming fella who never hears the word *no*." Her eyes keep forward as her lips press together in a thin line, biting back a smirk.

"I didn't ask a question that required hearing the word *no*," I say as her head bows down to her side dish of maraschino cherries.

Something a damn twelve-year-old would order.

"You never need to." Her head angles my way, peeking through her lashes, and piercing haunted emeralds raid every breath of oxygen as they look through my soul. "You smile like that and women throw themselves at you. As if they're doing *you* a favor."

Max snickers from the truth in her sass as he wipes down an already clean counter. I hold back my amusement and let the amber liquid burn through my chest. Sassy and intelligent. Thoughts of making her beg once I have her at my mercy play through my mind. I want her against the wall, dripping wet and arching herself into me as she begs for the release of her arousal. My wicked smile grows, and Max shakes his head, reading my well-predicted mind. She looks bored as her delicate fingers pop a cherry in her mouth without a single sexual innuendo. Yet my pea brain imagines her fingers wrapping around my cock as her lips pop over my tip.

The fucking male brain is a curse to live with at times.

I take note and survey her naked fingers. There's no sign of an engagement ring and she's showing no interest in my charm. She's either a lesbian or about to be engaged. I can't imagine she'd stay single for long. She could be batshit crazy, and even then, her looks could manipulate a sucker.

"You're strikingly beautiful." She turns her face directly toward me, and I confirm that wasn't a lie.

Her blonde locks waterfall softly down her back. Her plump lips look so kissable on her innocent face. I then take in her youthful features. It is possible she just turned twenty-one and is too young for me. Her blue dress hugs all the right curves, making her body look more mature than she possibly is. Her face is free of makeup except for long, dark lashes. The lack of face paint in comparison to most girls I take home should be a red flag. Clearly, I've mistaken her for my usual *type*. But those eyes. They're a vortex sucking me in, as if she's hiding secrets to the world but desperate to hand someone the key.

"You have the type of face I'd have a hard time forgetting," I try again.

Her shoulders shrug as her eyes crease, showing a hint of humor. "That is where our problems would start."

"I take it you have a boyfriend?" I tip back the rest of my drink, my eyes never leaving hers. "Waiting for true love?"

"Never." Her mouth articulates dramatically without actually making a sound.

"Lesbian?" I try to lighten the weight of our conversation that's clearly not going my way. "Fugitive on the run?"

"Not tonight." Boredom laces her voice and her eyes return to being fixated on her drink.

God, asking someone to give away their dog seems like an easier job than getting this woman to show the slightest bit of interest.

Max clears his throat, trying to save me from humiliation. "Can you hang that photo before you head out?"

I reach behind the counter for the hammer and a few nails before heading over to the wall. My mother and sister came up with the stupid idea to have a wall full of our favorite portraits from our family travels. Tacky if you ask me, but what Kelsie and my mother say design wise, it's always accepted by my father. My knuckle meets the wall as I listen for the hollow sound to stop on a stud. I enjoy tasks like this. They aren't in my CFO job description, but they make me feel normal.

Well, as normal as I can feel growing up in a *luxury* hotel in downtown San Francisco.

Out of the corner of my peripheral, I catch a glimpse of Blondie eyeing me with raised eyebrows. I feel judgment radiating off her smirk as she pops another damn cherry between her teeth, holding the stem between her fingers until she decides to pull it off. As if waiting for me to fail, her arms fold against the bar top as her eyes taunt me. Her doubt is clear that a man in a tailored Armani suit can't hang shit. I hold the nail in place as her tongue darts out to wet her lips. It's more than likely to lick the cherry juice off instead of an innuendo, unless she's playing the innocent card. But it's enough for my pants to grow tighter.

Holding the nail in place, I keep her eye contact to show her I'm fucking capable. Except I swing the hammer before I confirm where it's supposed to hit.

Fuck!

Throbbing.

My breath halts as pain vibrates to the tip of my thumb. I grit my teeth, taking a sharp breath in, and grunt as my thumbnail starts to turn black. Dammit, I look like an even bigger idiot now. I walk over to Max, who already has a cup of ice in hand.

"That won't work too well." The pain pulsing through my hand mutes my ears as Blondie speaks.

She follows me behind the bar and grabs a thumbtack from a small jar of random things by the cash register. I don't bother protesting how she's not supposed to be on this side. Max steps aside as her delicate fingers take my hand to examine the blackening thumbnail. She holds my hand close to the sink and turns to Max.

"Grab a cloth, please. This could get messy." Her tone holds a leveled assertiveness and sounds beyond her years.

"Ow, fuck. This fucking hurts."

"No shit, *Charmer*," she states with an eye roll. "You have blood pooling. Once I release it, the pressure will ease up." She places my hand back on the counter as she grabs the lighter we use for certain drinks, and heats up the end of the thumbtack.

Oh, hell no.

"Trust me," is all she says. "Max, have a clean cloth ready if the blood flies. Charmer, move your hand in the sink when I relieve the pressure." She ignores my questioning eyes burning through her as she continues to warm the sharp metal.

"I don't think—"

"Shut your delectable mouth for five damn seconds and hold still." Her voice drops an octave, shocking me, and I nod with compliance.

Once content with the scorching metal, she picks up my thumb while rolling her lips inward to focus. The heat of the tack pushes into my nail, melting it. Blood flies up, releasing the throbbing pain. The water has a cold bite as she holds my hand under the stream for a moment. As if I'm not capable of doing this task either.

"I got this. Thanks." I pull my hand out from hers, and she makes her way to the customer side of the bar. It's then I notice her height. I stand six foot three, and she's well over the average height of most women I know.

"You'll want to take extra-strength pain meds if it hurts *that* much."

She handled this situation astonishingly, but there is no way she is old enough to be a doctor. "Delectable, huh?" I smirk to shut out the pain.

"It distracted you for a moment, right?" And we're back to the cold shoulder.

"Max, her drinks are on me tonight." I hold her gaze, trying to figure out this enigma. "Vodka cranberry?"

"Wrong again, Charmer." Her bottom lip brushes against the rim of the glass before unhinging her jaw and downing the rest of her drink in one gulp. "Is that what your *lobby friend* drinks?" She picks up a cherry and tosses it at me.

"Are you jealous?" I plaster on my last fighting smirk that works with every damn woman. "How about we get out of here, and I can thank you properly?"

A soft laugh resonates in her chest and she pushes her empty glass toward Max. "Oh don't go and get attached just because I made your *boo-boo* feel better." The barstool screeches as she stands. "Thank you, Max, for the Shirley Temple."

Yep, like a damn twelve-year-old.

"Do you live around here?" I make my way around the bar, needing to be close to her for some fucking odd reason.

"Aren't hotel lounges a hot spot for all the locals?" The sarcastic wittiness rings through her voice, and I instantly want to shut her up with my mouth. "I have an early flight. Good night, boys."

"Will you be back?" She heads toward the lobby, and I follow behind like a damn puppy.

"If I'm hired."

"What's your name?"

"There's no point in remembering it." Do dream girls exist and have I just met mine?

"Well, then. Thank you again for my thumb, Blondie."

Her eyes soften as she nods. I feel like a dick to keep pursuing this woman who clearly isn't throwing me a goddamn bone. I watch her walk to the elevator, but I am well aware that her hips are purposefully swaying the way Miranda's were. Her arm lifts as she runs a hand through her hair and stops midscalp to fluff her curls.

I know that *is* intentional.

"Make sure you hold on to that innocence." I respect she turned me down, but I'm confused with her hot and cold angle.

She jolts with an abrupt stop from my words, and her head slowly turns back to me with her chin resting on her shoulder. A twisted sultry smirk plays on her lips as her narrow eyes hold humor. My dick responds in ways it shouldn't as I try to figure out what the fuck this means. Her emeralds dip to my thumb for a moment, then connect back to mine. Blondie's tongue darts out over her bottom lip tracing the edge before her teeth clench on to it. Is she debating us tonight? The lust in her eyes vanishes with one last look at my hand.

"Good night, Charmer." With that, she steps into the elevator, and my contracted lungs can't find the power to seize oxygen.

Am I embarrassed to know I was rejected because my sore thumb could maybe interfere with my bedroom skills? Slightly, yes. Honestly, Blondie is probably right, considering she's the reason I'm not at the hospital right now. I walk back into the lounge bar, straight toward Max, who already knows my question.

"The only information I gathered is that her ID is from California and she's twenty-four, dude."

My thumb continues to pulse as I piece together how I have gone thirty years without meeting a woman who won't give me her name.

I've gone all these years without caring to know a woman's name.

Until now.

Chapter 2

Lauren

Two months later
"I'm proud of you." Lloyd, my final foster person, wraps me in a brief hug. "Marsha would be too."

Marsha, his wife, died my second year in their care. Cancer sucks, but at least we had time to prepare for it. After she passed, Lloyd and I kept to ourselves. What else would a twelve-year-old girl and widowed old man talk about anyway? We held a basic routine where most of our communication was done over dinner. He wasn't a cook. My youth and adolescence consisted of packaged and frozen foods. But I was fed and thankful to not be transported to another family. Or add more demons to my hellish past. The real advantage of being placed with Lloyd was how he allowed me to stay with him through university.

"I'll give you a call when I arrive." I hit the interstate anticipating the eight-hour drive from a small town outside of San Diego to San Francisco.

My best and *only* friend, Rachel, had me questioning why I would give up the sunny south for misty skies and concrete hills. It's where I was born. I never left the hospital with my womb supplier. I've known nothing other than life in the foster system.

I feel drawn to find what was so appealing about this city to my mother, aside from the drugs of course. I pull into a hotel six hours later, not wanting to navigate downtown San Francisco on a Friday night.

The lobby is dim as jazz pours through the lounge. It's not as classy as the one a few blocks from the new condo I am moving into, but it's still nice. The piano player calms my nerves as I order food and lose myself in the rhythm of the ivory keys. I have no idea how to play and probably never will. I'm drawn to the alluring way chords can strike so much emotion. How certain chords resonate with how I feel.

Each rhythm can hack the encrypted emotions I've mastered to suppress. I call it an early night to prepare for San Francisco bright and early the next morning.

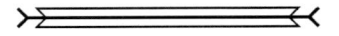

>=====<

My bachelor condo has more room than any other living space I've called *mine*. Shared foster bedrooms or dingy plain rooms hosting a single bed and dresser are all I've known. Now, I'm in a brighter box with a city view. It doesn't take long to unpack my three suitcases full of possessions. I've been conditioned to never need much, though it's trendy to coin the term *minimalist* nowadays. The bonus of this place is that it came furnished. My stomach grumbles, signaling me to venture into what the nearby streets offer to eat.

The streets are packed. Large sidewalks are filled with locals trying to push through the sea of confused tourists. The muttering of conversations, car engines and distant music make up the white noise of this city. I follow the smell of fresh grilled food and reach a market around the corner. Warmth hits my chest, pushing forward my smile that I've spent a lifetime suppressing. Having this market close is convenient since I don't cook beyond scrambled eggs and oatmeal.

My legs burn by the time I reach a coffeehouse. The layered city hills look fascinating, until you have to walk up them to get anywhere. I'm not lazy. I do prioritize the gym after a twelve-hour shift, but these hills might just replace the gym. Cars honk as I watch a driver nearly hit a pedestrian too busy looking at his phone and walking into the street. Driving and finding cheap parking in this city is too overwhelming. I decide at this moment to sell my old car and take a cab to work. I can use the car money for a special project I'm holding dearly to my heart anyway.

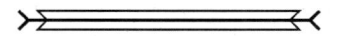

>=======<

"Welcome to San Francisco General, Lauren McAllister." I look up at the gray-haired registered nurse practitioner. "You will be working alongside me today."

I look *up* at her.

For once, I am not the tall one among the girls. "I'm Velma." She glances down at my nametag and gives me a puzzling look.

I know what's about to come out of her mouth just like everyone else I run into when the subject of jobs arises. I look too young to be in my job position, and I am younger than most.

"You must be a smart cookie." She smiles. I worked my ass off through high school to be qualified as a practitioner as soon as possible.

"I like to learn." I smile and follow her down the emergency room hallway.

"You'll be working the opposite shift to me, but Tessa is a great nurse and a hard worker. I think you'll get along great." Velma smiles as the wrinkles on her eyes crease.

The next few hours are spent proving my knowledge of trauma cases. I'm due for a coffee by the time I take a break. I walk the break room, and a small brunette pokes her head out of the doorway. Her straight pigtails barely reach her shoulders.

"You must be the new girl, Lauren." Her smile reaches her brown eyes. "I'm Tessa."

She's short. Almost doll-like from the anime shows that my best friend Rachel watches.

"Hey, Tessa. I heard Velma talk very highly of you." My five-eleven lanky frame towers over her.

"I have a mouth other than mine to feed. Can't risk losing my job." She laughs and shows me her phone. "That's my son, Dylan. I got pregnant at nineteen, but my parents help out a lot. I can't believe he is starting kindergarten in the fall." She pauses, expecting more than just my smile.

"He looks just like you," I reply, always unsure of these moments.

The moments where people spill their personal information or life story and expect you to do the same. My story isn't going to change her life, and honestly, I try and bury my past daily. What matters is the current moment we are in and the job I am here for. Be friendly and smile, but stay disconnected. I've witnessed the pain people go through when a friendship, relationship or loved one is no longer in their life. I'm social and happy, but a deeper connection is unnecessary.

I finish out my next few shifts strong. Work has been mentally exhausting, and every night when my shift ends, I pass out after my shower. Tonight is different. Maybe it's the glow of the city lights illuminating through the raindrops on the cab window or the fact that I haven't hooked up with anyone in a few months. A rarity for me. I played the good girl until my senior year of university. Now, I've hooked up with over a handful of men in the last year and a half. Rachel calls it making up for lost time, while some would probably label me as a straight-up skank.

The cab passes by the large hotel I previously stayed at. In the glow of the rain, it's even more inviting with the yellow lights and dark velvet entry. I ignore the calling of my bed as I walk into my condo. The warmth of the shower clears my head before I walk three blocks over to the hotel bar lounge. I wonder if I should have kept my car on nights like this, but the goal for my future project is worth a short walk in the rain.

The faint perfume through the hotel air vents subconsciously adds to the higher-class appeal. The black countertop reflects a warm glow off the lights and the empty piano. The royal-blue, diamond-tucked booths sit unoccupied. The lounge seems dull for a Thursday. Even though this place is empty, for some reason, I feel underdressed. I glance down at my leggings and a flowy silk tank top.

Maybe I should have chosen a cocktail dress. I push the self-judgment aside and take a seat on the same barstool as before.

"Do you poison customers so no one returns?" Max lifts his eyes up from his phone as I wave my hands at the emptiness.

"You must have been a lucky one." A smile breaks across his face.

"Why is this place empty?" I take a seat, propping my elbows up to rest my chin on my hands. "You give out free dishes of maraschino cherries."

"There are a few shows playing tonight, and we aren't booked to full capacity." He shrugs, not making much eye contact. "Are you in this city for good?"

"As long as this city holds my interest, I'll stay." I smirk using a flirty tone.

"Shirley Temple *sans* alcohol?"

He remembered.

"With extra cherries, please." He has this brooding, chill vibe to him. "Also, if your food is safe to eat, order me your favorite thing off the menu."

He nods, punching something into the waiter tablet. "It'll be about ten minutes."

I stir my drink and wish I had chosen a nightclub instead. Max is attractive. He has a tall, lean muscular build with dark-blond hair styled upward at the front. I imagine it's silky soft when you run your fingers through it, but he's not throwing any flirty looks my way. His brooding blue eyes remain focused everywhere but on me. There are always more choices in men at a club or frat boys on a school campus. Frat boys are usually the best to get my fix from because they don't want you in the morning. Still, I always hold the fear that they have contracted some type of STD and the older men end up wanting more than just one night. The game is ruthless.

The plate clinks on the bar top, pulling me out of my thoughts. A giant burger and seasoned hand-cut fries sit in front of me.

"I hope you're not a vegetarian." Max laughs.

"No, this looks incredible." I am midbite as a voice ghosts from behind.

"Look who got hired." Charmer takes a seat next to me.

"My job perk is being able to live anywhere."

"Influencer?" Humor laces his deep voice. "Model?"

"The more you speak, the happier I am for you that you're at least attractive." Why so many questions?

"Ouch." He places a hand on his broad chest then smirks. "How about we get out of here?"

The nerve.

"If burger breath is your kink, then let's get to it." I take another bite.

He sucks in his cheeks to hold back a laugh. "That shouldn't turn me on, but your wittiness is refreshing."

I toss a fry his way and continue to eat in silence. I acknowledge his workout attire. The man is a beast in muscular width and well over six feet. His black shorts hang loose, and the fitted gray T-shirt doesn't do any job of hiding his very well-chiseled abs. He looks more like a professional sports figure than a man in the business world.

"Thanks again, Doc, for my thumb fiasco last time." His dark-brown eyes are hard to pull away from.

"Trauma nurse practitioner, to be exact."

"Practitioner?" Max leans forward, now interested in our conversation. "You seem young for that."

"I graduated high school with my AA." I shrug.

"Wait, what?" my attractive, annoying bar accessory chimes in.

"I received my high school diploma the same month I received my associate's degree from college. That set me ahead two years." I don't normally feel the need to explain myself, but tonight I felt proud of my accomplishment. "I didn't have much of a life in high school."

"Clearly," Max states, raising his eyebrows as the guys share a silent look.

"Your food is on the house tonight." Charmer nods, holding his drink up as if he's saluting me.

Max taps the bar and excuses himself.

"In case you aren't familiar with jobs and finances, my job pays more than enough to afford a burger." I hold the sarcasm strong in my voice.

"Are all your patients blessed with your sass, too? Or is that just for me?"

"Do you ever keep irrelevant questions to yourself?" I pick up a fry and break eye contact as I deliberately run the tip of my tongue up the fry to taste the seasoning.

I enjoy acting as if I don't know the effect it's having on him. I continue to let him think he's the only one with a game. The man will usually put more effort into his bedroom skills if he feels pride in finally getting your attention.

"You're right." Mr. Armani gym guy stands up from his stool and nods. "Dedicating that much time to school is respectable."

Is he respecting me? Hold up.

"I was just trying to say thank you. Enjoy your night." His stool pushes behind him and he stands.

He strides out of the bar and into the lobby. Now I'm following after him like a damn fish to a shiny hooked tassel. It's clear he's older than me, but his one-night stand bravado is strong. He must sense me trailing because he stops, and I crash into his solid back. His expensive cologne ignites my senses, awakening naughty thoughts of what I want to do to this man. He turns around as his brown eyes bounce from mine to my lips.

"I live a few blocks away if you want to thank me properly." I cut right to the point because I'm done playing games.

"You wouldn't tell me your name last time." His lips twitch to a smile but his eyes flash with caution.

He takes a step forward as I falter backward.

"I still haven't asked for yours." I regain composure and take a bold step toward him.

His chest brushes mine as his whisper hits my lips. "I have rules—" he begins as his fingertips feather up my bare arm creating a trail of goose bumps.

Get a *grip*, Lauren.

"You have rules for a brief hookup?" I arch an eyebrow at the ridiculousness of the situation.

His brown eyes darken as a primal gaze takes over. His hand encompasses my wrist, leading me to the elevator. Adrenaline courses through my veins with high hopes he can give me what I need tonight. The elevator doors chime closed and as I inhale, a strong hand meets my neck, pushing me against the wall. His lips press into mine with the same desperation I crave. Charmer's other arm rests on my hip, but he keeps our bodies apart. My heart hammers in my chest as my body pulses with need to feel him against me. I take the reins and wrap my arms around his lower waist to pull him flush against me.

His solid length pushes into my hip as my lower region throbs. He's so hard, I swear his dick is going to leave a bruise on my hip. My stomach flips up to my throat then drops, sending lightning to my core. There's a hum radiating off his body, and he's as eager as I am. Our frequency level soars to heights I've never experienced. The doors chime open to a hallway with only two doors. We stumble into a hotel penthouse. I'm panting too hard to care.

Chapter 3

Adam

The moment her innocent act dropped, and I knew she was serious, I snapped. Her cherry-flavored lips sent me into an intoxicating spiral I hadn't imagined. Her sweet floral scent is driving me fucking insane as her body crowds mine. Her boldness of pulling me against her in the elevator gave a prelude to her racy side I've yet to discover. It's all fucking hot. Her breathless moan rings through my ears as I carry her to lie on the nearest chaise lounge chair.

Her eyes drop to my healing thumb as her chest heaves with labored breaths. My brain floods with the need to prove myself. My fingers grasp the waistband of her leggings and she arches her back to lift her ass as I slide them down. The need to make her beg evaporates as my need to taste her takes over. I lift both her long legs up and meet her eyes before I go any further.

Even though she's wide eyed awaiting my next move, part of me still holds values.

But part of me is trying to piss her off more with anticipation. "You're on board with all this, right?"

Her head leans forward. "The more you talk, the more orgasms I'm going to tack on for you to accomplish."

And instantly, her sass spikes my need to make her plead before fucking the brat out of her.

I lower my head between her legs and inch up kiss by kiss from her knee to the inside of her thigh. Her legs spread wider as she tries to arch closer to me. It takes everything to not devour her soft, throbbing pussy. I regain the strength to control myself and take my time kissing up her aroused swollen folds until she can't take it anymore. Blondie attempts to move herself to connect with my mouth. Breathlessly, her hand weaves through my hair and grips it tight, trying to angle my head where she needs it.

"Tell me what you need, Shirley Temple." I glance up and receive a glare.

"If you don't already know, then you deserved that slap from your *lobby friend*." Her words come out hoarse.

"Oh, I know what you need." My tongue quickly feathers over her clit for a brief second and her hips jolt. "I just want you to tell me how bad you want my lips to devour your pulsing pussy."

"Just fuck me with your mouth already, Charmer." Her voice pitches higher and higher with each word she speaks.

My lips part, gently sucking in her clit before I pull my mouth up and release the suction with a pop sound. I flatten my tongue and taste all of her before I slide two fingers in, hearing her gasp from the width. My large fingers suit my six-three frame. Maybe I should have started with one, but her moans tell me otherwise as they fill the room. I curl my index finger upward as my middle finger pushes in deeper.

Her hand tightens in my hair as a pleasured hiss escapes her pretty lips. I slide them out then enter again as my tongue keeps the slow rhythm on her clit.

Blondie's hips buck and my forearm drapes across her lower abdomen. I make sure to press down on the center of her lower abs, just below her hip bones. I know hitting her outer G-spot will intensify her orgasm. Her hips rise again and start to circle, so I quicken my tongue pace with more pressure. With hitched breath, her body straightens and her soft walls tighten around my fingers.

"Let go, Blondie." My tongue goes rapidly as her body starts to shake. "Take every ounce of pleasure you want." Her hands have probably ripped out half my hair by now as she rides out her orgasm.

I won't let up until she physically can't take it anymore. She scoots back, breaking the contact. Her chest rises with ragged breaths as her green eyes lock onto my shorts like a shark to its prey. Her tongue darts out to wet her lips and verifies what's on her mind.

"There's not a chance I'll be able to fuck you properly right now if you follow through with that thought."

"Then get naked before my patience runs out and I fuck myself." She reaches for the bottom of her shirt and lifts it over her head, exposing her braless, perfect handfuls.

Damn, this girl can talk dirty.

I oblige and reconnect our lips. Her tongue tangles with mine as I lead us to the minibar and bend her over. She lets out a surprised squeak as her flesh meets the cool countertop. My hand slaps her ass before I enter a finger into her pussy and rub her juices around her folds. I am so hard I swear the simple task of rolling on my condom will make me come.

A condom is only useful to prevent me from coming too quick, but no one needs to know that story.

My foot kicks her legs wider as my teeth drag along her shoulder blade. Blondie gasps and I smile with pride knowing she is unable to speak when my hands are touching her body. My hand comes around her front to circle her clit. As badly as I want to hold her down on the counter and pound her senseless, I take my time. I grip the back of her neck on the bar counter and slowly, I ease in leisurely.

"Give me more." The agitation in her voice grows, and I let her back all the way into me.

"Your hungry pussy wants all of me, doesn't it?" I grunt and slam into her with force.

Her noises become incoherent as I feel her constrict my cock. I reach forward, weaving my fingers through her long curls to yank her head back. My hand grips her hip hard enough that she'll have a bruise as her waves of pleasure soar through. "You're painting my cock beautifully, Blondie."

I pull out as she turns around, eyes full of sated lust. Her hands rest on my shoulders before she jumps into my arms. My grip on her ass tightens as she tilts her hips forward, sliding down on my dick.

"I'd say you're decent." She shrugs with a smirk. "Was that your go-to best move, Charmer?" Her thumb and index grip my chin, tilting it to connect our lips.

I sit us on the chaise as she starts to ride me. My eyes close as my head falls back, begging myself to hold off as long as possible. Her hand grips my hair pulling my face between her tits. I reach up to squeeze her full breasts before my teeth take a nipple between them. Moaning, she grinds into me harder. Her hand takes mine, bringing it up to her throat while her other hand travels south to circle her bundle of nerves.

What a fucking show. This woman's confidence in knowing what she wants is more than any past woman I've fucked.

"I'm coming," she whimpers and I tighten my grip on her throat.

I keep my hand in place and guide her to lie down while keeping my dick still inside. Her arms lift to wrap around me, but I shove them above her head, needing dominance. I lean down and devour a spot behind her ear. She sucks in air so strong I swear she's about to come from it. I make each thrust count as I grind my pelvis against her clit and feel her start to tighten around me *again*.

She's intoxicating.

I don't want to stop.

Every moan, breathless whimper, and *"Oh god, Charmer."* I want them recorded to memory and played on repeat. Euphoria travels down my spine and I can't hold off any longer. I let myself go as she cries out, throwing her head back. My lips meet her exposed neck wanting to taste her a little longer. I rest my forearms at the side of her head to catch my own breath. I've never cared to put this much effort into a hookup before, but damn, she possessed me.

Her palms rest against my chest, pushing me up. Her lean frame sits up as she inhales. "No wonder your lobby friend didn't want to leave a couple months back." A soft laugh cuts through the room.

Sex wasn't what Miranda was after, nor were our hookups ever as intense as this was. I shake my head and pick up my shorts as I make my way to the kitchen for a glass of water. "Now, can you at least tell me your name?"

Her teeth toy with her bottom lip as she gets dressed. "As long as you promise not to ask for anything more."

Well, that's a first from a woman's mouth.

"I promise. I don't *need* anything more." I smirk, reaching for my shirt.

"I don't *want* anything more than what just happened."

What the hell happened to make her not want more?

"Blondie, Shirley Temple?"

"It's Lauren." A Cheshire smile widens across her prominent cheekbones.

"Well, Lauren, thank you for tonight." I wait for her response to ask for my name.

"Thank *you*." Her eyebrows rise in surprise. "I didn't have to give out one preference pointer."

"I wouldn't take offense if you did." I shrug.

I am well aware every woman's body is slightly different, but her confidence was hypnotizing to watch. So, why the mystery?

Her eyes linger on the panorama floor-to-ceiling windows over the city. "I mean, against the window would have been quite a thrill." She nods toward the chaise lounge chair, giving me a side-eye. "Taking you in my mouth upside down on that chair would have been fun too. But I don't do relationships."

As my gaze heats at the thought, she gets up and makes her way to the door. I test the water to see how uncommitted she really is. "Why? Having a partner to make memories with and endless sex sounds like it would be enjoyable."

Her laugh is boastful as it echoes in my entryway. She slips her shoes on and shakes her head. "That is why we wouldn't work. Fun yes, but getting attached beyond orgasms is not worth it." She walks out the door. "Thank you for tonight, Charmer. But I'm not what you're looking for long term." Her finger lights up the elevator button as I feel my willpower siphoned.

Damn, and I thought that my view was harsh.

"I'm wrong again," I speak louder than needed. Her attention is back on me. "I called your bluff. Most women say they're fine with friends with benefits. Until they think they can change me."

She ignores the open elevator doors, giving me her full attention.

"Yet, you were turning *me* down."

"I don't want to be your friend. Guys can get attached, and I have valid reasons for not *wanting* anything but an orgasm."

"I don't *need* you, but I might need your body again," I reply honestly.

She summons the elevator with a smirk. The doors open, and I'm not sure I'll see her again. "Maybe I'll see you around, Charmer. I suggest my place next time, so it's not as echoey." She disappears behind the closing doors without asking my name.

Yep. Yep, I'm fucked... in every way.

>=====<

My mahogany desk displays stacks of paperwork, and every spreadsheet is open on my computer. I blink at the screen a few times as if that will complete all of my daily tasks. As the CFO of my family's billion-dollar hotel chain, I feel like my job is never caught up. My mind keeps wandering to Lauren and her elusive demeanor. I want to hire somebody to get more information about her, but I know that's wrong, considering she's not a threat. I've lost too much sleep, wondering if she's off with another man or why she is that guarded with feelings.

A nurse practitioner who doesn't harbor feelings is one hell of an oxymoron. Her lack of reaction to my hotel penthouse was nothing more than a straight face glance around. Is she from big money too? And my place is not that *echoey*.

Why didn't she want my name? Fuck, I should be thrilled about that.

My eyes rest on the family photo on the wall. It brings me back to my childhood years at our family cabin. The only simple times I've gotten to experience the rawness of this world. Every Christmas was spent there without talks of work or distractions. The cabin holds memories of endless board games and communication face to face. The trees rustling on plush redwood hills speak to my soul more than hills of concrete, horns, and revving engines. Our memory making became less frequent once I and my two siblings became old enough to work. I'd give all of this up to live in the past. To live in that damn quiet cabin *now*.

The heavy wooden door echoes as knuckles tap on the other side. My father's head pokes in. "Do you have a minute?"

"For you, always." I shuffle paperwork around to make room for another folder of something I'll probably dread opening.

"We received more marketing budgets." His aged smile meets his wrinkled eyes. "I've added a few things to make our hotel stand out among the rest."

"That's great." I force a smile and hope he can't see through my will to spend days chopping wood instead of chopping numbers. "You and Grandpa have a knack for putting our hotels above the others."

"Look over this tonight if you have a chance." The whoosh of air from the red folder drops on my desk, mimicking the sacrificial breath of how my time is spent on earth.

A pang of guilt hits under my ribs for wishing I wasn't born into the world of wealth that many people strive for. "Of course, I will."

"I knew I could count on you, son." He nods and closes the door behind him.

I don't hate my job. I'm blessed to have it. But finding meaning in something the world doesn't need is hard to wrap my head around. It's already late afternoon and I'm nowhere near finished with deadlines.

I refuse to cancel my class tonight. I need the stress relief. My class is one of the few things I hold myself accountable for. People pay and rely on me for a service. Gathering my work for tonight, I sigh and push back my chair. These four walls are too suffocating to concentrate. I mentally prep myself for another all-nighter before closing for the day. I walk a few blocks over to my favorite coffee shop for another espresso. I'll sleep when I'm dead.

Chapter 4

Lauren

"I'm heading out," I call over my shoulder to Tessa.

"Good work this week, Ren. Enjoy your days off."

I smile as if I have any energy left to do so. I've worked overtime every shift, and the number of resuscitations we have had has been beyond what I saw back in my town. Tonight's work trauma triggered thoughts toward my own womb supplier. How lucky I was to be taken by the hospital and not meet a horrible fate like others have. I don't have the utmost expectation to find my womb supplier. After everything I've seen with that lifestyle, the chances of her still roaming the streets for the past twenty-four years seems unlikely. The chances of her remembering the name she gave me at the hospital or what year I was brought into the system are slim. But there are some people who do get clean.

The lump sitting in my throat grows on the cab ride home. I focus on my favorite breathing pattern to calm my anxiety as a result of this work shift. *Cardio*. I need to forget as much as possible. Multiple yawns take over during my shower, so I fight the sleep urge and turn the water to cold. Tessa mentioned the perfect stress relief class at the gym around the corner. Which apparently is filled with attractive men who can *give* stress relief. Charmer and his stupid skills have now ruined men for me. Seriously, I lost count of how many times that man had me coming. I'm annoyed with him even more than before. He and his attractive brown eyes and tall, wide frame.

The chill of the night hits me as I step onto the street. I'm brought back to this afternoon and my stomach turns as I walk the few blocks in the dark.

After registering with the front desk, I focus on the smell of rubber mats to calm my mind. The stale humidity with a hint of chlorine is faint coming down the hall. Gyms have that distinct smell about them. I walk down the hallway and turn right into the classroom, and halt. I need to turn around and leave before I'm spotted, but my mouth speaks before I can stop it.

"No, no, no. No, you can't be here." I grab the attention of Charmer as he turns to me with his signature sinful smirk. All six-three of him in a gray muscle tee and black shorts. The same ones he wore the other night when he—

Keep your focus, Lauren.

"You're a stalker." I cross my arms over my chest as he takes a bold step closer.

"I was here first, *Lauren*." He says my name in a deeper part of his chest. And now, I stand here imagining what it would sound like if he growled my name while bending me over his bar counter. "I've called dibs for years here."

"Ha. After today's shift, I need this class more than you." Is that enough to make him leave?

"Well." He smirks, rubbing his hand on the back of his neck. "I'll be sure to leave you breathless." He turns and claps his hands to command the room.

He makes his way to the front of the classroom as people pipe down their conversations and give him their full attention. My body wants to melt to the floor in embarrassment. The glint in his eyes shot a clear message of how satisfied he was with my reaction. *He's the instructor?* Charmer goes over the different circuits and begins a brief warm-up. I remove the baggy sweats I wore on the walk here and smile inwardly as his eyes burn through me. My short spandex shorts and a loose shirt tied in a side knot are a wicked tease for what's underneath. What he knows he can't touch in this current moment.

I manage to avoid him on most of the circuits and pace myself well until the last station. Long, weighted ropes meet their challenger, and an internal cry cuts within. Arm strength is my weakness, but there's a strong gnawing need to prove myself to *he who still remains nameless*. I bend my knees and feel the ropes burn my shoulders as much as my legs. My abs ignite with fire and I release a breath. The pain turns into an addictive need to push myself. The heaviness grows with each lash as Charmer approaches.

I had high hopes I could actually finish this class in peace.

"More," he encourages.

I feel the sweat pool at my forehead and channel my annoyance with him into the ropes.

"Come on, Blondie." His voice lowers as he leans in closer. "I know you can pant harder than that."

His breath hits my ear, challenging me to feed his ego.

My eyes focus forward in the mirror and recall the past few hours of my shift. The pain. The anger. The helplessness I harbor is one of the main reasons that drove me toward my career. I try to focus on beating the ropes instead of the defeat I faced today. My stomach turns as the room blurs. A voice says something, but I can't make it out as I continue to beat the ropes through a cloud of stars.

Then, everything goes dark.

Cool water trails down my forehead and over my eyes as I squint. *What the hell?* I hear a faint voice as my eyes adjust to the fluorescent lights above me. A large figure appears over me, and I rub my eyes. Deep-brown eyes look down at me as he takes a knee and brushes a loose strand of hair off my forehead. The stubble from his five o'clock shadow shouldn't have me wanting to reach out and touch it, so I fight the urge.

"When I said breathless, I didn't mean to go and pass out."

I sit up as I watch the other classmates start to clear out of the room.

"I only ever give it my all," I reply and accept the hand he offers to help me stand.

"Let me buy you some pizza. I know a great place." His tone is genuine. "You worked hard at whatever was going through your head."

For some reason, I find myself smiling and nodding.

We eat in silence at a small pizza joint that most people wouldn't find unless they really know the area. Hands down, this is the best pizza I have ever had. Not that I'm a pizza connoisseur beyond frozen boxes from a grocery store or a slice from childhood Chuck-e-Cheese's birthday party. Charmer fixates his eyes down or off to the side giving me headspace. Yet at the same time, trying to watch and wonder what the hell I'm thinking about. His eyes scream the brief moment they meet mine, desperate for an answer. If he wasn't so hot, it would be pathetic. But he doesn't ask. He lets me think.

I wrap my arms around myself as the chill from the bay rolls up a hill. Though it's July, San Francisco's temperature drops with the sun. We cross the street and reach a grassy park on a hill overlooking the city lights. The lights glow to a blur as I let my eyes soften their focus. My lungs expand as calmness washes over me for the first time today. I've never gone to therapy, though I'm well aware it could help with my past and job field. I've managed to find ways of coping with my darkness and cluttered mind. The cool wind hits my face, and a car beeps its horn, pulling me from my trance. Charmer keeps his gaze ahead, but I can see his eyes drift to me every few moments.

I still don't know his name. Part of me likes that he is at a distance. An acquaintance at best, who has bought me food and dished out orgasms. Oh, and brought me back to consciousness after I blacked out.

My mind flashes back to work and I feel anger resurface, building in my gut. I focus on the lights again. Charmer takes slow deep breaths, probably on purpose if he's so magically in tune to sense me. I mimic his breaths, desperate to feel light again. The words flow out of me before I can stop them.

"A newborn was found today and brought in."

His forehead scrunches, but his face remains forward.

"She was found in an alley and heavily drugged. We couldn't save her." I lower my voice an octave in hopes my voice won't break.

His eyes wince as I watch his throat constrict, trying to force a swallow. I keep going, as the weight lifts.

"We only know what she went through from assessing, but I know this baby went through hell before she took her last breath." I turn to him. "You have *no* idea how bad I want to go after the people who did this to her."

"That must have been quite the sight to work on." He shakes his head.

I debate how in depth I want to taint his mind with the sick things people do to each other in the alleys. "Abuse beyond stomaching."

We stay silent. His eyes search mine, unsure how to respond. I expect him to reach out or say something most people would want to hear, but he doesn't. Maybe this guy is the first who is on the same page. I don't need hugs. I just needed to tell someone about my day and move past it. My stomach swirls as my throat closes, blocking all oxygen from escaping. Nausea waves through me, and I inhaled sharply to resist the contents of my stomach expelling. I fail miserably. My hands instinctively reach for my hair as I double over and paint the grass. This guy hands me a napkin from the pizza leftovers bag without a word. I wipe my mouth, surprised I'm not embarrassed. I thought he would be the one to vomit, to be honest.

"You must see a lot of horror in your field," he speaks.

"It's not always *that* terrible." I shake my head and regain strength. "I don't hold on to feelings outside of my job, but patients, especially children, really get to me."

"Noted." His smile is soft this time. Understanding. "I'll walk you home, Lauren." His hand rests on my back as he leads the way.

And I let him.

What the hell is in this city air and my vulnerability? Men have tried to break me down over the years, and yet here I am vomiting out everything—in every way. Maybe I admire the way he stuck to his promise and hasn't asked for *anything* beyond my name. Finally, a guy who gets it. So why do I feel like I owe this man the respect to address him properly?

"Okay." I break our silence as we wait for the crosswalk light to change. "What's your name?"

His smile lights up his beautiful eyes and the city lights reflect in them. Air escapes my lungs. God, he is handsome.

"Guess," he challenges. "If you're right, you can have all the leftovers."

"You'd let me have them regardless. You're still a gentleman deep down."

"Lauren."

"Fine. Augustus? William?" I follow him across the road as he shakes his head. "Arthur?"

He stops at the corner, cocking one brow up as if I'm insane. "Really? Arthur?"

"I don't know." I shrug. "You seem pretty prestigious, and wealthy people tend to have fancy names."

"No, they don't."

"Important royal ones do," I tease and pull his arm, leading him around the corner to my block.

"It's Adam," he states as we arrive at my building.

"Adam." I find a giggle escaping. "That's so generic. But thank you, Adam, for helping me out tonight." I nod and reach for the take-out bag. "Thank you for listening."

His arm lifts to grab the back of his neck. "If you want someone to show you the best-hidden gems besides a hotel bar, I'm open to being nothing more than a tour guide."

"I don't *want* more than a tour guide." I smirk.
"I don't need anything more than a pretty view." He winks.
"I'm off for the next three days."
"I'll swing by around three, after work tomorrow."
"Good night, Adam."
"Lauren."

Chapter 5

Lauren

I jolt awake and know the time is 5:08 without checking the clock. I swallow my consistent nightmare as the sun begins to peek through sheer white curtains. I twist, feeling my lower spine ache from the couch. How tired was I last night to not walk the extra ten feet to my bed? I yawn, yearning to crawl under the heavy duvet and sleep for a few more hours. I decide to break my one rule and slide into bed. Life is too short to lie around. My muscles burn as I move toward the bed. Those ropes did a number on me. I chug the bottle of water on my nightstand and stare at the buildings through my giant windows. They are what enticed me to rent this place. The view of this layered city is artwork itself. Magical.

Hours later, I decide on a sundress. My body ached too much to add different garments. So, a flowy green dress it is. I'm not one for fashion since most of my time is spent in scrubs. I didn't grow up with a fashionable budget to keep up with trends. Skinny jeans and a flowy tank top are my usual go-to attire. And flat shoes. Heels are not my friend since I already feel like a giraffe.

I head downstairs at three and see Adam waiting. His muscles beneath his black V-neck make my mouth water. My lower region picks up its own heartbeat, tempting me to drag him upstairs and forget about touring anything other than his body. His eyes meet mine. I feel my cheeks flush at the thought as his charming smile appears. Damn boy could read my mind. Am I blushing? *What the hell, Lauren. Get a grip.*

He offers his arm to loop through his, but I walk past it because we are not a couple. "Where to first, Charmer?"

"Can you stop calling me that since you know my name?"

"I suppose, Adam."

The streets are loud. Each sound fighting for its turn to speak, like a disturbed echo of white noise. Crowds of people push past us until we walk a few blocks over and approach a packed tour bus. I see a sign up ahead. "Lombard, that sounds familiar."

"I'm sure you've seen this on *Full House* growing up." He chuckles.

"Nah, I was more of a *Charmed* fan." I laugh. "The crookedest street." I look at the red pivoting road heading downward.

A car beeps for tourists to move out of the way and I link my arm with Adam's. I deem this acceptable since I hate crowds and don't want to get lost.

"Come on." He smiles. "We are almost to my favorite place."

The new area isn't any less overwhelming than the other streets. Pizza shops, gelato, and cafés awaken my senses as he tugs me to a little café on the right. "Welcome to North Beach. The little taste of Italy."

"Have you been there?"

"I've been to Italy a few times over the years. This place has the best espresso and gelato." We pass the few small bistro tables set up outside and head to the counter. "Do you like ice cream?"

If he only knew my obsession and goal, it would scare him off.

"May I have a hazelnut latte and a chocolate gelato, please?" I order, but my credit card is pushed away. "This isn't a date, Adam."

"I don't care. Ciao Tony, avrò il solito, per favore." He smiles at the short Italian man who opens his arms and nods in approval.

"Bella signora." Tony smiles and starts our order.

I halt, looking between the two men, feeling clueless and more turned on than I should be in public. Adam rolls Italian off his tongue with ease, and I wonder if that's why his mouth skills are impeccable.

"What did you order?" I bring myself back to the current moment.

"I told him the usual." Adam leads me to a small bistro table out front.

The crowds of people are within a couple feet of us walking by, and I wish the city made these sidewalks larger. "Teach me something in Italian." I give a warning look. "But it better be appropriate."

"Non ti voglio." He smiles and relaxes back in his chair. "It means *I don't want you.*"

"That can come in handy." I repeat the phrase a few more times as Adam fights a smile. "What?" I see a shadow cast over me and look up to see Tony holding our coffees.

"He is beautiful! Why don't you want him?" He sets the coffee down and shakes his head. "I thought maybe he was interested in the other team. You're the first lady he has ever brought here and you say you don't want him."

"I'm just a tour guide, Tony." Adam laughs. "And I am most definitely team woman."

I stir my gelato a few times without having a single taste. I drink my latte and receive questionable looks from Adam, but he doesn't say anything. Thankfully, with this heat, my gelato quickly becomes the perfect mix of thick and runny. A yogurt consistency, if you will. My smile reaches my eyes as I take the first bite. This gelato is perfect. The smooth glazed texture hits my tongue like silk. I shut my eyes, assessing like I do with all ice cream. The temperature is cold but not shocking. This flavor is not syrupy and overly sweet like the kind you buy in a cardboard box. This is pure heaven. I open my eyes to a puzzled but amused Adam who can't bite his tongue any longer.

"Why?" He tilts his head.

I offer him a taste, and he scrunches his nose. "It tastes best like this." I smile, unashamed of my odd preference.

"It's melted. You could have ordered a milkshake."

"No, it's not the same." I shake my head. "And it's not melted." I hold up the spoon as part of it falls off in a lump. "This is perfection. My goal is to try every ice cream place by the end of the summer."

"That doesn't seem healthy." He leans back in his chair as I finish my gelato.

"Well, it's part of my main food group." I scrape the bottom of the cup. "It's good I love cardio."

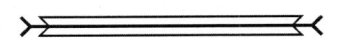

>=====<

We knock off a couple main tourist sights on a streetcar before getting off at Alamo Square. The grassy area hosts many picnic blankets, families and dogs running about. It's a nice park as we walk to the top of it. I see why he wanted to take me here. Adam clears his throat as we walk farther on the grass.

"I know you said you're more of a *Charmed* fan, but this is still cool to see in person."

We make our way through the grass approaching the infamous Postcard Row. It's a strange feeling after seeing it so many times on television and now it's tangible. "You're right, it is cooler in person. Is the *Charmed* house here too?" I ask as my voice pitches with excitement.

"Nah, that one is in Los Angeles."

"Bummer. I used to live much closer to it before." I narrow my eyes at him as we take a seat on the grass. "I thought you weren't a *Charmed* fan."

"My older sister knows every word to every episode." He sighs. "Our parents only had one TV growing up. My sister hogged the damn thing every time the show aired."

"Come on, at least the witches were hot. I'm sure you didn't hate watching it that much."

"I may have beat off to Phoebe back in the day," he shamelessly admits as I roll my eyes.

"Do you have any more siblings?" I don't know why I'm asking because it's irrelevant, but conversation flows easily with him.

"A younger brother. I've got quite a few years on him. He's studying abroad right now." Adam shakes his head, staring ahead. "He's twenty-six and still working on his master's. It's a degree that doesn't have much to do with his profession after graduation. I think he wants to live off the freedom that I crave to have."

"What will his job be?"

Adam sighs, staring ahead to give thought to his answer. As if telling me will cause trouble. "The Wheaton Hotel you frequent? My family owns that. Along with a few other hotels across the country."

"Adam Wheaton," I test out the name to debate how well it suits him. "Your family seems tight knit and dedicated to their business." I wonder how much freedom he actually craves growing up in a family who literally can afford anything.

"Devoted to work, no doubt." His voice falls flat. "My father and grandfather work hard to keep our name prestigious. The three of us children are the *siblings of heir*."

"You seem thrilled." I let the sarcasm be known.

"I respect my brother as much as I resent him. I think everyone craves choice." Adam keeps his eyes focused on the picture-perfect postcard homes in front of us.

My craving for freedom doesn't seem too far off.

Freedom to answer to myself.

Freedom to choose a relationship.

Freedom to not be told how to live my life.

Cold liquid splashes on my shoulders as I jolt back to reality. Adam and I jerk forward as a small voice speaks behind us.

"Sorry. I tripped." A small boy gets up off the grass as his mother runs over.

"No worries, little guy." Adam smiles, turning around. "Are you alright?"

Watching him interact so calmly and naturally with a tiny being isn't something I expected from a big tough guy. Adam picks up the soda cup and hands it back to the child. The boy's mother wears an apologetic look.

"Dean, I told you to be careful with a full cup." She bends down to our level on the ground. "I am so sorry."

"It's not like there was acid in the cup." Adam chuckles. "We're fine. I'm sure Mr. Speedman was just excited to catch up with his friends."

The mother's face softens. "Again, I am sorry."

"Accidents happen." Adam holds his fist out so the young boy can bump it. "I know you didn't purposely spill soda on us."

As they leave, Adam rises to his feet extending his hand to help me up. "We need to shower before the bees get us."

"I haven't seen one bee here yet, Adam." I smile at the worried tone he's trying to hide. "Are you scared of a little bee?" I tease.

"Have you been stung by one? One stung my eye years ago, and I swelled up like an orange." He shuddered, and I tried not to laugh. "They're tiny but mighty."

I shake my head and follow him to my place.

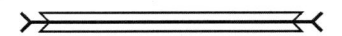

>=====<

"You're right." Adam stands in the center of my condo taking in the small surrounding. "It's not as echoey. I like it."

"Come on." I laugh. "It's no penthouse suite, but the water view is nice."

"You have everything you need. The human species over-consume."

"I only have what I need." I shrug my shoulders as the sticky beverage starts to irritate me. "Shower?" I raise my eyebrows.

"Do you really have to ask?" He stalks toward me. "I've been staring at your ass in that dress all day."

I smirk as I lift my dress over my head, handing it to him with an innocent smile. "This dress?"

His hand brushes over his jaw as his eyes track my body. His hands rest on my hips when his primal gaze meets mine. Something clicks in his mind as an agitated sigh fills the room. "I didn't bring a condom."

"I don't have any on hand." I roll my eyes and curse myself for not grabbing a box the other night. "I'm also not on the pill because it messes with my hormones too much."

I take the dress from him and hold it against my chest. As if covering myself up will make this situation better. His next sentence throws me.

"I had a vasectomy back in college. My best friend and I both did." His voice wavers with the uncertainty of his suggestion. "It's reversible if I ever changed my mind. With my family's financials, I wanted to cover the ground if a false claim ever came about."

I lean against the counter and wait to see if he will keep talking, but he doesn't. "You're true to your word," I state and look into his dark-brown eyes.

"I have to be. My sister is the only one who knows. I don't want the risk of bringing a child into the world without consciously doing it."

"But you still wear a condom?"

He shrugs. "People don't know my personal choice unless it's needed."

"So why tell me?"

"You're different." His eyes search mine for an answer he can't find. "You have your own secrets and I just... trust you. My job title is the first thing people ask for if they don't already know it."

"So, you don't care if we use a condom," I state and feel my pregnancy anxiety peak, even though I believe him.

He takes my hands. "I'm clean, but if you don't feel comfortable or trust what I've told you, that's okay too. Nothing has to happen today."

"If you're lying and I do get knocked up, you'd support whatever choice I have without a question?"

"Without question." His eyes don't waver from mine. "I'll request a paternity test if you decide to follow through with the pregnancy though."

He stands there waiting for my approval on our current situation. I've never gone bareback in fear of being faced with the choice of having to terminate a life or own up to my mistake and raise a child without the knowledge of how. There is also the dreaded possibility of emotional connection from oxytocin. Adam's tone and assured face tell me he's not lying. He's been open about his past. He and I are on the same page. A rarity in my book.

His honesty shows he is being a good guy. Yet the tension in his jaw proves how much he wants to pull me against him. I reach out and grab his wrists, pulling him closer. His lips meet mine in a desperate manner as his hard length pushes into my stomach.

He bends and reaches behind my thighs to lift me as my legs wrap around his waist. My fingers grip his hair as he walks us toward the bathroom. I'm thankful the bathroom has a large walk-in shower for us both to fit in. He reaches in, turns the shower on and breaks our kiss for a moment. I grind my hips forward, touching the tip of his hard erection. He growls as his fist tightens in my hair, turning my neck to the side as his teeth run along the curve.

I gasp as pleasured lightning courses through my veins with the need to feel his skin against mine. Orange soda consumes my senses and I straighten my legs, dropping to the floor. Adam's one arm reaches behind his neck and rips his shirt off the way only men do. My mouth waters as I mentally count his abs as if last time wasn't real. He kicks his pants aside and grabs my hips, backing me into the shower.

It's then I realize I didn't remove my thong since being in an admiration trance with his defined abs. My back hits the cool tiles as his fingers dig into my hips. Adam sucks my bottom lip with an aggressive perfect tug and I hear a tear. He tosses my thong aside and I gasp, *not* from the hot gesture, but because of that particular thong.

"That was *La Perla*." I tighten my arms around his neck bringing him closer.

"Now, it's on *La Floor-a*," he jokes and nips at my ear. "I'll replace it, Blondie."

I hike my leg around his waist and reach for the shampoo. I run my hands down his neck and over his shoulder muscles. I roll my hips forward and start to drag my nails down his chest. Adam spins me around like whiplash, and the cool tile shocks my breasts but causes heat to pool in my center. Such an intense combination. His hands trace the curve of my body with soap until one grasps my hip while the other teases my inner thigh. I reach down, bringing his hand where I'm begging for release. He complies and lightly circles my clit, miraculously knowing how much pressure I need. I bow into him away from the tile and he slips his finger inside while his other hand rolls my nipple.

A breathless moan escapes as the heel of his hand brushes my clit every time his two fingers pump inside me.

"Fuck, you're so wet," he growls in my ear. "Your pussy loves my fingers, doesn't it, Lauren?"

My body is on fire. The heat of the moment with the showerhead hitting my body sends sparks building as my stomach tightens. "I'm gonna come." I pant as he speeds up his rhythm and grinds himself on my ass.

My walls tighten around him as my orgasm pulses through my body. He holds me close until the wave slows. I spin around and meet his lips, desperate to feel him everywhere. He lines himself up with my entrance and holds my gaze for one last approval. I'm paralyzed in the moment. I can't find the strength to nod or lift myself forward, allowing him to enter. Immediately, I drop to my knees and look up at him. My hand grabs his cock as I lick it from base to tip. My thumb sweeps over his precum and his breath hitches. I meet his wide eyes and slowly take him into my mouth.

"Show me how you want to be sucked." I keep a steady rhythm and place his palm on the back of my head allowing him to control the pace.

"God, I didn't think you could get any sexier," he purrs. "Do you want me to fuck your mouth till you choke on my cock, Blondie?"

Damn, his filthy words are the match to our dynamite. I hum in acceptance and drag my nails down the back of his thighs, pulling him in deeper.

"Take every ounce of pleasure you need from my mouth, Charmer." I kiss the head of his swollen dick.

He loses control and starts to thrust in, hitting the back of my throat. I let him use my mouth and hold eye contact as my eyes water. He pulls out as I take a few deep breaths and flatten my tongue, unhinging my jaw to pull him even farther down my throat. His expression changes and I know he's about to finish if I continue. I suck him in as deep as I can and reach my hand up to roll his balls.

"Fuck," he grunts and goes to back up. "I'm going to paint your face with my cum."

I grab onto his ass to keep him thrusting.

"Lauren, this is your last warning." His voice is strained.

I don't back down to his polite gesture. Warm liquid hits my throat as he grunts. I swallow and he pulls out. His head is still bowed down to me as his arm supports him on the wall. I stand back up as pride gloats through me. I don't dish out blow jobs often, but when I feel someone deserves my talent, they sure as hell get it.

Vasectomy or not, I don't feel I can risk it. I also don't know him well enough to trust *he* won't get attached.

"That was an incredible surprise." He shuts the water off and hands me a towel. "There are women with no gag reflex, and then there is *your level* of no gag reflex."

"Just have to relax the jaw." I smirk and shrug.

We head to my bed, and I pull out clean clothes, realizing his shirt is covered in soda.

"I have an old university tee that might fit you." I hold up a long navy shirt.

"I'm fine walking a few blocks without a shirt."

I pull a shirt over my head and grab fresh panties. I feel my wet hair start to seep through my tee and wonder if I look like a drowned cat. I've always hated how I looked with damp hair all clumped together.

"Thank you for the fun afternoon." I smile, pulling my hair into a messy bun.

I watch his eyes drop to the hem of my rising shirt that exposes my panties.

"Yeah, I'd say I am a pretty good tour guide."

"You don't need a map, that's for sure." I keep a flirty tone as I bite my lip and noticeably let my eyes wander over his chiseled body.

"I'll gladly give you another eventful afternoon if you decide you want more explorations." He takes a step forward and the air leaves my body.

I want him on me.

Under me.

In me.

Now.

I can feel my underwear grow wet even though I just had an orgasm. His presence does this to my body. I feel my heart pick up and my lips tingle with the need to feel his on mine. Adam grabs my elbows and I know his smirk confirms he's reading my thoughts. I stare into his dilated eyes and wait for him to grab my neck and throw me on the bed, his lips painting my body as I moan his name. He needs to be the one to step away because I won't be able to resist letting him inside me without a condom this time. He takes a deep breath and clears his throat.

"Rain check those thoughts, Lauren." He steps back. "I need to go get some work finished."

"Maybe I should make a friend at some point," I think out loud.

"I could be your friend." He pauses. "We're on the same page. Friends with benefits?"

"You're being so cliché right now, and I'm about to kick you out of my place." I cross my arms trying to hide my smile.

"Who are you and where have you been all my life?" His hand meets his chest over his heart.

"Stop." I swat his arm and push him toward the door.

"Seriously though. You really don't want a relationship?"

"Do I seriously need a neon sign above my head saying *guarded?*" I sass.

"Maybe I'll buy you an open sign and you can let me know when you're available." His banter makes me laugh. I can appreciate quick wit.

"If we can keep us on a strict friend, better yet, an *acquaintance,* level, then this might work." I glance around the room as if it has more answers. "But..."

"But if either one of us begins to have the slightest urge for anything other than orgasms and laughs, we call it off." Adam steals the words right out of my mouth.

"I'm putting a lot of trust in you to not *need* me like you preach." I point my finger into his chest.

"Blondie, don't *want* something you'll never have." He grabs my finger, giving the tip of it a soft kiss.

"You can leave now." I open the door. "Let me give you my number so you can be my tour guide again."

He enters it into his phone. "I'll text you later."

"Any dick pics and I'll exile you," I call out down the hallway.

"You know my dick is too large to fit on your screen," he calls out and continues walking down the hallway.

Chapter 6

Adam

Relief flows through me when I manage to get everything finished for the week. I look down at my phone and have two hours until Lauren arrives. We are barely on a friend level and I want to keep it that way. Orgasms and laughs seem to be a great combination, so I'm glad she agreed to come over. My gut drops at the fear she still has an ulterior motive, like a snake knowing its victim and waiting until the right time to strike them down. My past is hard for me to ignore. I hope she is true to her word, but twenty-four is still young enough for the mind to change. I make a mental note to dive into why she is hell-bent against a relationship.

The lounge has soft, distant chatter from a few booths over as I make my way to the piano. Max nods from the bar as I pull out the leather piano bench. My fingers stretch before they rest upon the smooth keys. It's been a week too long since I've played. I open with a light riff then straight into classical jazz. The melody takes me back to my childhood with every note I play.

I've never had a lesson other than with Theo, our jazz pianist, who played here for years. I remember running around the hotel as a child and hearing the melodies. The sounds resonated with me and lit up my ears, drawing me in. The melodies became the only way to tame my hyperactive self. I'd sit in the back booth every chance I could when I managed to sneak down at night. I'd spend hours hiding until I fell asleep and got caught. Eventually, Theo taught me the basics, but the rest was by ear. My parents didn't show interest with my piano obsession. They assumed I was a busy boy, just wanting to smash on the keys instead of taking the time to listen. I would wait until no one was in here to be able to play. Every chance I could, I'd be on this bench.

My foot lifts off the pedals and I still embrace the elation that washed over me when I was finally tall enough to reach them. My parents were too busy with work to realize I kept up with playing. I don't boast about being a pretty kick-ass piano player. It's too personal to share and the only thing I am shy about.

I play a few songs and glance toward the bar. My fingers nearly fumble on the chords. There's a drink in Lauren's hand as she leans on the counter, talking to Max. If she spotted me playing, she didn't acknowledge it. I ease off the keys, slowly ending the song. I try to be discreet, standing to move away from the piano before she turns at the stopping of the music. Her head tilts back, laughing at something Max says. Jealousy pumps through me with the way he made her laugh. She pops a shiny plastic cherry in her mouth from the bowl.

I watch a few heads turn her way and their eyes linger. Her leggings hug her sculpted ass and instantly my dick twitches, wanting to run my tongue along the curve of hers. A flowy tank top hides her toned stomach. Her blonde hair is pulled up into a ponytail and I can't wait to wrap my hand around it. I shake my head and make my way to the bar, thankful how the dim light hides my growing cock.

"Do you always need to hit the alcohol before you see me?" I give her hair a light tug, causing her to squeak.

Cute.

"Extra cherries have me tasting sweeter."

My eyes widen at her boldness, and she clasps a hand over her mouth.

"Oh my gosh." She looks around to see if any customers heard her. "I hope you know I meant my lips."

So, Blondie does get bashful. I hold my tongue as long as I can and don't break eye contact so she knows exactly what's going through my mind. Her eyes narrow, warning me not to speak.

"Oh, both types of lips are sweet, Blondie." I watch her face match the color of the cherry bowl.

"For fuck's sake, guys." Max shakes his head, backing off.

Lauren clears her throat and slides some money across the bar to Max. Her stool pushes back, catching the attention of a few men as they tilt their heads to get a better look at her ass. I shoot them a glare and square my shoulders. Not that I really need to look any bigger than I am. Lauren has the supermodel height, but still, the top of her head rests at my chin. I place my hand on her back and she stiffens at the touch but doesn't knock my hand away.

On top of her intoxicating scent, I'm more worked up after watching other men want what isn't even fucking *mine*.

I restrain myself from pushing her against the door of my place and claiming her right here. I should at least feed her. Nodding toward the kitchen, she follows and takes a seat on the island. Her hands rest on the edge of the counter as her feet dangle.

"What do you feel like eating?" I step into her as she raises her hands to rest on my shoulders.

"Chinese takeout?" Her long legs wrap around me, but I grab her calves to tilt her on her back. "Or, you?" Her voice rasps with seduction.

"Takeout makes me feel like trash." I crawl on top of her. "How about I make you the best beef and broccoli you've ever had?"

"You're gloating to the takeout connoisseur here. Are you sure you're up for the challenge?" Her arms wrap around my neck and pull me to her lips.

She tastes sweet, like plastic cherries, as my tongue swirls with hers. I can't stomach eating them, but the lingering notes off her tongue have created a new kryptonite. My lips trail across her jaw and down her throat, stopping at the end of her shoulder. I grind into her as our breathing becomes heavy.

"I picked up condoms today," she whispers, leaning up to nip my ear.

"I did too." I pull out of her grasp and stand back up. "Let's eat first."

I take the ingredients out of the fridge along with a jar of maraschino cherries I purchased just for her. Lauren's eyes gleam with happiness as I hand her the jar.

"Do you have chocolate ice cream as well?" Her voice laces with hope.

"I don't. You can call room service if you want some brought up."

"I guess if I call it in now, it'll be the right consistency after we eat."

"You mean melted? Are you sure you don't just want a milkshake?"

"No one understands how it doesn't taste the same. I've accepted the fact that most don't eat it that way." She laughs as I send a text down to Aaron, our chef.

"It'll be up shortly." I set my phone back on the counter and start to prep the food.

Her teeth toy with her bottom lip, making me practice restraint. "Do you want help?"

"Only if you want to." My knife slices through vegetables as she hops down.

"Who taught you how to cook?"

"I did." I shrug. "I was sick of relying on others to bring meals to me."

"I never learned." I think that was a sigh as she reaches for a knife. "Lloyd only cooked frozen meals, and I was always so wrapped up in school assignments or my job to learn."

"How do you manage to stay skinny with a diet of plastic cherries, ice cream, and takeout?"

"Malnutrition, minimal food, and neglect through formative years can fuck up your metabolism." She twists the thin gold band on her pinkie finger, and it takes everything in me not to ask who the hell Lloyd is or any further questions about her confession.

"How about I give you your first lesson?"

Her smile returns as I spend the next twenty minutes showing her how to properly hold the knife and how using minimal ingredients doesn't make cooking as overwhelming as it seems.

Out of all my furniture options in my penthouse, she sits on the floor against the wall of floor-to-ceiling windows. Her spoon glides through the melted ice cream as her feet curl under her. I take a seat beside her. I haven't sat by the window admiring the view in years. Cars outline the streets like lights traveling through a circuit board. I wish I could find the same glimmer of enchantment that's passing through Lauren's eyes, but the city isn't for me. She rolls her shoulders back as her neck cracks.

"The gym kicked my ass today. I signed up for more classes."

"You didn't pass out on the coach, right?" I smirk.

"There's only one Viking stature man I can rely on to catch me." She laughs and I shake my head.

"In high school, our mascot was a Viking," I begin. "Every year, I'd dress up as one for the mascot during sports games. Which landed me any girl I wanted, and one teacher, might I add."

Her head shakes and the scent of her perfume fills the air. She sets the empty cup aside and turns to me. Her gaze seems lost. Her emeralds dim and the haunting look returns. As if she's replaying a memory or suppressing a question. I give her a moment to speak, but she doesn't.

Chocolate rests under the side of her lip. I bring the pad of my thumb to her bottom lip and trace the outline. Her breath hitches as my middle finger tilts her head and I grip her chin to pull her forward with my thumb and index finger. My body gravitates toward hers with the need to lay her down and cage her under me. Lauren smirks, catching me off guard. Her hands meet my chest as they firmly push me down. I look up with my famous grin and enjoy the view of her straddling me. As her hands reach up to let her hair down, I quickly flip us with hopes of hearing the little squeak she makes. Mission accomplished.

"I guess I'll just lie here bored."

"Yeah? You won't make a single sound or movement when I do this?" I whisper before licking the shell of her ear, and she gulps. "Or this?" My hand trails down her chest and I ghost my fingers along the exposed skin of her stomach.

"Wow, so gentle." Her voice goes flat, but I didn't miss the way her stomach tremored as my finger danced across it. "Is this how you took virginities back in the day?" She gives me a wicked grin and winks.

"I promise this will be more eventful than when you lost yours."

She tenses at my words and the grin wipes off her face. Only for a split second does her eyes glaze with a look I can't read.

It happens so fast that I would have missed it if I blinked. I try not to focus on what she never says.

"Then you better be able to make me come before I beat you to it." Her hands cup my face as she closes the space between us.

Her hand slides down her body into her leggings. As she lets out a moan, it distracts my plan to pin her arms up. Damn, she's clever. Or my pea brain is easily amused. I love how she's fighting for dominance. I'll let her have it after I'm finished making her come a few times. I break the kiss and pull back. My hand covers hers over the leggings when Buzzkill Number One knocks on my penthouse door.

A knock I know too well, and the timing couldn't have come at a worse moment. Lauren's eyes widen as her head snaps to the door. With a groan, I stand and readjust myself in my pants. I take a deep breath and give Lauren an apologetic look.

"I'm not expecting a visitor, but I can't ignore this one."

Puzzled, she nods, smoothing out her shirt as I open the door.

"Shouldn't you be in bed? Does your mother know you're at my door?"

Giant brown eyes stare up at me as she clutches her stuffed bunny. "James keeps getting out of bed and I haven't seen you all week. Momma said I can stay here since you don't have work tomorrow."

"Mallory, I'm a bit busy." I sigh but have already accepted the fact that telling my six-year-old niece *no* is a losing battle with her logical wits.

Mallory walks through the door under my arm and assesses Lauren. Her tiny head of brown curls bounces as she makes her way over.

"Wow, Uncle Adam." She turns back to me with an approving grin. "She looks like a princess."

Lauren smiles at her. "I love your princess pajamas. Who is your favorite?"

"They're all plausible for their own reasons, so I can't choose." Mallory takes a seat on the couch. "Come sit next to me. My uncle will make us popcorn and the three of us can watch a movie together."

The rank this child knows she has in my life is well used. I look toward Lauren, about to apologize, but her face holds utter shock, like most people when they hear Mallory speak. Lauren nods at Mallory with an impressed smile.

"Come on, Uncle Adam." Lauren takes a seat next to Mallory and points to the kitchen. "We'll choose a movie while you make the popcorn."

I'm dumbfounded. Loss for words with what is happening right now. Most women, when they have a brief encounter with Mallory or, lord forbid, enter a situation like this, see her as an annoyance. They'll smile and be polite, but I can see clearly through their gritted smile and raised eyebrows that they're lying. I don't fault them for it either. Mallory holds a place in my heart, but they aren't with me to deal with *her*.

"Are you sleeping here, princess?" Mallory snuggles into Lauren as if she's known her all her life.

Lauren lifts her arm to let Mallory snuggle in. I watch closely at Mallory's comfortable body language. She has always been very picky about who she lets in her *"personal space"* but welcomes Lauren instantly.

"No, I have my own place. My name is Lauren, and unfortunately, I'm not a real princess."

"You're going to miss out, Princess Lauren." Mallory chooses to ignore the princess rejection. "My uncle makes the best French toast ever!"

"You'll have to eat an extra piece for me then. With lots of syrup." Lauren giggles and I throw my hands up in defeat.

"I'll have you confirm that with him." Mallory laughs. "And I know a princess in disguise won't blow her cover. Your secret's safe."

I hurry to the couch, mortified by the many things my niece could say to scare Lauren off. Her filter lacks when it comes to embarrassing situations. I set the popcorn on Mallory's lap and lift my arm on the edge of the couch, beginning to rub the back of Lauren's neck. Mallory picks up the remote, looking back and forth between Lauren and me.

"I'm going to hit play. If you need to say anything to each other, please do it now," she directs as if she is about to start a meeting. "I don't want to keep pausing this."

"I'm sorry, I could have walked her back if you didn't sit and make conversation." I feel a pang of guilt on both ends for the girls.

I know I've been neglecting Mallory this week and I know Lauren doesn't do well on a personal level. But if this situation is bothering Lauren, then she is one hell of an Oscar-winning actress. I still don't know her well enough to know if she has an ulterior motive.

"You can't kick this adorable child out. She wants time with her uncle." A laugh radiates in Lauren, and I commit the beautiful sounds to memory. "Also, she'd probably win any debate you throw at her."

"Mamma says I'd make a good lawyer." Mallory smiles.

"You do whatever makes you happy, Mals." My tone is serious when she talks about her future. The last thing I want is for her to end up even more indoctrinated in this life if her free-spirited soul doesn't want it.

"A job isn't worth doing if it gives no joy or purpose to you," Lauren adds and gently brushes the hair out of Mallory's face.

How maternal for someone who doesn't *want* love.

"I'm pressing play now." Mallory digs into the popcorn and becomes transfixed by the screen.

Thirty minutes later, Mallory is passed out against my arm. I watch her even breaths as her bunny is clenched to her chest. With her daily high energy, I'm surprised she made it until eight thirty. Lauren brushes Mallory's hair out of her face again and smiles at me.

"I'm going to head home. Thank you for the food and laughs." She stands up and I go to move. "I can let myself out. I don't want her to wake up."

"Sorry again for the interruption. She's very persistent."

"It's a good quality to have. Please don't ever apologize for putting a child first. She has clearly missed you this week." Her smile is warm and hits me hard in the chest. "I'll text you tomorrow if you want to get together." She winks and heads out the door.

I carry Mallory to the guest bed and call it an early night myself.

>=======<

I picked up the box my cousin left at the lobby counter. I sent a thank-you text for the favor since I didn't want to wait on shipping. The overcast sky dulled everything besides my attitude. Lauren was beyond sweet with Mallory last night. I smile as I enter the ice cream shop and replay my morning with Mallory. She repeated on a loop how much she liked Lauren. Mallory had spent all morning until she left, going over her plans to tell everyone in school how she met a real princess. I pull out my phone and wait for an answer.

"Hey, are you home? I'm walking around the corner if you want to hang out."

"Yeah, I'll buzz you up." Her voice seems rushed.

She opens the door, standing fresh faced with her hair piled on top of her head. Her smile is sleepy as my eyes drop to her long bare legs and T-shirt, covering just below her ass. I question if lingerie will even turn me on the same way this has got me going. Her knee bends forward and her hip pops to the side as she opens the door wider. I walk through her place, unapologetically eye fucking her as I set the items on the counter.

"I woke up from a nap and didn't have time to get ready." Her cheeks hold a tinge of red as she tries to fix her lopsided hair.

Her blush is fucking adorable. My hands rest on her hips and I shake my head. Her sweet scent engulfs my senses. "You look hot as hell right now. Don't apologize. You work tomorrow night, right?"

"Yeah, I have four shifts this week."

"I picked up some ice cream on the way here."

Her teeth clasp down on her bottom lip, but I refrain from tugging on it. I watch curiosity fill her green eyes as they linger over the smooth silver box and ribbon. I smirk as her mouth parts when she realizes where it's from. She doesn't say a word.

"This is for you." I hand over the box.

"I-I can't accept this." Her fingers brush over the La Perla letters. "You really don't have to replace my underwear."

"I wanted to. I'm well aware how much our shower cost you. Plus..." I flash my charming smile. "It's a gift for me too, if you choose. Though right now, you're looking extremely delectable like this."

"Adam." Her voice was laced with concern.

Her fingers play with the satin ribbon as if she's debating whether to open it or hand it back.

"It's just me being a man of my word," I assure her. "I told you I would replace the panties, and I did. I also came across another item that matched perfectly. Please, just open the box."

Her eyes go wide as she pulls out the delicate emerald-green lingerie set. The smooth fabric lies perfectly as she places the bra and panties on the counter.

"You really didn't have to." Her head shakes and I know right then, she's not using me for my money. "They're beautiful, but I don't need any gifts. Especially at that price."

"The green matches your eyes." I bring my hands up to cradle her jaw. "I had to replace what I ruined. As for the other piece, consider it a birthday gift."

"My birthday isn't until next month."

I smile, satisfied at the win and her jaw drops.

"What day?" I press as she walks backward out of the kitchen, shaking her head. "Come on, you can at least let me buy you a Shirley Temple or melted ice cream."

"The end of August. But I'm scheduled to work that day anyway." She rolls her eyes and I lean down, tasting her sweet lips on mine. "Did Mallory enjoy her morning with French toast?"

Mallory? My damn chest warms again with Lauren's thoughtfulness.

I pull back and search her eyes. Is this a personal interest or friendly acquaintance question?

"She did. Her younger brother is going through a sleep problem or something."

"Hmm." She drags her fingers down my chest and brings her lips to my ear. "I haven't been able to sleep well in a while either."

There we go. My hands latch on to her waist and I walk her backward until the back of her knees hit the edge of the bed. I lean forward, giving her no other option other than to bend and fall down onto the bed. I crawl over her body as my forearms cage her.

"Too much built-up tension keeping you awake, Blondie?" Her teeth sink into her bottom lip with hunger as she nods. "I'm sure you've taken matters into your own *hands* a time or two."

"My bag of goodies doesn't expel my energy the way you do." She leans up and takes my bottom lip between her teeth and tugs.

Fuck, I need her.

Fuck, I want to savor her.

Fuck, why am I thinking this much?

"Bag of goodies?" My eyes dart around, looking for their hidden home as I picture Lauren getting herself off.

"Another day." Her legs wrap around me as the heels of her feet attempt to push my shorts down. "Right now, I need *you* to deplete my body of energy."

I capture her lips in mine and kick my shorts off. My hand feathers up her leg, bypassing her pussy. My thumb presses into her hip as I tighten my grip. A breathy moan passes through my ear as her teeth nip at it. Our erratic breathing syncs and we haven't even hit the tip of the iceberg. I reach under her shirt and cup her breast, feeling her arch into my touch. I roll her hard nipple in my fingers, capturing her gasp in my mouth.

"I take it I'm not boring you?" I smirk and travel my fingers down the valley of her breasts, continuing south until they brush over her panties.

"I'm somewhat engaged," she fibs with a flushed face and skin painted in goose bumps.

The wetness of her underwear coats my fingers through the fabric. How responsive she is to my touch is a turn-on in itself. My teeth sink into her neck as I gently drag a finger up and down her wet slit. A small whimper escapes her lips as my finger flicks her clit over her panties. Her body jerks as I connect with the right spot and her knees spread open wide. A wicked grin forms on my face as I kiss my way down her body, never breaking eye contact. I skim my nose along her folds, breathing in her scent. Her hands reach for my face to pull me up.

"Dammit, Adam!" Her ragged breaths are hoarse as her pupils dilate. "I need you to fuck me right now. Give it to me mercilessly." Her begging twitches my cock as it throbs. "I need to feel you."

"Oh, believe me. I'll live up to merciless." My thumb moves her panties to the side to expose her swollen mound. "After my tongue has you all over it."

Before she can protest, my mouth covers her pussy. My intention to take things slow goes out the window when she grabs my hair and releases a loud moan. I've only sucked her a few times, but her hips buck and her back arches off the bed. Her orgasm flows through her body and I push her hips down, continuing the steady motion with my tongue. Incorrigible sounds fill the room and she trembles, ripping my hair from the roots. My adrenaline runs high as I'm fueled by how much her body reacts to my touch. I'm throbbing so bad it hurts, but I don't let up until her heel pushes into the bed and she breaks contact. Her hands fly above her head as her heaving chest continues.

"Fuck, you should see how sexy you are right now." I don't miss a beat.

I roll a condom on, throw her legs on my shoulder, and thrust in.

"God, that's deep," she moans as I keep my steady rhythm.

Her legs bend and I let them fall to the mattress. I lean forward and hiss as her hands rake down my chest. It's a euphoric mix of pain with this pleasure. A squeak comes out of her mouth as I grab her wrists, pinning them above her head to use for support. Her hair is half out of her bun and splayed out around her. I watch mesmerized as her breasts bounce with each thrust until she tightens around me.

"I'm—" I swallow her words with my mouth as her body locks.

She whimpers as her lips still against mine. I slow my pace as she rides out the euphoria. I pull out and she flips over, opening her legs and backing her ass up against me.

"Good girl," I purr, grabbing her hips up as my dick rubs against her ass. "You know just how I like it."

"Try to fuck me like it's *not* your first time, okay?" Her head peeks over her shoulder, sporting a devilish grin.

Fuck, this woman can keep a man humble.

Blondie doesn't know what she's asking for.

I thrust hard and grind myself upward to her ass, stretching her out. My fist spins around the loose bottom strands of her hair as I pull her head back, showing no mercy. I know she won't be able to take one step tomorrow and not think of me. Lauren lowers onto her forearms, but I push her head down to the mattress as her arms move to her sides.

"My god. You're good. At. This." She manages to speak between each pound. I bury myself deeper than I've ever been with a woman, and I watch her hand move underneath to rub herself. I want her to have one more orgasm before I let myself finish. I ease up on my pace and bend down to her ear.

"You're so fucking wet for my cock, Blondie. Take what you need from me." I drag my tongue up her neck and bite behind her ear. "Be a good girl and spread your legs wider. Show me how well you can rub that swollen clit."

She whimpers and hikes one leg higher for more access. "That's a good girl. Surrender to the pleasure it brings you."

I pick up the pace as my hand slaps her ass. Hard. The sting makes her yelp, but she tightens around my cock. Her head turns to the side as a silent scream exits her mouth. I feel my balls tighten and I let myself go.

Slowly, I slide out and drop beside her on the bed, catching my breath. She turns to me with a sated smile and tired eyes.

"I thought our first time was mind blowing, but..." She rolls onto her back to look up at the ceiling and I watch her full breasts rise as her chest fills with air.

"I know." My eyes dart back and forth from her breasts and her face while trying to decipher whatever is going through her mind.

"Yeah, you—" She clears her throat. "I think I should be able to sleep tonight."

Chapter 7

Lauren

"You had to sit through a kid's movie and didn't receive an orgasm after?" I tuck my feet underneath me as my best friend Rachel's voice flows through the phone.

"I didn't mind." It was the truth. "You should have seen how happy she was to see her uncle. I wasn't going to ruin her night."

"You know you have other peen options that don't have family members to kill the mood. Keep your options open, Ren."

"Believe me when I say he made up for it the next day." I *could* go for any guy, but our arrangement works. "I'm busy with work. I know he's on the same page with not asking for more."

"I'm just saying, I would have put her to bed and still took a ride on that stallion." I can picture what she's doing on the other end of the phone, shaking her head and biting her thumbnail as her short red hair sways.

"I wouldn't have sex with her so close. I'd wake her and she'd be traumatized." I feel my cheeks heat at my own words.

"Yeah, you're pretty loud. It's great." She laughs. "I am taking a weekend trip to see you soon. There are a couple clubs I want to hit up."

"I bet there is." Rachel was notorious for all types of clubs. "I may pass, depending on what you have in mind." I've seen everything from gay bars, sex clubs and some involving dressing up as aliens and dragons.

"You know what I always tell you—" she starts.

"You can't judge a peen before it aims to make you scream," we both say in harmony.

"I've found my lane, thanks to you." I smile and try to suppress my surfacing dragon experience.

"I still feel you left the dragon club too soon to judge it."

"Rachel, I'm going to hang up."

We finish our conversation and I reach for my yoga mat. I need a good stretch from my intensive workouts and from Adam. I lean forward, grabbing my feet and wince. When I told him to go hard, he flew past the home run and branded my body in the best way. I know he will pass through my mind with every step tonight.

The problem with alternating day and night shifts is your body never gets to adjust to a proper sleep routine. I hope I can switch to all days soon. I finish stretching, take a shower, and gather my scrubs and food for work.

My phone buzzes as *Charmer* lights up the screen.

Charmer: I hope you're ok for your shift tonight.

Me: Why wouldn't I be?

Charmer: Wasn't sure after yesterday.
Me: I know, I thought I told you to go hard.
Charmer: Hey, that says more about you than me. We both know the size tool I pack.
Me: Shut up. Heading to work. –
Yes, you'll pass through my mind with every step. Not that your ego needs to be stroked.
Charmer: I'll give you something to stroke
Me: You're on your own tonight. *Attached racy bikini photo*

By the end of the week, I'm wiped.

"Lauren," Tessa greets me in the hallway. "You alright, girl?" I take it she sees the dark circles on my exhausted face.

"After a twenty-four-hour shift, a twelve-hour recovery wasn't quite enough." I force a laugh and it turns into a yawn. "I am so happy this is my last shift." Thankfully, double twelve-hour shifts don't happen too often, or I'd switch to clinical.

"Are you seeing Adam again on your days off?"

I have been filling her in between patients about how our arrangement has been.

"Oh, shoot!" I pull out my phone. "I forgot to text him back. He asked if I wanted to swing by after my shift."

"Just acquaintances, huh?" Tessa smirks and watches me text a reply. "You've worked your ass off the past few days and yet still will find energy to get laid."

"I thrive with a full schedule." I look at my phone and see he asked me to bring a comfy change of clothes. "Plus, his bedroom skills are worth giving up hours of sleep." I'm glad

I always keep a change of gym clothes in my bag just in case I deal with a trauma that triggers the need to burn off steam. It saves me not needing to swing by my place after my shift.

A night with Adam has been playing through my mind all afternoon and has been powering me through this last hour. I finish up with patients and grab a chart to wrap up an earlier patient. I'm already off the clock, but I like to release my patients if it is within a reasonable time. I glance over the results confirming what I expected.

"Ava Rose." I smile, walking into the room. "That's a beautiful name for a beautiful little girl." The nine-year-old gives me a half smile. "It appears you have a urinary tract infection, sweetie."

She glances at her guardian, who bluntly informed me earlier that Ava is a foster child. "I will write Ava a prescription and she needs to take it for seven days. Does she have any known allergies?"

Ava holds her panicked gaze at her foster guardian.

"No allergies." The woman shoots a pointed look at Ava as if giving her a warning.

Ava swallows and her feet swing off the bed as her guardian returns to looking at her phone. Am I sensing tension, or am I just too tired to focus? It's quiet as I write the prescription and look up for a final word.

"Do you have any other questions?" I look toward the guardian still staring at her phone and annoyance boils my blood.

"Do I get to sleep here tonight?" The young voice is almost hopeful.

"That's not necessary. Your antibiotics should make you feel better by morning," I assure her.

Her foster guardian stands and takes Ava's hand to help her hop off the bed. Ava stiffens at the contact and my heart drops. I remember the feeling of a foreign touch. I still have yet to cuddle or accept tender touches from someone.

"I promise you'll feel better. Go get a good night's sleep and drink lots of water, sweetie."

She silently nods with eyes filled with pain and hurries out.

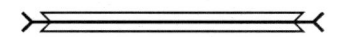

I'm twenty minutes later than Adam expects as the cab pulls up in front of the hotel. I sling my workbag over my shoulder and attempt to fix my messy bun as I walk through the hotel lobby. I instantly regret not changing out of my maroon scrubs at work when I spot Adam talking to an older gentleman in a tailored suit. His tall stature and dark-brown eyes give me one guess who the man is. An older clone of the man I'm toying around with. I don't meet parents. But with the desperate look on Adam's face asking for compliance, I walk over because his dick is hard to turn down.

"Crazy shift?" Adam raises his eyebrows as his eyes trail over my body.

"Try a crazy week. My shift ran late again and I didn't change." I adjust my bag on my shoulder in an attempt to slow my words down. "I might fall asleep in the elevator."

I realize I forgot to remove my badge as the man squints at my chest. "Practitioner," he muses and assesses me. "That takes years."

"I'm a fast learner, sir."

"You look too young."

"Age doesn't measure competence, sir."

"Well, you're interacting with my *son*—" He stifles a laugh and it comes out as a grunt.

"Who speaks nothing but highly of you," I cut him off and raise my eyebrows.

He pauses, holding eye contact until a small smile turns upward. "Call me George." He nods. "I hope you keep my son in line with your quick remarks. Good night, you two."

Adam takes my hand, jolting me to the elevator as if he can't escape the lobby fast enough. His eyes roam over me, trying to decipher something, or maybe I've grown two extra heads. I sense he wants to talk but keeps rubbing the back of his neck instead. We enter his suite and if I wasn't so tired, I'd call him out on the weirdness.

"I really need to shower, if you don't mind." I glance around the perfectly decorated cream walls and expensive furniture.

"Yeah, take as long as you need. Did you have a chance to eat?"

I shake my head.

"I'll whip something up for you. Go clear your head from today." His smile shouldn't make my stomach flip.

I shower in his guest room and change into my workout gear. My body aches but I am determined to make sure I have no energy left to spend. Hopefully, I'll be able to sleep past 5:08 tomorrow. I follow the smell of grilled food into the kitchen as Adam sets a wrap in front of me, along with a large glass of water. I take a seat next to him on a barstool.

"Did you actually make this?" It looks like something room service would bring.

"Yeah, it's a grilled chicken and veggie wrap." He takes a long sip of his beer, still in his suit. "Do you not like them?"

"I do." I smile and take a bite. "This just tastes and looks so good that I thought a chef made it."

He chuckles and the sound resonates in my core. "Cooking is not as hard as you make it out to be."

"You look a lot like your father."

"I'm sorry you had to meet him unannounced." He shakes his head. "I don't introduce many people to him, and I know our boundaries."

"You didn't introduce me. You looked mortified." I silently giggle, recalling his eyes moving back and forth between George and me.

"Lauren, you held your own in a respectful manner and didn't take shit from him. That was fucking sexy."

"Does that mean I get an extra orgasm after our workout?"

"I admire your ambition, but you don't need those clothes for tonight."

"So, I get an orgasm first?"

"Remember how I mentioned I like to hike and see the coolest clouds when I called the other night?"

I recall a brief mention when he called after one of my long shifts but was too tired to really care. I feel my face scrunch and try to piece what he's not saying. "Adam, just tell me the plan so we can move on to orgasms."

"I'd like to take you hiking early in the morning up Mount Tamalpais. There are only certain days the special fog will cooperate, and tomorrow is supposed to be one of them."

"Special fog?" *Weirdo.* "So you want me to crash here to ensure I wake up in the morning?"

"Yeah." He leans back, prepared to flinch from my unknown reaction. "Is that too much for us?"

"No, that's fine, numbnuts." I hop off the barstool and put my plate in the sink. "You could have logically told me that instead of baiting me. I would have brought a sweatshirt and snacks too."

"So, you're not mad? We said no sleepovers."

"This is a bit different. We know the rules and where our feelings stand." I fight my yawn. "I can also sleep in your guest bed when I'm ready to pass out."

"Do you want to lie in bed and we can watch a *Charmed* rerun?"

"Putting you through *Charmed* is something a girlfriend would do." I wink. "Let me *give you* a memorable show." I turn around and begin to leave a trail of my clothes on the floor as he follows me to the guest room.

The weight of a heavy arm holds me in place in my dream. Or am I awake? I feel a hard length grind against my ass as a hand cups my breast. Nope, definitely awake. I am still processing the moment. I don't share a bed and I don't cuddle. Teeth meet the shell of my ear and hitch my breath. He doesn't seem mad that we fell asleep in the bed. Which could be bad. The last thing I want to give up is orgasms this good too soon.

I should jump out of bed, but as his hand travels south and his crafty fingers brush over my folds to spread them, I feel my top leg lift to allow him more access. Slowly, he circles my clit without saying a word. His motion is steady until my labored breathing becomes erratic. I reach my arm back to tangle in his soft hair. A breathless scream leaves my mouth as I come, and seconds later, his fingers stop.

"Good morning." He sits up and reaches for his sweats.

"We shared a bed."

"It appears we both fell asleep, and you slept through the alarm."

I don't try to hide my eyes trailing over his chiseled abs. *A fucking statue of a man who should be carved in marble.*

"I never sleep past five."

"Well, you did."

I check the clock myself with disbelief.

"Luckily, my personal wake-up call worked." His grin is wicked and if he hadn't thrown a hoodie in my face, I'd be riding his. "We have to hurry if we want to make it in time."

I groan and fall back onto the pillow. "What if I don't?"

"Trust me, you do." He offers his hands and I take them.

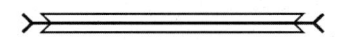

We don't speak the first twenty minutes of the climb. Adam seems lost in thought, but I'm on high alert for wild animals and rattlesnakes. Yes, even in the damp morning I'm terrified a snake will be slithering about. I wanted to give up the first ten minutes of this hike. My body and lungs felt like they were going to tap out. Almost an hour in, I halt our steady pace and sit on a large rock and reach for my water. The cold, damp mist seeps through my leggings and chills my bones.

Adam senses I've stopped and turns back to me. If his fit ass has a tired, flushed face, I can only imagine how unattractive I must look. He pulls his water from his bag, props his leg on the rock and takes a long drink. If someone snapped a photo of him, it could easily be used in a magazine or a scene for a sports commercial. He hands me a granola bar and eats half of his bar in one bite. What a sexy beast.

"I am thoroughly impressed, Blondie." He grins. "You hiked farther than I expected without stopping or complaining."

"You mean that your other play toys didn't make it as far as me?"

"They won't even walk on the grass." He winces. "Don't call yourself a play toy."

"You're not feeling more for me, right?" My eyes scan his face as my heart picks up again.

"No." He rushes his words. "I'm saying you're more respectable. You work for what you want, you know what you want in life and hold yourself accountable. You don't worry about ruining your shoes by walking on grass. I only need you for sex, but it's a bonus that you're a cool person."

"Good." Relief gushes through my chest and I relax my shoulders. I take one last sip of my water and stand. "Let's keep it that way."

We continued our hike for what seemed like a lifetime. Okay, I might be exaggerating a little. I have no idea how I'm going to make it back down, but I don't dare complain. We reach a landing as Adam stops. He turns around with a smile.

"We are right around 2,500 feet above sea level." He is beaming more than I've ever seen.

"Okay, it's foggy." I don't understand.

"You're about to become a fogaholic."

I don't bother replying and just follow him to see what this is all about. Not long after, I'm frozen in place. My eyes fool my brain and I don't believe what I'm seeing. I stand above the fog as if I'm in an airplane looking below. The most beautiful waves of fog dance through the tips of the trees. I'm transfixed on the thick ocean-style waves encompassing us. It's another world up here. A breathtaking one I never knew existed. I glance around and land my eyes on Adam, who is staring down at me. The altitude must have kicked into high gear and steals the breath from my lungs.

"Would you say you're a fogaholic yet?" His eyes soften and hold mine.

"It's unreal." I shake my head as my eyes magnetize back to the rolling fog waves. "Definitely a *deathbed* memory."

"A what?"

"I've seen more people take their last breath than I can count. They all mention something they wish they had done or think about a moment they'll never forget." I shrug. "This moment is mine to commit to memory."

His hands cup my face, and he looks to my eyes for approval. My arms instinctively wrap around his neck as I bring my gaze to his lips. Adam smirks just before gently pressing his mouth to mine. There's no urge. No hunger. Just a soft, still kiss and I lose track of time. It's probably out of pity after that weird deathbed truth bomb I dropped on him. But up on this mountain surrounded by magic, I accept it. He pulls back without a word and looks around. I focus over his shoulder as his head follows. There are a few people with their cameras and tripods set up in the distance. One guy waves us over with excitement.

"Do you know him?" I ask and walk in their direction.

"I'm part of a San Francisco fog group in order to know the best hiking times to see this. I'm sure he's part of it."

"Yo, dudes." The photographer points to his screen. "Do you mind if I submit this online?"

I look at the small screen and my heart jumps. It's one of the coolest pictures I'll ever be a part of. Anyone who doesn't see this for themselves would think it's photoshopped. There Adam and I are, on the edge of a mountain. A beautiful silhouette as his mouth claims my face. The fog rolls through and exposes the tip of the trees just as the sun starts to glow in the distance. I'm speechless. Adam leans down beside me, taking in the image. A grin spreads wide across his face and he nods.

"I'm cool with it if she is." Adam nudges me.

"Yes, please send that in. Any place would be crazy not to use it." I shake my head. "I would really like a copy of that to hang in my place."

"Yeah, I'm having an art expo in a couple weeks, and it would be great if you both could join." He hands over his business card. "You two make a great couple."

"Oh, no. He and I are just friends." I feel my cheeks heat, unable to look at Adam. "Acquaintances, actually."

"See you in a few weeks, *just friends*." He chuckles and starts to pack up his gear. "I photograph weddings too."

"Acquaintances!" Adam calls out as we walk away.

Despite the altitude stealing my breath, I catch him staring at me on the hike down. I make a mental note to make sure we stay nothing more than acquainted friends.

Chapter 8

Adam

Two days pass and I haven't heard from Lauren. By the time our morning meeting ends, it's well into my lunch hour. I head down to the lobby and see Max entering. His ball cap is backward and he wears a content smile. A grocery bag slung over his shoulder and my nephew, James, sits in the stroller. For a guy who works until one a.m. and commits to teaching a kickboxing class at nine in the morning, I wonder how he's not burned out. If he is, he doesn't show it.

"Hey, Mr. Mom," I greet my best friend.

"Feels like it some days, but Kelsie needs all of our support." The three of us grew up together and lately, Max has been filling in to help with my sister's kids. He walks toward me as James leans back trying to climb out of his stroller. Max unwraps a granola bar and hands it to him, buying us a minute to talk. Everything seems so natural to this man. Except James isn't even his child.

"Hey James." I ruffle his brown hair and look up at Max. "Where's Kels?"

"She had a meeting today with the lawyer to go over her and Benson's custody. I took this little guy to the gym day care while I taught and then picked up food to throw in the Crock-Pot for his mama." He smiles and changes his voice to a kid-friendly tone, even though my nephew's only concern is his snack.

"I thought Benson was signing over parental rights?" My heart leaps to my throat and my urge to punch her ex in the face grows.

"He has a few requests before he commits to severing ties."

"Why does no one keep me informed about this shit anymore?" I know I haven't been giving enough attention to my sister or her kids lately.

"You've been busy tasting Shirley Temple and consumed with your constant workload." He shrugs like it's not a big deal. "I'm single and it's Kelsie. Since the elevator fiasco as kids, you know the promise I made to her."

Is she *still* using that moment to her advantage?

"I'm just saying, best friend or not, you shouldn't have to rearrange your day for someone else's kids." This man never sleeps and still manages to smile and fill a parental role.

"Come on, they're like family to me too."

I vow to not associate with Lauren for the next couple of days and focus on family. She wasn't supposed to take up this much of my free time. Yet, I enjoy my time with her. That would be a red flag if I knew she wasn't as strict as me with our rules.

"Why didn't my mom watch the kids?"

"Helen went with Kelsie, and you had your meeting."

"Thanks, Max. Kelsie better know how lucky she is to have you as a friend." His eyes flash something unreadable for a moment but my stomach grumbles and I don't care to ask. "Mallory and James love you. Sometimes I wish you were our brother instead of Emmett."

"Emmett will come around. He just needs time."

"He's had plenty." I don't bother to hide my annoyance. "I'm grabbing lunch. Do you want something?"

"Nah, I better get this little guy down for a nap before Mallory gets home from camp." He heads to the elevator.

I make my way across the street to grab a sandwich. I order and take a seat reflecting on the past years.

If there was any guy out there too good for anyone, it would be Max. I've never asked why he hasn't settled down, but I don't need him asking me that question either, even though he witnessed my main reason. I think back to the days we'd go to clubs or on my parents' yacht to party it up with college women. Kelsie would turn her face up in disgust and lecture us about being better. He started to leave me to party on my own while his friendship grew even stronger with my sister. That was also around the time Kelsie met her piece-of-shit husband.

The door chimes, pulling me out of thought as my grandfather enters and takes the seat across from me. Meeting here has been our weekly tradition since I started working for the company. I stir my coffee, knowing his next sentence verbatim.

"You ordered my favorite, right?"

"Pastrami on rye, no onions." The staff knows our order without us having to open our mouths. Over the years, it's never changed.

"You missed last week." His eyes crinkle inquisitively. "You've never rescheduled our lunch a day in your life."

"I promised a friend to be a tour guide." I choose my words carefully. "I didn't want to cancel since they're new to the city."

"Ah, yes." His smile has been passed on for generations and I know why Lauren calls me Charmer. "The princess practitioner."

"Lauren." An odd warmth waves through me as her name leaves my lips. "And she's nothing like a princess."

But my list of past women had been princesses. Thinking that their prestigious family names entitled them to be waited on. The women expected to be spoiled for the lame-ass reason that they *deserve* it. Lauren gives her time to people. She wasn't worried about having a full face of makeup or needing her hair and outfit done to the nines in order to walk outside. She wore confidence as her sex appeal and holy fuck does it work. Even though her taste in lingerie is pricey, she isn't flashy in the least.

"You really like this woman." My grandfather leans forward with a smug grin.

When did our food arrive?

"It's not what you think," I defend and pick up my sandwich. "She's barely even a friend."

"It's exactly what I think."

"And that is?"

"Now, what kind of wise old man would I be if I told you?" He stares through me, reading more than I think I can hide. "I need to start traveling again. The legacy we've created needs to transfer responsibilities."

This is either about our new Aspen building or the dreaded great-grandchild talk again.

"How about the days when we used to not focus so much on work and expansion?" I changed the subject. "Remember when we'd all venture to the cabin a few times a year? We don't need more responsibility *transfers* yet."

"You're right." He clears his throat. "We need to connect as a family again."

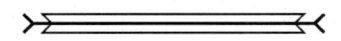

>=====<

The smell of rubber and the clanking of weights surround me as I make my way to the fitness classroom. I set up the different circuits for my class as a blonde ponytail and long legs catch my attention passing by the door. I peek my head around the corner. A yoga mat is tucked under her arm and I can't fight my smile when I noticed the oversized hoodie she's wearing. The one she swore she would return. Lauren catches up with one of the females from my class. The short one that my niece could surpass in height next year.

"Lauren," I call out, but she doesn't turn around.

The tiny one looks my way and points, confused. Lauren's friend turns with a smirk and tugs on Lauren's hand before making her way over. Lauren slowly turns and reluctance fills her stride. Is she avoiding me? I head back into the room to finish setting up. I should really get better at learning people's names, but people are always alternating in drop-in classes. The red tinge on Lauren's cheeks is either from yoga or blushing. The fact she was reluctant tells me it's the second. But why? She's had no problem telling me exactly what she wants in the bedroom and now she won't even say hi.

"Whatcha thinking so hard about, coach?" The tiny one cuts through my thoughts.

I need to get a grip. That's the second time I've zoned out about Lauren today.

"Hey!" I smile. "I'm trying to go over each circuit."

"It's Tessa, by the way." She laughs and sets her bag down. "I work with *Lauren*, who has only taken this class *twice*."

"I'm Adam." I don't know why I gave out my name.

Her eyes go wide and dart back and forth between Lauren and me. "No. No way you're *that* Adam." She clearly reads the mortified confirmation across Lauren's face. "Why would a hotel heir teach here? I take it you do it for stamina and not money?"

"Okay." Lauren raises her hands. "I do not talk about you except when Tessa asks a brief question at work." Someone's getting defensive and it's the cutest thing I've seen in a while. "And I answer brief."

"Nice hoodie." I ignore her defense and flash a wicked grin. "I remember the moment before I tossed it to you." Her mouth drops and fuck me if I'm not enjoying every moment of this. "Are you cheating on me with yoga, Blondie?"

"After the hike and various activities, I needed something easier on the body this week."

Tessa chuckles. "Yeah, coach doesn't seem like the *easy* type."

"Okay." Lauren turns and looks over her shoulder at the door. "I'm going home."

I can't focus the entire class. I jog past Lauren's on the way home and see her light on. Should I knock? She would have texted or invited me if she wanted to see me. I do mental calculations of the time frame we've fooled around and conclude it's that time of the month. A time I have no idea about besides bitchiness or a crying sister through the years. I'm well acquainted with the cravings and mood swings growing up with a sister who's barely a year older.

God, I feel fucking dumb right now. I should just go home and sleep because work is going to be hell tomorrow. Instead, I find myself jogging down another street to collect a few things. I reach her door with a tub of gelato and three different bags of potato chips. She gave me the code the other day so I didn't have to keep buzzing up. Her eye covers the peephole when I knock, and a moment later, she lets me in. Her fresh face smiles in confusion. The black sleep shorts match her tank top and instantly I want to run my tongue along her exposed collarbone. She ties her wet hair up and my eyes drop to the sliver of skin as her tank top lifts. I clear my throat. That's not why I'm here.

"Unannounced booty call?" she states, confused.

"Nah, I just came to drop this off and apologize if I humiliated you tonight."

"You didn't have to buy me ice cream." She smiles and takes it anyway.

"I've observed my sister long enough."

"What?" She laughs.

"Math is my job. My calculations have me thinking it's that time of the month."

"I guess that's why they pay you the big bucks." She giggles and instinctively I want to wrap her in a hug.

I refrain.

"Anyway, it's late and you work tomorrow, so I'll let you sleep." I reach for the door handle.

"Isn't doing this something a boyfriend would do?"

"I wouldn't know." I shrug. "Obviously I don't mean it in that way. I'll call this my daily act of kindness."

"Anything to fill your ego, Charmer." She smirks and steps forward, crowding my space.

"When you brand me with a name like that, it's only right I live up to it." I place my finger under her chin and tilt her lips to mine. Despite the fact I know what's happening in her panties, my dick responds to her soft kiss. "How does period sex work?"

She pulls away, shaking her head. "That's one experience I'll never know."

"Noted." I open the door. "Night, Blondie."

Chapter 9

Adam

"Please ask her, Uncle Adam." Giant brown saucers plead for the umpteenth time today.

"She has a busy work schedule, Mallory."

"It's my *birthday*. I want a princess to come to the cabin with us," she huffs and paces the floor. "One, you haven't even asked yet, and second, this day is not about *you*." She stops in the center of the room and places her hands on her hips. "Dare I ask Martin to pull up her contact information?"

How the hell she knows Martin is our guy for background checks and clearing employees beats me. The child is six, going on thirty-six with how she handles business. Fucking family genetics run through and through.

"Okay," I sigh. "I'll give her a text." She doesn't seem convinced.

"I can take her number and deal with the arrangements." God, she's crafty.

"Fine. I'll write her number down for you." I send out a warning text before handing over Lauren's number.

Me: Warning, your pint size biggest fan will be contacting you sometime.

Cherries: You're too well endowed to call your *Deep-V Diver* pint size.

"What's so funny?" Mallory leans over my phone as I actually laugh out loud.

"Nothing. When are you calling Lauren?"

"Once you or mom lend me your phone." I glance at the time; Lauren should be getting off work any minute.

Me: I'm glad you enjoy him. ;) Mallory has been nagging for the past two hours to contact you. I said you're busy for a few days, but she's adamant to ask a question.

Cherries: I can swing by if you're home. Just waiting for a cab.

"She will stop by shortly." I sigh, unsure of how I feel about Mallory's request.

My heart picks up pace as I contemplate Lauren's reaction to this family event. Our rules have been strict from the start, but we haven't followed everything by the books. It's not a huge deal considering we are both on the same page with how the other feels about relationships.

I sip my beer as Mallory and James pretend that they're dogs barking around my living room. They stop at every furniture leg and pretend to sniff it before communicating in barks. I guess this animal version is better than when they pretended to be monkeys and James somehow ended up swinging on the table chandelier. I had literally left the room for a second to take a piss. No wonder my sister asked for a couple hours to herself tonight.

Mallory bolts to open the door as soon as there's a knock with James trailing behind. Lauren is in her maroon scrubs that hug her body enough to make me consider sending myself to Emerge. Mallory wraps her hug as James copies. Lauren stands with open arms and an unsure expression.

Fuck, these kids are probably too much for her. Lauren glances at me, clearly surprised as if she doesn't know what to do. Her smile is soft but her eyes hold exhaustion.

"Guys." Both kids look back at me. "Let Lauren make her way in before you scare her back down the elevator."

"Princess Lauren has her own voice to tell us what she would like," Mallory sasses.

"Mallory Elenore." I lower my voice an octave and she lets go of Lauren.

Lauren bites her smirk and follows the kids into the living room. "I heard you have been asking your uncle to talk to me."

"I have, but we will get to that after. Why are you wearing dentist or doctor clothes?"

"I work in the hospital. In the emergency room." Lauren takes off her tag and hands it to Mallory.

"So, you're not a real princess?"

"She's better than one," I chime in. "Are you hungry, Laur?" The nickname rolls off my tongue, surprising us both. "We have leftover lasagna."

"You have to try it." Mallory runs to the fridge. "We made it from scratch." She talks a mile a minute and that's exhausting in itself.

"I guess I'll try a small piece," Lauren agrees as I cut a piece and hand her the plate. "Are you babysitting tonight?"

"My sister should be here soon. It's been a rough few weeks with custody paperwork and she needed downtime."

I pull a beer out of the fridge to offer her one, but her nose scrunches up.

"Understandable." She takes a bite of the lasagna.

Her eyes close and a soft moan passes through my ears, making my dick twitch. I'm seconds from sending the kids back home so I can bend her over this counter.

On cue, Mallory walks up to the counter.

"Do you like it?" she asks.

"It's one of the best things I've put in my mouth."

"I'm turning seven on Friday." Mallory hops up on the barstool and starts swaying it back and forth.

"That's so exciting." I watch as Lauren's chair sways, mimicking my niece's.

"I really want you to attend my party that evening if you're available." Mallory grins with eyes full of hope. "It's going to be at the family cabin with a giant ice cream cake!"

That got Lauren's attention. "A giant ice cream cake? That's pretty hard to refuse."

"I'll let you have an extra piece if you say yes," Mallory sings and leans forward, arching an eyebrow.

"Goodness, you know how to pitch a sale. I'll see if I can get my shift covered for Friday."

"If work needs to valiate the event, they can call me." Mallory nods.

"Do you mean to validate?" I ask.

"Look, I only started speaking like four years ago." She yawns along with Lauren. "Can James and I go back to see mom?"

"Go get your shoes on." I lock eyes with Lauren as the kids run off. "If you don't want to go to the party, that's completely fine," I whisper. "I know you're working and it's hard to tell Mallory no face to face."

"Do *you* want me there?" I pause at her question, wondering if this is some sort of test.

"I enjoy you when you are around, but I don't *need* you there. This is for Mallory. The entire family will be at the cabin." I smirk. "The party would be less dull with your pretty face, but I am well aware our rules were no family. So, this is completely up to you."

"Ice cream cake or a trauma room," she debates. "I've already met some of your family, so that wouldn't be breaking another rule, right?" I shrug, leaving this up to her. "Are you all staying the night?"

"No. They most likely will but I have a class to teach Saturday morning as a fill-in."

"I'll see if I can make it."

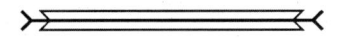

>=======<

I pull in front of Lauren's place Friday afternoon. She holds a sparkly pink gift bag and a giant princess balloon. My heart warms with how thoughtful she is. I get out and pop the trunk for the gift.

"You look beautiful." Her light-pink top and dark jeans hug her curves the way I want to. "You didn't need to bring a gift." I debate parking the car and carrying her upstairs so I can wrap my hand around her side braid.

"We should get going." I know by the look on her face she can read my thoughts. "If today goes well, maybe you'll get a gift *too*." Her finger slides down my chest and drags across my waistline. "Now, open the damn door for me."

"Yes, ma'am." I step back and open the door. "Isn't this a couple thing?"

"Manners are manners, smart-ass."

The drive north passes quickly with light conversation. We round the bend to a familiar secluded dirt road leading up to the cabin. Redwoods surround us as the weight lifts off me. I should come here more often. I crack the windows filling the car with the fresh forest air. Lauren remains quiet, staring at the nature surrounding us. Her raised eyebrows and parted lips tell me the family *cabin* is more of an understatement.

A large deck wraps around the two-story, four-thousand-square-foot chalet. Large triangle windows meet at the peak of the angled roof. Pot lights trace the roof line and shine down, giving the cabin a warm glow. I put the car in park and take a deep breath.

"You sure you're ready for this? It may be loud and chaotic."

"Cabin my ass, Charmer!" She shakes her head. "I'm very curious to see what the *little getaway* looks like on the inside." She undoes her seat belt. "Let's go. We know Mallory is probably going to chew us out for being the last ones here."

I smile and follow her up to the door. The giant balloon is almost the same size as my niece. I shouldn't be surprised Lauren agreed to come. She did say she has a soft spot for children. *Maybe I'm overthinking too much.* We can still have fun together and stick to the other rules.

"You're here!" Mallory bombards us and throws her arms around Lauren. "Is that for me?" Her eyes light up toward the balloon.

"Yes, it is, birthday girl!" Lauren hands over the gift. "You only turn seven once." She reaches into her large purse and pulls out a stuffed dinosaur. "This is for your brother."

We make our way in and I shoot a warning look in the direction of my mother, whose eyes are full of bombarding questions. All eyes are on us. A wave of energy flows through me and I can sense nerves starting to radiate off Lauren without turning my head. She doesn't flinch this time when I place my hand on her lower back to guide her forward. I feel her back expand as she takes a deep breath before stepping out of my touch. My sister smiles and goes straight for a hug.

"I'm Kelsie. Thank you for coming tonight. It means a lot to my daughter."

"She had me at ice cream cake." Lauren laughs.

I let the girls get acquainted and head to my parents by the kitchen bar. They quietly sip their wine, eyes squinted with soft, knowing smiles. Whatever they're thinking, I don't want to know. I can already read their thoughts about settling down and pumping out grandkids. I know if I want to keep this thing with Lauren, I need to lay down ground rules with my parents. Fast. I give my mother a kiss on the cheek and give my father a nod.

"She's beautiful," my mother chides. "Naturally beautiful, unlike the others we've seen leave our lobby."

"A smart one too," my father boasts. "Quick wit is a trait I truly admire."

"Your younger brother is coming back in town tomorrow with his girlfriend from Italy." My mother smiles with an implication that I've yet to settle down with someone and give her more grandbabies.

"Look, she's nothing more than a friend and I don't want you to scare her off with wedding suggestions or implying she give you grandchildren." I hold my mother's eyes with a pointed look. "She's new to the city and not one for big family events. She came for Mallory, so behave."

"Got it." My mother gives me a dramatic thumbs-up. "Your relationship is still too early, and you don't want me to ruin things."

"Not too early. Just friends." My father clears his throat in that tone to signal someone's arrival.

I turn to see Lauren making her way over to us. She holds out her hand to shake my father's. By the rise of his eyebrows, she must have given a proper firm shake.

"Good to see you again, Mr. Wheaton."

"Call me George, my dear." My father points behind him. "Mr. Wheaton is behind me playing with his great-grandchildren."

"I'm Helen," my mother chimes. "Mallory doesn't stop talking about you."

"I don't think I've done anything to leave an impression. I can't imagine what she even says about me."

"All good things, dear." My mother smiles. "May I get you a drink?"

"A coffee would be great," Lauren replies.

Lauren goes off with my mother as I scan the room for my sister. Her face is glued to her phone as her mouth droops. Whatever she's reading isn't partyworthy. I take a seat beside her on the couch and hand her a glass of wine. Even with makeup, the circles under her eyes look dark. Her phone screen clicks off and she takes a shaky breath. I keep quiet and let her make the choice to start talking or not.

"I don't want to ruin Mal's birthday," she starts. "I just got the paperwork from the lawyer. Benson is completely terminating his parental rights." Kelsie looks up at the ceiling and blinks before chugging a fifty-dollar glass of wine.

My gut caves in as the air leaves my lungs. That fucking asshole. How can someone never care to see their children again? How can you not wonder what new things they'll learn, what they'll look like, how they've grown into their own? I feel my nails start to indent my palms from clenched fists. I wish I was at the gym tonight to get my frustration out. I shake my head and finish off my drink.

"Fucking hell, Kels. I'm sorry it's ending this fucking shitty." My brain tries to rack up something more meaningful, but I fail. "At least you have family to stick by you."

"Max said I need to take up kickboxing in case I ever see that prick again." She smirks. "Maybe I'll have him show me a few moves."

"I'm sure Max and I would rather get to him before you do." The bastard used our family name for success and publicity and is now running for the high life of models and his yacht.

"I don't doubt that." Kelsie stands. "I need more wine."

The evening passes with ease. I give Lauren a tour of the chalet. Just like my penthouse, if she was blown away by the extravagance, she didn't show it. She wore a humble smile the entire time and made easy, light conversation with everyone. After presents and a second piece of cake, we hit the road. Dark sky surrounds us with the glow of the dashboard. Much like our drive up, we're quiet for the first bit.

"Your family is fun. I can tell how much you all love each other." She's first to break the silence.

"We have our bickering moments, believe me." I tighten my grip on the wheel. "Did you have fun?"

"It beat being in a hospital for twelve hours." There's a pause. "That cake was incredible." Her sentence ends in a quiet tone, making me feel as if she's dodging what she wants to talk about.

I remain quiet and let her wind down from her thoughts.

"I don't get why you're different." Her questioning voice holds no conviction.

"Different in what way?"

"Your family seems stable. Happy. I don't know why you don't want to share the joy of family with another person." Her thoughts are valid, and I know she's not implying that I commit to her.

On the outside, things look great. They are, for the most part. My father and grandfather are definitions of how to treat a woman in a relationship.

"I don't want this life. The business side of it, I mean." I wish the words would go back in my mouth but my mind wants to vent. "As selfish as that sounds to people who wish more than anything to achieve it, it lacks human purpose to me. I'm participating in society, but what value am I really bringing people?" My hands grow wet against the wheel and I keep my eyes ahead. "If I don't want this life, why would I bring a child into it?"

She places her hand on my leg and I feel my heart rate ease. Her gentle touch creates a lump in my throat and for the life of me, I have no fucking reason why the emotion is in full force. *Maybe because you've never admitted that out loud, dumbass.*

"That was beautiful." Her voice barely whispers above the road noise. "Have you told your family how you feel about your job position?"

"I was born into this, Lauren. They worked their asses off to make something for their family. I owe them this. It would be selfish to leave them when they've given me the best opportunities in life."

"If they really love you for who you are, you should let them know how you really feel."

"They *need* me."

"What do *you* feel *you* need out of life?"

No one has ever asked me this. Most of my alternate life thoughts have been spent staring through a large window over a concrete jungle. I'd watch the morning fog as it clouded over any dream I've had. When the fog dissipates over the bridge, I'm greeted with endless paperwork and calculations. I take several deep breaths and answer as honestly as possible. What do I want?

"I want silence. I want a smaller living space, a decent-sized piece of land, and to be a part of a community. Maybe with my math wits and business skills, I can help with a nonprofit organization. *Not* the kind most run for a tax write-off. That's another scheme in this elite world." I feel the weight lifting off my chest and keep going. "I've never wanted a wife and kids in my current world, and I have no idea if I want that in my wishful world."

I glance her way as she nods. "All of that is a want. I don't *need* another life even if I want it. My sister and her husband were in love at first. Now, he's gone and signing over his full parental rights to Kelsie." She tenses at the last part, and I realized I let that personal information slip. "Sorry, I'm really opening up too much."

"No." She shakes her head. "I respect your honesty. You should remember that sometimes you *need* to put yourself first. It's your life." Her hand gives my thigh a gentle squeeze. "I feel terrible for your niece and nephew, but at least they'll be surrounded by a family that loves them. That is one gift so many take for granted."

If you say so.

"I didn't scare you off?"

"Unless you say you *need* to wife me up, then we'd have a problem." Her giggle is light and brings a smile to my face. "I do have one last question though."

"Yes, you can move your hand up higher." I give her a smug smirk. "Fine, one last question, then no more until I take you home and make you moan my name."

"It's hard to believe you've sworn off relationships when you grew up with such a loving family."

"This isn't a trick question, right? You won't end our arrangement based on the past?"

"Ha, you have no idea why I'm the way I am. So no, I won't judge." She twists her pinkie ring and looks down. "We've all got our reasons."

Even though I've been vulnerable tonight, there's no need for me to push and make her feel this way too. That would be too much like a couple. And we are nothing like that.

"I was in love once," I start, recalling the memory I've worked so hard at suppressing. "It was the year before graduating university." I see short brown hair fill my vision and a sinister laugh rings through my ears, haunting me to this day. "Britney was her name. Our highs were high. We really only had highs since she painted this perfect vision of us taking on the world. We had come up with a plan to help build my family business and travel to third world countries helping build homes for orphans in our spare time." I laugh at my naive self.

"I know it sounds over the top, but she was very into my family's business. Or so it seemed. During my final semester, my family wasn't too fond of her. She didn't make the best impression when I brought her home for Christmas, and she knew she wasn't on their good side. A month later, she told me she was pregnant."

The car is dark but I see Lauren's green eyes are soft, full of acceptance. I pull into the underground parking of my hotel and stare straight ahead.

"I was scared shitless even though I knew I had the funds to support the child. In that moment, I knew I had to do the right thing. I told my family, and much to their concern, I still bought a ring. A few days later, I saw her in the library with her friends and overheard her bragging about my money and family name. She was thrilled at how I was so easily suckered into her scheme and how I wouldn't even know what hit me until it was too late. Her friends laughed, saying I was only good for my money anyway and how brilliant Britney was for planning all of this. I was a bookshelf aisle over and cleared my throat, feeling completely heartbroken. The look of horror on her face brought me satisfaction in a sick way. I flat out told her I would not pay for anything until a paternity test was done. By some fluke, she lost the baby a few days later after I refused to *take her back and love her*. Women after that seemed to only want me for my last name too. As you witnessed the evening that I met you."

I dumped a lot on Lauren to process. She nods, toying with her bottom lip and uncertainty fills her beautiful green eyes. There's a softness to her face, almost an understanding of rejection. For all I know, she could have had a perfect life up to some point. Whatever made her switch off emotions must have been pretty shitty for someone with a stable career and looks that any Hollywood actress would pay for.

"That's a shitty gut punch she gave you." She takes a deep breath that turns into a yawn. "I promise I don't need your name fame. I'm content with orgasms and *maybe* allowing you the joy of buying me ice cream."

"Yes, orgasms and melted ice cream." I laugh, catching her contagious yawn. "Weirdo."

"I am sorry Britney was a greedy bitch."

"We all have to figure out how cruel the world is at some point in life, right?" I shrug.

Her eyes shoot down and her soft smile tightens. She clears her throat and her brows scrunch together. Her cheeks suck into her teeth as she bites them. Whatever is going through her mind drops my heart. I reach over and give the back of her head a gentle rub. What event changed her demeanor? Someone her age should believe in love. I don't press because, like Max, maybe she's from a divorced or broken family too. Our frequency shifts.

I can feel the tension of whatever she's not telling me. Anxiety radiates off her as her face hardens, her eyes darting around the car. She doesn't want to remember. I place my hand gently on her forearm.

"I've unloaded too much, haven't I. Do you want me to take you home?"

"You haven't ranted too much." She shimmies, trying to break her funk. "But I'd rather we go back to my place."

"Of course." I start the car back up.

"And Adam." Her voice pitches to a question as she says my name. "When we walk through my door, please make me forget."

And so I do. Three times that night. Whatever she needs to forget, I'll do whatever it takes to block it out.

Chapter 10

Lauren

The time lights up my alarm clock, 5:08 a.m., but not from the piercing sound. I haven't had to set an alarm once in my life. Relieved my inner wake-up call is nothing more than a haunting past, I lift my arms above my head to stretch my sore naked body and sink back into the mattress. Adam, without a doubt, took my request to *make me forget* seriously. I appreciated how there were no questions asked. The man just blew my mind and kept me panting for hours. It's a wonder I didn't sleep in for once.

But personal trauma calls.

It's supposed to be a scorcher today in the city. Rachel's flight arrives at noon, giving me enough time to throw in laundry and head to the gym.

As sore as my body is from last night, I still have steam to blow off. I enjoy the sun on my face as I walk the several minutes to the gym. I have no idea what I'm in for, but I figure with all the walking I'm doing around the city, I should learn how to throw a proper punch. The drop-in kickboxing class seems like a good enough start.

Max smiles at me, and I almost don't recognize him. His muscle shirt is a nice trade-off from his usual button-down at the bar and shows off his muscular arms. Wow, who knew how toned they were? His sweats give great definition to his ass that his jeans and shirt normally hide. I wonder if Kelsie has ever thought of him as more than a friend. I know I could never stay friends with someone like that and not run my tongue over their body. His blue eyes smile at me as he runs a hand through his blond hair. Oh, he is dangerous in an innocent, brooding way. He and Adam must have all sorts of wild stories growing up together.

I find a spot beside two older ladies gushing about his radiant blue eyes and smile. The class is quite empty for a Saturday. Then again, it's nine a.m. Wait, isn't Adam teaching something today? Max leads a warm-up and I follow his eyes every few seconds as he glances toward the door. Once everyone is set up with their known routines, he makes his way over to me.

"Good morning, Shirley Temple."

"Ugh, you and Adam both drive me crazy with that name." I roll my eyes with a laugh.

"I coined the name first."

"I guess you can have it. You have supplied me with enough *plastic cherries,* as Adam likes to call them."

"I have now given you your own category on the inventory list," he jokes, shooting me a boyish smirk. "I haven't seen you much lately."

"I'll come in one night just for you then." I walk closer to the little hanging punching bag thing. "I am sure you have very funny stories about you and Adam growing up."

"Oh, there's some we will take to the grave."

"I heard about the teacher," I dramatically whisper with a laugh.

"His teacher story, or mine?"

"What kind of school did you guys attend?" I shake my head. "They must have had their own curriculum."

"Old women taught us quite a bit back then." He clears his throat and I watch his cheeks heat.

"Did Kelsie get lessons too?" I taunt the moment as his demeanor changes.

"She sure as hell better not have. Adam and I protected her like no other even though we were a grade younger."

"Just a question." I put my hands up in defeat before taking a punching stance near the bag.

"Let me show you the proper stance." He repositions his feet and I mimic. "What made you take this class?"

"I figured I should learn how to throw a punch living in this city." I bring my arms out to copy his. "How long have you been teaching?"

"My parents, well, my father, owns this gym. Most of my childhood was spent raising hell with Adam in here." He gives my stance a once-over and shakes his head. "You want your hips at an angle." He moves behind and places his hands on my hips to turn them. "My balls would be gone right now if Adam had shown up." He laughs.

"Adam doesn't *own* me. He and I are strictly orgasms and sightseeing."

"Mmhmm, so he didn't wake up with you this morning?" His lips roll in to bite back a smile.

"No, he actually told me he was teaching a class this morning." I ball my hands into fists and take a punch at his arm.

"Ouch." His tone is dramatically flat and unamused. "You don't want your thumb poking over your knuckles." He fixes my hands, and I try again. "There, much better."

Another student calls him over and I make a mental note to drop by the lounge one night for a drink without Adam. I realize how much I enjoy talking with Max. He's attractive, but oddly, I don't want to sleep with him. What the hell is wrong with me? Is this how developing a friendship is supposed to be? I finish up the class wondering about all the hell that Max and Adam could have caused growing up in a gym like this. Clearly, having access to this place fed Adam's teenage ego. I wouldn't put it past him to have made a pass at the middle age yoga ladies. I chuckle to myself. Max, on the other hand, seems humbler. The quiet, reserved type. The type every woman *should* go for, but I won't.

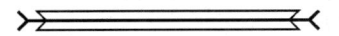

"Ah, there's my nasty Nordic!" Rachel wraps me in a hug as I greet her at the airport.

I cringe at the nickname and pray no one ever knows her reasoning for it.

"I've missed you, Rach." I pull back, taking in her hip-length extensions. "The hair looks great."

"Thanks! There's enough hair for two guys to wrap their hands around it while they ram me." Her nonchalant verbal diarrhea is mortifying for outsiders, but it's something I've grown accustomed to over the years. We drop her stuff off at my place then grab lunch at a little bistro.

"I can't believe it has taken a lifetime to finally see San Francisco." She takes a bite of her sandwich. "This city is so busy, yet so small. I love the layers."

"It's growing on me too. Everything is walkable." I no longer am winded walking a few blocks up the steep hills.

"So, tell me about your new dick daddy."

I used to look around mortified to see if anyone heard the things that came out of her mouth, but it never made her stop. The lack of a filter is just part of her personality.

"First, stop with the daddy thing. It creeps me the hell out." I shake my head. "Second, Adam is phenomenal. It's as if he was preprogrammed to know what makes my body tick, and then took it to the next level." I cross my legs feeling desire build at the thought. "His fingers are a masterclass beyond compare. The rest of his body and skills follow suit."

"So, he's made you come every single time." She smiles.

"I swear the first time we hooked up, I had four, no, maybe six orgasms. I stopped counting after three."

"Please share him." Her hand grabs my forearm with pleading eyes.

"I'm sure you have a few guys lined up here for this weekend." I laugh.

"You're right. Tonight, we are going to a bar and then there's a club I want to hit up. I found this group and we've been talking online. You and I can grab drinks at the bar first. I know you'll pass on the club event, but it's one I can't ignore."

"I'll take your word that it's great."

We make our way to union square and spend the afternoon shopping while taking photos for her social media. It's no surprise she has an account of random objects that can be viewed as obscene. It *is* surprising when she shows me her eighty thousand followers. Who knew that a dedicated, passionate geriatric nurse could be so eccentric in her personal life? A few hours later, we ended up back at my condo.

"This view is amazing, Nordic. I would love to be fucked against a window like this."

"I know, right?" I remember making a suggestion to Adam the first night at his place. "I still haven't crossed that off the list."

"Seriously? That would have been a top priority for me." Rachel laughs while pulling out her outfit for tonight.

"Please tell me I don't need a costume or special attire to go out for drinks." I look down at her fishnets and neon-green garter belt.

"No, this is nothing like the dragon thing." She waves her hand in the air. "Though, you did draw a lot of attention in the alien meetup."

"Stop reminding me." I shudder and pick out black dress shorts with a cream flowy tank. "I'm having a quick shower before we head out."

"I'll be doing my makeup by the window. This lighting is amazing."

I step out of the shower as a knock taps on the door. I'm not expecting a package, nor did I hear the buzzer. "Hey Rach, can you see who that is?"

I step out of the bathroom trying to catch a glimpse of whoever knocked. Rachel gasps and opens the door wider.

"Well hang me from a ceiling fan and clamp my nipples!" Her astonished voice travels through my condo as she allows Adam to step in.

His eyes dart around for me in utter confusion. Our eyes lock before his drop to the hem of my towel. I know I look like a drowned rat, yet his heated gaze makes me feel as if I'm irresistible. He snaps out of it and turns to Rachel. Rachel looks at me with wild impressed eyes.

"I hope you know this fella, because if this is a mistaken address, I'll escort this hunk home and let him ride me like the stallion he is." She sizes him up. "How tall are you?"

"Six-three." He clears his throat, looking at me as if he's scared to move.

"Adam, this is Rachel." I hold my towel with one hand and point with the other. "My one and *only* friend in my life."

I've never seen him speechless and somewhat scared besides the soda spill and possible bee encounter. He glances her way, trying to discretely observe her neon green corset, fishnets and leather collar.

"I can be a bit much for some people at first," Rachel explains, making her way to the couch.

"She's harmless." I walk toward the bed to grab my clothes. "She broke me out of my shell during nursing school."

"You're a nurse?" His jaw drops.

"Geriatric. And let me tell you, some of those oldies have the kinkiest stories." Her laugh boasts through the room. "I've learned a thing or two."

"I don't want to interrupt your girls' night. I'll head out." He turns to the door.

"No, come out with us." Rachel smiles. "We are going out for drinks but then I'm taking off to a club that Ren says she won't step foot in."

"For good reasons," I say through gritted teeth.

"It wasn't *that* terrible last time. I happened to love every minute." Rachel turns to Adam. "Don't make her come home alone. I'll be out until tomorrow afternoon."

"I'll join." Adam smirks. "Only if you tell me why you hated the last club."

"Yes! I love this story." Rachel goes back to doing her eye shadow.

"Can I get dressed first? I'll return in a minute."

"Just drop the towel and get changed," Rachel says with a sly smirk. "It's nothing we haven't seen or explored before." The implication of her words match her voice and Adam's eyes ping-pong back and forth between her and me.

"Sorry, what?" His jaw is slightly hanging.

"Could today get any worse?" I tilt my head back and want to lock myself in the bathroom for the rest of the day. "You get one story from me. Which is it going to be?"

"Let's start with the club."

"If it isn't obvious, my adventurous friend here is into trying every kink and sex club." I put down my clothes and decide to just sit on the bed in my towel. "It was a role-playing medieval-themed club with cages, chains, fire and dragon people. Aliens had invaded and captured us in cages." I pause and recall the members swooning over me with their fake wings spreading. "I got sucked into being an alien who was awaiting her new dragon lord to submit to." I shake my head, unable to look him in the eyes. "There were custom dragon strap-ons and egg toy implants. I ran out of the club as soon as the cage door opened."

"You missed out on a great night. Those dragon peens beat any man I've been with." Rachel laughs. "The club kept asking for her back because she fit the perfect description of a Nordic alien. Tall, skinny and blonde."

"I'm sorry, a custom dragon dick? How does anyone know..." Adam takes a seat beside me, his brows still drawn in. "No offense, but you chose Rachel as your *only* friend?"

I giggle and can't fault his question. I bring my damp hair to the side of my neck and begin the story.

"I had spent my life dedicated to school and nothing else. I was quiet, inexperienced and didn't quite communicate beyond sarcastic remarks." He smirks. "Rachel opened up my closed-off world and enlightened me." I clear my throat, careful of my words. "She showed me how to enjoy sex with a guy while protecting my heart."

"Showed you?" Amused brown eyes light up with curiosity.

"If you don't talk to me again after everything I'm about to unload, it was nice knowing you." I force a laugh. "I was pretty lost at twenty-two. She and a guy gave me a hands-on experience about how to be confident with what I need in bed."

"Watching her break through her past was quite gratifying." Rachel's eyes glass over as they lock with mine. "I am so damn proud of you for taking back your power, Ren. You can control sex and pleasure as often or as little as you want."

Rachel had gotten me drunk for the first time that night when I broke down about the weight of my past. If anything, Rachel should be the name I call out when anyone gives me an orgasm. Sex probably would have never been something I would have pursued, if not for her. We share a look of secret understanding before I clear my throat and stare down at my clothes.

"Well, I'm glad you led her to me, Rachel." Adam smiles and gives my bare thigh a squeeze. "Whatever happened in the past made her one of the strongest kick-ass women I know."

"Enough with the heaviness." I walk into the bathroom with my clothing. "Let's go have some fun."

The hip downtown nightlife doesn't grasp my attention the way it used to. As much as I have missed Rachel, all I can focus on is finishing out the feeling that sparked through me when Adam placed his hand on my bare thigh earlier. The fact that I am wanting to give up things in exchange for his touch should be a red flag. I remind myself how I still don't *want* him entirely. I want what he does to my body, and that is perfectly justifiable. Rachel grabs my hand, pulling me to the dance floor for a few songs until her group appears and steals her away.

Adam comes up behind me, pressing himself against my back. I feel the hard length of him as my arm snakes up around his neck. His mouth presses a kiss to the curve of my neck as my breath hitches. I grind my ass against him on the crowded floor shamelessly. His hands grip my hips, holding me tight against him. My core aches with the need for him to reach in front and touch me. My chest heaves with insatiable need. I spin around and he pulls one of my legs up over his hip, giving me the friction I desperately need against him. My nails dig into his shoulders, feeling the tension between my legs build. His possessive eyes are filled with desire as he brings his lips to my ear.

"Let go, Blondie. Soak those panties for me." His teeth nip the shell of my ear in hunger and I feel myself let go.

His hand grips the back of my hair as his mouth crashes to mine, swallowing my cry of ecstasy. My body is on fire. I'm in too much of a haze to care about what I just did in a crowd of people. The bass music pulses through me, extending my orgasm. I still need more. I've become insatiable to this man. I grab his hand as his possessive gaze burns with need. We need to get out of here. Pronto.

The short drive to Adam's penthouse is tantalizing in the back of the cab. Each second the driver casually taps his fingers against the wheel, I feel our bodies hum with pulsing need. A brief thought of living out my Chuck and Blair fantasy in the back seat passes through my mind. But getting kicked out of the cab and walking home would only prevent our activity longer. I squeeze his hand trying to ignore my need, but it's no use.

Adam pulls me through the lobby and I stumble on my feet to keep up. His elevator opens and my back meets the wall before the doors shut. His hand reaches to the side to type in a code, and we ascend- in more ways than one. My heart beats into my throat as I gasp for air, desperate for him to consume my entire being. I'm about one brush against my clit or a thrust away from calling out his name. It's pathetic how entrenched he's made me. My hand clasps around his wrist guiding his fingers down my shorts. His finger lightly strokes up my slit and I arch into him, desperate for more pressure. I'm giving Niagara Falls a run for their money. I've never been this flooded with need.

The doors open and Adam withdraws his hand. I whimper like a pathetic puppy and wonder if my eyes are as dilated as his.

"Holy *fuck*, Blondie." He bends to grab my waist, throwing me over his shoulder and carries me through the door to his bedroom.

As my back hits the bed, Adam is removing my shorts. My soaked panties should cause a blush on my face, yet I'm far from feeling bashful.

"I love how desperate your pussy is for me." Adam admires my panties with a heart-stopping grin and drops them to the floor.

His pants hit the ground and his glorious Viking cock springs free. I shamelessly spread my legs to expose my desperate, swollen core for him to fill. His eyes track my every move before he raises my thighs over his shoulders. The heat of his heavy breath nearly sends me over the edge before his mouth wraps around my clit, sucking me with need. A few flicks of his tongue and I'm gripping his hair screaming out his name.

As soon as I reach my release, he wastes no time and enters me. Punishing strokes pound through me as his hand reaches down to grip my throat. My nails rake at his chest, branding him with my desire before I gently rub my thumbs along the *V* of his lower abs. His abs flex with each thrust and define that sexy *V* I love to run my tongue over. I feel my next orgasm build as he grinds upward hitting my clit with his pelvis. His jaw clenches and his forearms rest on each side of my head.

"Lauren." The strain in his voice tells me he's barely hanging on. "Be a good girl and come on my dick with your tight pussy."

His way with words command my body to obey. My heels dig into his ass, pushing him into me deeper as I shake. His forehead drops to mine as our staggered breathing subsides. Slowly, he pulls out and I realize then why it felt different. His bare dick glistens with our release and my eyes go wide. I can't blame him more than I can blame myself. We were both too caught up in hormones to think. Am I worried about pregnancy? Not as much as the emotional connection I know bareback sex can create.

"Lauren, I'm sorry I..."

"I believed you when you said you had a vasectomy." I roll off the bed, needing the bathroom. "I've just never been one to go without."

"Neither have I. I should have realized that's why I couldn't hold off my orgasm as long."

"Ha! Your performance is a far cry from concernworthy. *Trust me* with that one." I clear my throat. "Let's make sure we wrap you up next time."

I walk out of the bathroom and Adam is casually sprawled out on the bed in a pair of gray boxers. One arm is behind his head, and the other is beckoning me to him. I pause for a moment taking him in. It's as if I'm transported into an underwear model photo. Only this is real life. I oblige and lay my head on his chest. His heart is still thumping relatively faster than normal. His hand ghosts up and down my lower back. I'm so spent that my legs barely walk me back to the bed. My body's bones couldn't hold me up. Even though he's a good 200-plus pounds of muscle, I feel like my deadweight could crush him. I take a deep breath and prepare to get up and head home, but my body decides to sink deeper into him on my exhale.

"Stay," he murmurs into my hair before placing a kiss on my forehead. "I promise I won't wake you up with a proposal."

"The answer will *always* remain no unless it's a three-carat oval cut with a rose gold band," I joke. *"Engraved, of course."* I feel him tense beneath me. "Relax. I'm joking, Adam."

"That was a very specific ring." His hand is no longer moving on my back.

"It was the first thing that randomly came to mind. You know I'm not flashy, besides my taste in lingerie." I rest my chin on the back of my hand that's placed on his chest. "I don't even want a boyfriend. Breathe."

He licks his lips as his eyes narrow. As good as I've thought I'd been about reading him, I'm at a loss. His eyes hold me captive and for the life of me, I can't avert them. His thumb and middle finger gently touch the sides of my knuckle on my ring finger. With delicate ease, his fingers brush up the sides of my finger and lightly pinch the sides of my nail before easing off. My stomach flips at the new sensation tingling within.

My mouth goes dry and I am hyperaware of what question is coming next. The question I know he deserves some type of answer to at this point. He's given me his reasoning for everything. I swallow the lump in my throat as his eyes scream for my truth. His fingers lace with mine.

"Who did you wrong, Lauren McAllister?"

"Since birth, I've known no right." Cast the millstone into the sea, because as the words leave my mouth, weight vacates my body. For the first time in my life, this outspoken declaration waves new emotion through my heavy heart. "Life was anything but promising. Attachment equals pain. I've seen enough pain in my life and career."

"There's good in your career as well, Lauren." His eyes burn his statement in my mind as his fingers lift my chin.

"I see people on their deathbeds, or I witness people hearing about loved ones' tragedies." I shake my head and take an unsteady breath to rid this feeling. "The amount of power people have over each other is crippling. Heart wrenching. I never want to allow someone the power to completely eviscerate me." I sit up to get my point across. "I've lived almost twenty-five years without an emotional attachment to anyone. Another twenty-five should be a breeze."

Oh shit, I've said too much. My eyes stay wide for too long and I start to feel them burn. My chest tightens as my breaths become short. Where the hell did that truth bomb come from? I've been sober since the night I first tasted liquid sin with Rachel. Now, I'm drunk on a life-altering dick. I brace myself for Adam to tell me he's the one to change me. That I should give him a chance to show me more. I start preparing my mind to end this arrangement and add him to my list of *Past Peen*.

He sits eye to eye with me and brings his hand to the back of my neck, gently curling his fingers around my hair. His lips don't meet mine like I expect them to. I toy with my bottom lip hearing my heart race through my ears. His face softens as his free hand runs down my arm.

"Thank you for your honesty."

I blink and tilt my head at his response.

"You are *so fucking strong,* Lauren."

That's new.

No *"I'm so sorry"* or *"I can change that for you,"* which past guys had felt challenged to do when I gave them the brief rundown that I don't commit.

I nod and bite back tears as fear lights up my blood, waiting for him to ask further in-depth questions that will ruin everything.

Please don't promise you can change me.
Please don't promise there's a happy ending for everyone.
Please don't promise you're here to stay.

"I have to be strong." My voice cracks and looking at the man in front of me, I almost doubt my own truth. "I know what I don't want."

"I don't know what you've been through, but if this arrangement is what helps get you through life, then I will pass it with you for however long we last."

"Nothing more?"

"You're aware of what I *need* from you too." He smiles and cups my face with his hands. "I think we've passed the acquaintance phase though. Are you okay with a second friend?"

I click my tongue a few times and rest my hands on his chest, pushing him back down. "As long as you hand out more orgasms than questions, we should be fine."

>=======<

"He didn't say sappy shit to send you running after you opened up to him?" Rachel gives me a side-eye.

"He didn't take pity. He called me strong and then gave me another orgasm." Part of me wanted to tell him more for the fact that he respected me enough to not ask.

Or he really didn't care. But the way he spoke and held me said otherwise. God, I am too fucked up with my past to be able to read any emotional signs.

I shove a big bite of Chinese takeout in my mouth and continue to stare out my tall window. It's late afternoon and Rachel and I had a very late start to our mornings. She was completely hungover with people she met the night before, and my morning was spent in another orgasmic state while eating my weight in homemade French toast.

I had woken up just after five this morning with a loud gasp. I saved my ass, saying I was having a nightmare and that I quickly forgot what it was about. *Having* said recurring nightmare wasn't a lie. But that wasn't his burden.

Rachel and I pass the afternoon catching up and swapping work stories.

"He's a good one, Ren." Her voice is soft and understanding.

"Pardon?" I feel my face contort.

"I know you're thinking about what this all means." She turns to face me and grabs my hand. "Even if he only wants sex. He still cares about you. I saw the way he treated you yesterday and the way he looked at you."

"Meaning?" I hate how she drags shit out when I have no idea how to read any type of relationship.

"He's not a clingy psycho like the others, but he's also not a complete dickwad who only calls you for a quickie."

"I knew *that*, Rachel. He's an amazing uncle too." I smile, remembering how much his niece and nephew love him chasing them around. "What?" I ask as her grin grows along with the glow in her eyes.

"Nothing." Her voice is nonchalant as she studies me.

"You can't do that. Why are you looking at me like that?"

"I'm just happy you *knew* what I told you." She turns back to looking out the window and I still feel like she's not telling the full truth.

"Maybe I won't miss you when you leave tonight," I joke.

"Bitch, please. You'd be lost without me."

When she's right, she's right.

>=====<

"Dylan loved the zoo. He pretended to be a tiger the entire weekend which drove me up the wall but at least he's using his imagination." Tessa shows me the photo of her son standing against the tiger cage with his claws out. "Have you been to it yet?"

"Not yet. I'm not sure that's my sort of thing." I haven't been to various places that most kids get to explore, but I wasn't going to open that door.

"I mean yeah, it sucks that they're stuck in the zoo instead of in the wild, but the kids love it."

I smile and toss my third coffee cup into the garbage. My last day of work never seems to allow the caffeine to kick in. Tessa swipes a few more photos in front of me. I enjoy children but I enjoy helping them more. That's one of the reasons I wanted this job. Social work was a close second. Doing my best to calm kids in trauma gives me firsthand signs a social worker could be missing.

It's not that I'm sour toward caring about Tessa's son or her life, but I've come across too many people already that I've connected with. I wasn't expecting Adam's entire family to warm my heart. Their welcoming arms and the fun characteristics of Kelsie's children are too hard to ignore. I enjoy being around them. So, for the time being I let myself. They are aware of Adam's lifestyle. If I want to walk out, it won't be anything new.

I fight off a yawn and quickly acknowledge that in an hour, I'll be on my way home and Adam has a movie night planned. It's the history of San Francisco, but he said I'll have a better appreciation of the city after I watch it. I look over a chart and my heart puzzles. I knock before peeking my head in and seeing the tiny girl holding her hands together.

"Ava Rose, we meet again." I smile. "I hope if we meet a third time, it can be somewhere like an ice cream shop."

Her smile doesn't reach her eyes.

"She was climbing and the nail sticking out cut her." The female guardian spoke instantly.

"Adventurous, are you?" I keep my eyes on Ava, waiting for confirmation.

She nods and glances at the woman.

"Where were you climbing, Ava?" I keep my voice light and casual.

"An old play structure in our yard." The guardian speaks up. "We told her to keep off it many times."

I turn over Ava's hand and see a clean horizontal slice below her two fingers. Vertical would seem less suspicious, but I don't want to make a scene. Ava winces as I gently touch her palm. I see fat coming out of the wound along with a good amount of blood. Assessing the sticky black Band-Aid residue around the area, I wonder when this happened.

"How long has this been bleeding, Ava?"

"Um." She hesitates.

"You're a smart girl," I encourage her. "I know you can remember."

"Yesterday." Her voice is soft. "The Band-Aids won't work."

"You're right. Look at this." I point to the sliver of fat exposed. "This must really hurt. You have a bit of fat and it looks like it's almost to the bone. You're going to need a couple stitches."

"Another wasted day in the emergency, Ava." The woman sighs.

"It's common to see kids getting hurt. Broken arms and legs are the main event here this summer." I grab my files from the table. "I'll be back shortly to fix your hand." I keep the door open wide as I leave.

After stitching up her hand, I'm still not fully convinced with the story. I made a quick note to look into this further and file a report for the social worker. My heart clenches with the hope of this being the last time Ava needs to come back here. I have done my part in reporting my concern, so hopefully she's in the best hands.

I head out of the hospital with my grumbling stomach. I feel my mouth water as I wonder what Adam is cooking. This arrangement could go on forever and I'd never get enough of it. It's been refreshing to have someone on the same emotional page with perks of friendship, orgasms, and food. We don't need to be in a relationship to enjoy companionship or feel as if we are tied down to each other. I don't tend to see him during my working days, so seeing him on the days I do work is a treat.

Choosing our time instead of being with each other as an emotional default is a much better way to get through life.

Chapter 11

Adam

By some fluke, Lauren and I managed to fall asleep in the same bed. I don't feel like her panicked mumbling is a fluke yet again at five in the morning. She gasps, sitting straight up and I swear I see the pulse in her neck protruding. Her deep breath in is sharp as a hand rests over her bare chest. I place my hand on her back and she flinches, her eyes wide with panic.

Huh.

She looks down at me and attempts to play it off with a forced laugh.

"I guess having a hot guy next to me still doesn't scare the monsters away," she jokes, but I feel like there's an underlying truth.

"I can fight all the demons in your conscious world, but I lack the ability when they're in your unconscious mind."

"I'm fine," she lies through her smile and I let her.

"How could you not be?" I lighten the mood. My arms go above my head, exposing my flexed body. "You get to accidentally wake up to a man who knows your body better than its owner." I flash my smug grin in hopes of clearing her mind.

"You've got quite the chip on your shoulder."

"Oh, I think I've earned it."

"Hmm." She moves to straddle me and rolls her hips, angling the tip of my cock at her entrance. "Just because you have a cock, doesn't mean you need to be cocky." She narrows her eyes and gives a strong smirk. "You're not the only one who can get me off."

Smart-ass.

I sit up, pushing Lauren on her back and cage her underneath. Her legs fall open and expose her glistening pussy. My plan to grab her legs and feast on her sweet, addictive mound halt. Her fingers push into her mouth slowly before they trail down her body. Her eyes lock with mine and I'm torn between following her hand or keeping eye contact. Naturally, my eyes give in to her hand. She brushes her fingers down her slit and lets a soft gasp escape. Her middle finger lightly traces over her clit, pulling me into a trance. A front-row seat to a show I've only dreamed of witnessing again since our first night.

Her fingers dance in a delicate motion until her breathing increases. Her opening is slick as she inserts her middle and fourth finger. A sultry moan escapes and I'm done for. This woman could command anything from me, and I'd do it. I burn this moment into my mind and pray to never forget it. I grunt and can't ignore the throbbing of my dick anymore. My hand slides up and down my cock as I watch her touch herself. Every time I'm with this woman, I don't think I can be any more turned on than I was the last time. This goddess proves me wrong with each encounter. I watch her teeth sink into her bottom lip as her back arches off the bed in ecstasy. My balls tighten at the sight, and I unload.

I'm speechless as she lies there panting. A beautiful sight of messy blonde curls, a fresh face and the sexiest performance I have witnessed.

"Don't say I don't know my body ever again." She sits up. "I choose to let you help with my orgasms. I don't *need* you to."

"Yes, ma'am." I flick her nipple just because they're right in front of me. "Let's get ready. I have a tourist day planned for us."

"I swear, if it involves climbing another mountain then you're carrying me up."

The sky is a beautiful blue as we walk to the Embarcadero downtown. Despite being a large tourist attraction, the waterfront strip of piers has always remained one of my favorite spots in the city. We start at Pier 14 and walk out to a perfect view of the Bay Bridge. Sailboats pass in all directions among the lunch cruises and brave kayakers. Lauren's faint perfume travels through the air as the breeze picks up. The end of the large pier over the water has a noticeable temperature change.

Although I'm not one for fashion, her red sundress hits above her knees and adds a picture-perfect aesthetic in contrast to the whites and blues surrounding us. She faces out to the water, and I place my hands on the rail caging her in.

"Have you explored downtown yet?"

"I've been too busy exploring you." She leans back on my shoulder, and I bring my lips to her neck for a quick kiss.

"I love this view, but I can't wait to show you the rest of the city," I admit without thinking. "I feel like a kid again."

"Let's get to it, Charmer." She gives me a playful smirk and takes my hand, leading us back to the road.

We walk among families on bicycles, tourists sporting giant cameras, and a setup of tents by the giant clock tower ferry building. Fresh produce fills the tables as the locals get their groceries. The noise of cars, conversations, boat horns, and street music brings the city to life. We stop in front of street musicians and I can't fight my smile. I toss a few bills into their jar as the steel drums transport us to the Caribbean.

"This is amazing." Lauren grins as my heart skips. "I could listen to them for hours."

"They've always been my favorite entertainment." I give her hand a squeeze and realize we're still holding hands.

Is this too couple-y? Or simply two friends enjoying the day?

She'd let me know if there was a problem. Lauren pulls me out of thought as we continue walking past the street vendors. We pass a row of uneventful empty buildings before we reach the tourist hot spots.

"I bet all these kids will sleep really well after walking this strip." She laughs and watches a parent chase after a young boy.

"I bring Mallory and James down here sometimes when it's not too busy. Golden Gate Park is their favorite though."

"You're such a good uncle." She stops walking and I turn toward her. "They're really lucky to have you." Her dark glasses cover her eyes, but the hint of pain in her voice is noticeable.

"I try. Need to give them *deathbed* memories as you call them."

"We should go up that tube tower." She nods to the hill across the street.

"That tube is Coit Tower. We can go there at sunset."

We reach Pier 39 and are greeted with crowds and little shops. The mix of fried fish and waffle cones hit my nose at the same time, yet the scent combo works. Lauren stays wide eyed and quiet until we pass the ice cream shop.

"I'll need to stop in there before we head back."

We make our way in and out of all the little shops. Lauren looks to her right and raises her eyebrows. "I've always wanted a pair of cowboy boots." We stand outside a western shop and the smell of leather hits us.

"I'll buy you some if you promise to strut around my place in a pair of cutoff shorts and a button-up shirt that ties under your breasts." I'm not sure what sparked this fantasy, but picturing Lauren in anything had been a turn-on.

"I can afford my own boots, thank you very much." She pulls her sunglasses down the bridge of her nose, revealing a challenge in her eyes. "I'll wear whatever you want if *you* buy a cowboy hat."

"Not going to happen."

She reaches for a price tag on a large toy horse and smirks as I see an idea form. "Hey Adam, do you think my dildo will balance on this?"

"What did you just say?" I glanced around, relieved no one was in earshot.

"Well, it's not like I'll have a cowboy to ride."

The pull this woman has over me is getting unreal. Role-play has never been a kink of mine or even crossed my mind. The fact that Lauren threatened to get pleasure from something other than me, heightens something primal within. Her smirk and assertive remark have me questioning if I really want to call her bluff. She lifts her leg over the horse, pretending to ride it. To someone walking by, they'd assume she wants an innocent photo. The way she's deliberately making eye contact tells me she's serious about the fucking cowboy hat. I've seen her take matters into her own hands twice now. As hot as it is to watch, I don't want to be replaced by a fucking stuffed horse. I run my hand over my jaw and grab the first black hat I can find.

"Save the fucking horse, Lauren," I huff as she shoots me a grin. "But don't expect me to fuck you with this thing on my head."

"Wow." She removes my hat and sets it back on the shelf. "You really caved." She laughs and takes my hand, pulling me out of the store.

"As if I'd watch you fuck a fake horse." I shake my head.

"I wouldn't." She throws her head back in laughter and I can't help but grip her chin and place my lips on hers.

"You're a tease." I place my hand over my chest.

"Sorry your cowgirl fantasy won't be fulfilled." We make our way toward the carousel. "I don't even like country music."

"What music do you like?"

"It's not a normal genre people listen to." She reaches her arm out to grab a fudge sample from a tray. "I love pop songs that are slowed down and covered on the piano."

"Slow pop songs on a piano?" As a closet piano player, I am very much intrigued.

How come I've never thought to do that myself? For one, I hate Top 20 pop hits, even if the lyrics are decent. I just can't connect with songs that have a busy production. My favorites are jazz and the classics. I feel my fingers stretch out with the need to hit the piano keys. I have no idea what song I'd start with, but it's all my mind can focus on now.

"I know, it's not a generic first answer." She shrugs and stops in front of the carousel. "I've never been on one of these."

"I don't believe that."

"It's true. By the time I could, it was too childish and embarrassing to ride one." Her laugh seems forced.

"Well, you should go anyway."

"Let's bring Mallory and James next time. I'll feel less foolish." My heart warms and aches at her words.

What has her life consisted of?

"I enjoy piano music myself." I watch her bite her cheek to hide a smirk. "Jazz mostly. Do you play?" Does she know I do?

"I've never played and don't think I will. I appreciate the talent it takes though."

"You saw me the other day, didn't you?" My heart rate picks up with nerves, but if I'm being honest with myself, why would it matter if she saw me?

"Max said to pretend I didn't." She shrugs, looking toward the ocean. "Your talented fingers have many skills."

"Thanks." I feel myself become more at ease. "What pop songs do you listen to covers of?"

"I listen to 'Bad Habits' by Ed Sheeran and 'Blinding Lights' by The Weeknd *a lot*."

"I would never have thought of those as slow piano covers."

"You're missing out, Charmer." We make it to the end of the pier. "That's Alcatraz, right?"

"Yep. People also swim from the island to the shore. The city organizes races for those who want to compete."

She shakes her head in horror. "Count me out." The seals start their loud chorus and her head turns following the sound.

"Back this way." I lead us up the steps and turn down a small alleyway with swinging doors.

Two dozen floating docks serve as suntan beds to at least fifty seals. Lauren leans forward with her nose scrunched up. The smell of rotten fish takes some time adjusting to. One I'm not sure anyone is able to.

"They're so cute!" Lauren smiles and mimics their sound.

"You *did not* just do that." I laugh, watching her shameless, carefree side break through.

"Come on, you think it's totally sexy." She does it again and I feel my soul free up and join her.

A few people give us an odd stare, but the children a ways down the dock start to join us. Lauren's spirit is infectious. The stress of life, work and relationships melt away and I want this moment to last. I observe the sun's rays shining on her golden hair, the giggle escaping her belly, the smell of carnival treats and a soundtrack of seals. I commit it all to memory, burning it into my brain as a moment to replay during any spout of stress.

We have lunch at my favorite restaurant on the water and spend the rest of the afternoon lying on the grass looking at the Golden Gate Bridge in Crissy Field. I sit as her head rests in my lap. Dogs run back and forth among a few people playing frisbee. Our conversations haven't stopped until now. The quiet feels just as natural. A shiver courses through her as goose bumps paint her skin. The weather has dropped as rush hour dies down. My hand rubs her arm.

"I need to change if we plan on climbing that tube to watch the sunset."

"Let's head back then. I made lasagna yesterday if you want leftovers," I suggest.

"I'm going to take a shower before we head back out. As delicious as that sounds, I might just make scrambled eggs and meet you at your place after." She stands, offering me both hands.

"Make sure you dress warm. It gets windy." We walk to the end of the road and I flag down a cab.

Chapter 12

Adam

I beeline straight to the lounge piano as soon as I enter the lobby. There's still time before our piano guy arrives and I have over an hour before meeting Lauren again. I'm still trying to sift through my brain and figure out who she really is beneath her beautiful features and wicked smart brain. Not to mention what's beyond her sass. Piano covers to pop songs have my adrenaline going like a music junkie. I lightly tap a few notes to figure out the key and chords. I've always been able to figure songs out by ear. A few seconds to think about the song, and my brain unlocks each note before I hit the key. Lessons would have been great, but I never took the time to learn how to read music. I play around with the songs Lauren mentioned and notice a small crowd of young teens gathered by the bar door. I finish a few songs and close the piano lid to make my way upstairs.

"That was so cool!" A few young girls smile and clutch their phones as if their devices are comfort items.

"Yeah, I always thought those songs were for partying. Your version is something I could relax to."

"I'm glad you liked it." I nod with a smile. "Enjoy your evening." I head to the elevator, hearing them gush and snicker in the distance.

I take a long shower, throwing on jeans with a gray Henley. I grab my leather jacket and the keys to a vehicle I don't drive as often as I'd like to. Lauren steps out of her condo and it takes everything in me not to pick her up and take her back upstairs. It seems there's nothing this woman can wear that doesn't make my dick twitch. Her long hair is thrown in a messy bun and her black leggings cling to her toned legs. I can't fight my smile when I see her swimming in my gray hoodie that she's yet to return. Her mouth drops open as her head shakes.

"No." Her arms cross as she makes her way over to my street bike. "No way."

"I have an extra helmet. I promise I'll drive carefully."

"It's not *you* I don't trust. I work in the emergency room. Motorcycle accidents tend to be caused by cars."

"Live a little. It's only a few blocks over." I wave the helmet in front of her. "We aren't touching the highway."

She takes a deep breath as her teeth toy with her lip. "If I die, I'm coming back to haunt the hell out of you until you join me on the other side."

We zip through the streets and arrive at the parking lot within minutes. I love and hate how compact this city is. Everything is within a reasonable distance, but so many people are in one location. A few cars are parked in the lot facing the water. The sun is on the brink of setting as I lead the way toward the tower.

"It's closed, guys." A guy shouts out after us. "We wanted to go up top, but apparently they close before sunset."

"Thanks, man." I call back and Lauren pouts. Yeah, it's pretty damn cute.

"At least we still have a good view from here." She shrugs and I tug her hand up a set of stairs.

"It's closed to the *public*." I flash my charming grin I know she appreciates. "My last name can pull strings when I decide to use it."

"Adam Wheaton," she scolds playfully. "Did you bribe the city to let you up this tower?"

"I didn't have to do much bribing. You wanted to see the sunset from up here and it's something I've never seen either."

"I guess I'll accept how powerful your last name is *just this once*." She smirks and we head up.

She leans forward over the open cutouts and rests her chin on her hands. The sun is a dark orange as the sky above us turns black. City lights glow through every window and Lauren looks up.

"How did I not notice the top is open?" Her mouth gapes as her head tilts back. "Thank you for bringing me here."

"If you haven't *noticed*, you're hard to say no to." Her arms come up around my neck as her body pushes into mine.

"Probably because you're scared that I'll go buy that fake horse." She yelps when my hands squeeze her ass.

"That horse has nothing on me when it comes to pleasing your damn body." Our lips are so close to touching and I feel her heart pound against me.

Her breathing increases but her eyes are absent of their usual lust. Her body molds perfectly against mine and for the life of me, I can't remember how to breathe. Her eyes hold something I can't decipher and when I go to release her, my arms stay locked in place. Lauren's eyes fall to my lips as her hand runs through the back of my hair. She looks beautiful and nervous with whatever she can't say. Whatever it is, I can't find words either.

Something is shifting between us, but the red flag of danger is absent. Nothing about this moment with the stars above, her body consuming mine and my urge to kiss her feels wrong. The moment is silent. Her green eyes are transfixed on mine as she argues with herself to keep her thoughts quiet. Our arrangement is too perfect for one of us to ruin it. So together, we silently enter into a new beginning. A silent level up from general friends to friends who crave the emotional closeness.

I lean forward to taste her soft, plump lips. As our slow kiss continues, I gently suck her bottom lip between mine and tug to deepen the kiss even more than I thought possible. Lauren's soft moan sings through the tower. Her arms tighten around my neck, trying to get closer than she physically can with our clothes on. Our kiss remains gentle. Deliberate. Our lightning-quick rush of lust is absent for the first time. She pulls back and swipes her thumb under her wet bottom lip.

"Thank you for tonight." There's a softness to her voice before clearing her throat. "I can't think of anything else I could want in life today."

That's a good thing, right? I wait for the icy chill of my gut warning me to stay away, but it never happens.

"Yeah." I look out at the glowing city skyline and know we are still on the same page. "I have everything I need today." I kiss the top of her head. "Thank you for this *deathbed* memory."

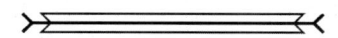

I walk past the lounge when I notice Max's alternative shift working the bar tonight. Grant is nice, but he talks too much about things I have zero interest in. I head to the elevator as the doors open to Max. His eyes avert from mine as soon as they connect.

Odd.

"Where are you coming from?" I toss the ball in his court, because I recognize the same suspicious look he sported back in the day.

The same look he had when bragging about a weekend he once banged his girlfriend *and* her mother. Our teen years held no lack when it came to exploration.

"James is sick. I took Mallory to swim lessons and helped Kels put the kids to bed." He walks past me then turns around. "You should try it once. It's exhausting."

"Max." I raise my eyebrows. "Kelsie is vulnerable as hell right now." I don't know why I have a weird gut feeling, but his look threw me off.

"Exactly." His tone is sharp. "She's a single mother now and doesn't have time to even brush her hair half the time."

"Kelsie has prioritized getting ready her whole life." My sister was big on looking the part to be productive in it.

"When was the last time she has looked *the part*." He has a point. "Her motherly role has taken over her kick-ass marketing role. Which would be fine if it didn't make her forget how badass she can be."

He's right. I need to start pulling my fucking weight in this family beyond job criteria. Kelsie should rely on her actual brother over the *adoptive one*, as my mother likes to call him.

"I'll stop prioritizing Lauren." I smile and wink to lighten the mood. "It's a relief to know you're not banging my sister."

"Dude, you're my best friend. Kels is someone I've vowed to always protect. Friends help each other." He spews off his response like rapid fire and shakes his head. "Good night, Mr. Lovestruck."

"Fuck off. I am not."

"Your face says otherwise, dumbass. Now, good night." He heads out of the lobby.

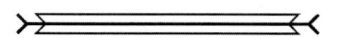

>===<

The office meeting drags out longer than it needs to. Our head of marketing needs to be fired for her unoriginal ideas. I don't know why my father has kept her around this long, if I'm being honest. I miss working with my sister. While I know she's going through a lot right now, James is old enough to be left with our mother, or at least enrolled part-time in a preschool. Max is right that Kelsie's divorce and extended "maternity leave" is taking a toll on her. I make a mental note to talk to her about coming back. Even if it's part time.

My pen slips through my lip and cuts my gum. I blink back to reality and curse under my breath. I could have skipped this meeting and put my time to better use. Our busy season is coming to an end, and I have countless hours to look over budgets.

"Son." My father's eyes are wide with annoyance as he pulls me out of my trance.

I swipe my eyes away from the building outside of our long windows and tap the end of my pen on my thumbnail. A telltale habit of my boredom.

"Father," I address him in a flat voice.

"Do you have anything to add?"

"Yeah, when is Kelsie coming back to work?" Irritation leaks through my tone. I don't give a shit anymore if I come off as unprofessional. "Katherine's marketing strategy is too generic for the Aspen location. We need to sell people on the feeling instead of an overpriced fancy chandelier and giant fireplace. It's standard in almost every damn luxury hotel."

If Katherine's glare could shoot lasers, I'd be severed in half by now. She stands up and straightens her spine as if it will give her more authority. If she's judging authority by height, I am the same size as her while remaining in my seat. My father clears his throat and his eyes waver back and forth between me and the few other team members.

"Kelsie will return when she's ready." *Or she needs a push to remind her how fucking brilliant she is with marketing.* "Leave your sister out of this."

"And jeopardize our business that you care so much about? If I'm wrong, tell Katherine how brilliant her tactics were during this meeting."

"Adam." His voice drops an octave, warning me to ease up before turning to Katherine. "Your presentation wasn't the best you've given us. If my son can come up with a better plan by the end of the week, you're dismissed." He nods and leaves the room.

What the fuck? As if I have time for another assignment. I'm not a fucking marketer.

I stand to head out for lunch and text Kelsie to meet up.

"You're a fucking bastard," Katherine mutters as I walk out.

I debate replying but Katherine is not worth my breath. She is well aware of the high standards this company upholds. If she can't cut it, she can't cut it. I don't have time for this crap on top of my own work. I also can't ignore how something better can be done for our newest location. I exit the building and buy the closest thing to eat for lunch.

I sit on a bench but no longer have an appetite for my burrito. My brain sorts through ideas as a pair of long legs I've grown to memorize catches my eye. Lauren smiles and takes a seat with her bag of groceries.

"You're alive." Lauren nudges my arm.

"It's been a crazy few days." I lift my arm and drape it over the bench.

"What's new with work?" Her body shifts toward me, giving her full attention, so I explain.

"Hmm." She purses her lips. "Well, that should be easy for you. You know marketing is about the feeling and connection. You, of all people, know the longing to have family together under one roof to make lifelong memories. Families need to put their phones down to enjoy the *social* without the *media*. Pull from that."

She throws around a few more ideas and damn, I almost dropped to my knee and proposed. Social without the media. That has to be worked into a tagline somewhere. Guests are heading to the mountains for a reason. Obviously, social media is great advertisement, but she is onto something. I start forming a commercial storyboard in my head.

"Or not?" Her voice cuts through the air and I watch her face scrunch up.

"You're brilliant, Lauren McAllister." I stand and cup her face, planting a dramatic kiss on her lips. "Any chance we can hire you to replace our marketer?"

"I'm sure sleeping with an employee is frowned upon."

"Your boss wouldn't protest." I smirk and instantly picture her bent over my desk.

"I'm happy with my career." She stands and takes my hand. "I don't mind helping out on this project, if you need any."

"Then come right this way, Blondie." I lace our fingers and lead her back to my office.

>=======<

Lauren sits on my lap as we hunch forward, staring at the computer screen. We have made great progress the past two hours on this presentation. I know she's starting to get uncomfortable sitting like this, but if her body shifts against my dick again, I'm going to hike up her sexy little sun dress and bend her over my desk. I should have fucking knocked that fantasy off my list before we started working. I know she can feel my dick pressing into her back each time she moves. Lauren clears her throat and continues to act oblivious, which only fuels my need to fuck her into submission.

My thought halts as a knock echoes on the door. The handle turns and my father's head peeks in. His eyebrows shoot up with surprise as he scans the layout of Post-its on my desk and the pretty lady on my lap. Lauren goes to stand, but my grip tightens on her thigh. The last thing my father needs to witness is the clear effect this woman has on me. Thankfully, she understands the mental memo.

"Sorry to interrupt." He steps into my office. "Adam, if we could have dinner together and go over this morning's meeting, that would be great."

"About that. I ran into this pretty lady on my lunch break and she threw out a brilliant marketing idea." Lauren has a wavering smile of nerves and I lean forward to kiss her soft cheek. "Too bad she turned down the full-time job offer."

"Hmm, I look forward to seeing what you've produced," my father entices. "Depending on how well Katherine pulls her act together, the marketing position can pay very well."

"It's not about the money, sir." Lauren shrugs. "I really enjoy the job I have."

Warmth. There's a warmth to my father's face that I have not witnessed since the birth of my sister's last child. Every time my father sees Lauren, he becomes more delighted. I don't know what it is about her, but she calms the silent storm between me and the person who created me.

"Care to join us for dinner?" my father asks her. "We can hold off business talk until the morning."

"Thank you, but I start work soon and should get going." Lauren stands and places a hand on my shoulder. "I enjoyed getting a glimpse into the corporate world today. It was fun." A giggle bubbles in her chest and warms my own damn heart.

"I forgot you have a night shift. I feel horrible knowing I'm the reason you didn't get enough sleep." Her lips press in a fine line to bite back a smirk.

"Lying isn't attractive on a man your age, *Charmer*." I hear my father grunt a quick laugh as Lauren's eyes send me the true message. *'You've never had a problem keeping me up before.'*

"Let me know how much money you want for your time helping with this project today. It was a great idea, Lauren." I stretch back in my chair and want to call it a day.

"Don't be ridiculous." Her face scrunches as if I've offended her. "Consider it my treat after the strings you pulled for Coit Tower." She turns to my father. "I wish you the best with your marketer. I'm routing that she pulls through, for the business's sake."

"Good day, sweetheart." He closes the door after she leaves and places his hands on the front of my desk.

"I'm glad I didn't walk into what I did eight months ago." Humor laces his voice but the accusation is sharp.

I lace my hands together and lean forward. "Nothing happened today. But if it did, the door would be locked." I never bothered to lock it before with Miranda. She always dropped in when I needed a quick fix. I respect Lauren's body too much to risk exposing it to others.

"She's a nice girl." My ears perk up at his remark. "Don't ruin her more than life already has."

Of course, he's done a full background check on her. It's nothing new with people who frequent our hotel.

I put both hands up and shake my head. "I don't need to know anything more than what she wants me to. Her past is for her to tell." I do wonder if my father knows why she wakes up some mornings in a panic. "We aren't together. We're strictly friends."

"You've told me." He stands and runs a hand through his dark hair. "What strings did you pull at Coit?" Why the sudden interest in my personal life?

"She mentioned it would be cool to watch the sunset on top of the tower." I tap a pen over the top of my thumb. "So, we did. It was great."

"I hope Katherine can save her ass with a new strategy, because your *friend* turned down the job."

"Dad, you're so picky about working with what your degree qualifies you for." Which confuses the hell out of me with Emmett's choice in philosophy. "She's not qualified. Why would *you* offer her the position?"

"She took a semester of marketing in high school." He nods with the same shit-eating grin that I use far too much myself. "You are not one to rave about people's skills, so I take it seriously when you do."

Honestly, I could spend the next hour raving about her *other* skills. Her mouth, to be specific. My father's clearing of his throat and knuckles tapping on my desk tell me he can read my thoughts. I interlock my fingers and push my palms down to give them a stretch.

"I need to wrap up these accounts before I call it a night." I turn back to my screen.

"Enjoy your evening." He nods and heads out.

I skip dinner and spend the rest of the evening blowing off steam in the gym.

Chapter 13

Lauren

My phone pulls me out of my sleep an hour before my alarm should go off. "Hey, Lloyd." If it were anyone else, I'd let it go to voice mail. "How are you?" We haven't spoken too much since I arrived.

"Good, hon. I haven't heard from you lately and wanted to see if San Fran is treating you right." The chuckle in his voice is hoarse from years of smoking.

"It's treating me really well." Despite anyone being able to see me, I sit up and pull the sheet to cover my chest. "I've met a few people and I'm getting to know the ins and outs of this city."

"I'm sure a lucky fella will sweep you off your feet in no time." He replies with such confidence in his voice. He knew I was quiet and reserved under his roof. Boys were not a thing we ever talked about.

"I'm in no rush for that." I keep my tone light. "How has the world been treating you the past few weeks?"

"I joined a board game group." I smile, knowing he'll do great since it was the only thing we really bonded over. "Heather beat me the past two weeks, so I owe her dinner." I can hear the smile through his voice.

"Heather? Is she a new lady friend?"

"We may have an infatuation with each other. Lauren, I think I'm ready to get back out there." It's been years since his wife passed. The pain he went through losing her has been embedded in my mind forever.

"Why?" My voice goes quiet. "After losing Marsha, do you really want to risk losing another?" I'm sandpaper when it comes to the pain of losing someone. Loss only happens when you allow someone to weasel into your heart. I was born never knowing love. The feeling of loss will never exist to me. I don't know how people voluntarily allow it.

"Lauren," Lloyd takes a deep breath and I wait until he forms an answer. "I know life has thrown you in the wringer. Marsha and I were probably the only brief example of a stable relationship. But the way that played out was heart wrenching." He clears his throat as I picture him reclining back in his corner chair like he always does while talking on the phone. "I promise one of these days you'll have a moment. You and someone will click, and everything will change. You'll feel it."

I felt a shift in Coit Tower, but that could have been the higher elevation...

"Feel what, though?" I blurt out louder than intended.

"You'll look at someone and your soul will tell you that every high with them is worth *any* alternative the world throws at you. Even if it's for a moment in life, that person will complete a part of your soul." The line goes quiet as he takes a long breath. "You won't know how much your life needs them until... that *moment*." He trails off as I watch blood stream down my thumbnail as my middle finger continues to pick the skin.

"How poetic of you." My throat tightens, anxiety forming that I didn't know was in me. "I'm sure I won't ever have that *moment* because I've seen how much pain it can cause."

"What's life without happy moments?" Lloyd drops his voice into a parental tone I've never heard. "You're young and your life is worth making memories. You deserve to share a special bond with someone. The experience will brighten your life. Trust me."

"I have happy memories. I don't need to feel the pain of what they could cause," I defend.

I hear the screen door open as he sighs. "I just want you to have what you deserve from here on out. A new city can be a new life. Use it to your advantage, sweetie." The car engine of his old green Pontiac rings through the phone. "I'm going to meet Heather. You take care and give me a call next week."

"I will. Enjoy your day." I end the call as my shoulders feel heavy.

I fall backward onto my pillows.

For the first time ever, I call in sick to work.

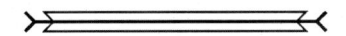

>=====<

I wake as the sun is setting behind the skyscrapers and still feel in a slump. Lloyd's words drained me with the basic fact of how I can't let anyone in. Not that I've tried. My reasons are too good for anyone to argue with. In an act of desperation to prove him wrong, I change into my workout gear with a one-track mind. I need to immerse in cardio and show myself I do not want the man who increases my heart rate. Tonight, there will be no *moments* Lloyd spoke of. I will strictly focus on fitness.

There's still slight daylight left, so my feet hit the pavement as I jog a few blocks to the gym. I sneak in the back of the packed class since they've already started the warm-up. I hope to go unnoticed, but my tall blonde ass tends to stick out in a crowd. Adam smirks at someone to my right causing anxiety to coil around my gut. I'm scared to let my eyes follow. We agreed to be casual, but side partners weren't part of the deal. I follow the crowd doing jumping jacks and glance to see Kelsie hyperfocused ahead. Relief lifts the weight off my lungs when I realize that was why Adam was smiling. I wonder how the hell she has energy at the end of the day after solo parenting. As if she feels my eyes on her, she turns and waves, drawing my attention to her brother.

Adam finds me and a flash of question crosses his face. I give a faint smile and avert my eyes, waiting for further instructions. When it comes time to partner up, Kelsie flies to my side.

"Hey stranger." She smiles and places her hands on her hips, taking a few deep breaths. "I told my brother if he makes us do those partner wheelbarrow things, then Mallory is spending the entire weekend with him."

"I hate wheelbarrows too." I laugh and glance down.

Unlike her father and brother, Kelsie is much shorter. Where her brother's shoulders are broad, hers are delicate. Their brown hair and eyes are the Wheaton's family signature. She also has killer curves that I've always wished for on my lanky, lean body. I mentally scold myself at the self-sabotaging thought because we all need to embrace the way we were made.

Adam pulls out boxing gloves and long pads with the handle. I'm excited to throw some punches. I wonder if Max told him I took his class the other day. My stomach flips with slight excitement thinking about showcasing my proper stance and punch to Adam.

Get a grip. Remember why you're here, Lauren.

"I'm so ready to throw a few good punches." Kelsie laughs. "Mallory has been nothing short of an attitude since she came home and my patience is running thin."

"I imagine she doesn't back down from many things."

"I am adamant about her critical thinking and throwing out a good debate, but I didn't expect her to throw me under a bus with logic at age seven." She shakes her head as Adam walks over.

"Who's watching the kids?" Adam asks, looking sexy as sin sporting a loose black tank and red basketball shorts.

"Mom was over, but the kids kept bugging Max to stay. So, he was guilt-tripped by Mallory to paint her nails and Mom said she was leaving shortly after me."

"Max is." Adam's demeanor changes as he replies sharply and shakes his head. "That's all you had to say. Women always elaborate on things that don't need detail."

"Right, I forgot how small the male brain is to process information," Kelsie bites back and grabs us gloves.

"Aren't you supposed to be at work?" He spews my way as his jaw tics and his posture remains tense.

"Aren't *you*?" I place my hands on my hips and nod to the rest of the class who have silently been watching us.

With a huff, he turns back to direct the class. "He's been in a mood all day." Kelsie sighs and starts throwing punches as

I hold up the mat. "Something about an extra work project he now has to deal with."

"The marketing?"

"He didn't go into detail. There's also something going on about the new Aspen location. He and my father keep arguing about it." She takes a few more hits before Adam circles back around to us.

"If you're going to be sassy, you can skip over us and move on to the next group." I square my shoulders and look him dead in the eye.

"I am *not* sassy." He takes the foam square from me and drops it. "Gloves on." He holds up his hand.

"You're not using a safety mat? That's a little cocky." The irritation in my voice proves his attitude is affecting mine.

I'm also ready to wipe the *"I'll show you cocky"* smirk off his face.

"I haven't needed one for students in this class yet." He shrugs. "Haven't you been watching the rest of the room?"

"I've been too busy hearing your childhood stories from Kelsie." I taunt, watching his eyes narrow at his sister. "I'm kidding. I don't care about your perfect childhood." I am well aware part of that is my own jealousy because my childhood was traumatic.

I look at his open palms and take a step to the side to give me a clear shot of his arm. Positioning myself quickly, I throw all my weight into the hardest punch I can deliver. It wasn't hard enough to knock him over of course. The man is a freaking marble statue, but it was enough to make him stumble with my unexpected force. Little did he know, I've been practicing daily in case I need to use it on the street.

His jaw tightens but his eyes light up, impressed. I know he's fighting back a smirk because he wants to stay pissed for some damn reason. I narrow my eyes and point with my glove toward the mat.

"Pick up the damn mat so you're not out of *commission* later." My attitude takes him by surprise and his eyes darken with racy thoughts he can't pursue in this moment.

His tongue darts out to lick his lips and I wish I could blame my shortage of breath from the workout.

"As you wish, *Blondie.*" His gravel voice hits my stomach, channeling me to throw my sexual frustration toward the mat.

Adam drops the mat and lets his eyes travel down my body before heading to the next group.

"Hot damn, girl, the sexual tension between you two is insane." Kelsie tightens her ponytail. "It would be hotter if it wasn't my brother, though."

"Hey, I don't know how you and Max are just *friends.*" I smirk and watch her cheeks tinge pink. "That man is wicked hot in a boy next store kind of way." I laugh. "I'm into your brother, but I've seen Max at the gym. Who knew all that muscle was under his brooding bravado?"

"He's not brooding." Kelsie laughs. "He doesn't open up to a lot of people. I've known him since I was Mallory's age. My mother calls him her *adopted child*, since he was always over and raised as much hell as Adam." Her voice projects all the reasons not to act on him. "He knows all my weird quirks and little tics, so it would be weird to breach a friendship."

There is some type of emotional response I pick up when she talks about him. But I can't pinpoint what she's feeling just yet. I've never been good at deciphering someone's emotions since I've spent a lifetime avoiding any of my own.

"And watching him help out with your kids, that's enough to make any woman's ovaries explode." For some reason, I'm enticed to see if there's a spark between them. Like they're my own real-time reality show. "I'm shocked he has never made an attempt toward you and your gorgeous ass."

I think they call this women's intuition or whatnot.

"Adam is amazing with the kids too." She doesn't take the bait. "I'm sure that sparked some baby daddy thoughts."

Damn, she is good.

"It's sweet to see." I shrug, noticing our class grab their belongings and file out of the classroom. "Adam and I are extremely casual though."

"And Max and I are just *friends*." Her eyes go wide as her head tilts forward, as if she's trying to convince herself of that too. "Good night, Lauren." Kelsie picks up her bag. "Bye, Adam, don't be an ass tomorrow." Well, that got me nowhere.

Adam and I are the only ones left in the room. I walk to pick up my bag as he picks up equipment. Taking a sip of my water, I feel it. My skin litters with goose bumps as my breathing picks up from his close proximity. I watch the light dim as his shadow towers over me. A hand rests on the wall, half caging me in. I'm annoyed how this dominant dick move still turns me on. Every. Damn. Time. Still irritated with his attitude from earlier, I swallow my water and turn around with an eye roll. His head leans down, pushing my back against the wall. His breathing is labored as his jaw tightens. I can't peg if his anger is at me for punching him or if he's pissed about whatever the hell went on before class.

"Aw, who ripped your Armani?" My teenage self would be proud of the amount of attitude in my voice.

"Who ripped your La Perla?" His voice purrs in a seductive invitation, transporting my mind back to us in the shower.

Ass.

"Just some random quick fix." I turn my head to look past his arm at the empty hallway. "I barely remember it."

His free hand tilts up my chin and for a moment, he remains silent. His hungry eyes burn into me, obliterating my ability to speak or form a thought. The ache between my legs sends my body humming as our electricity burns rapidly. His breath hits my face and his scent consumes me. If I continue staring into his eyes and watch everything he wants to do to me, his stare will harness the power to make me come. His lips brush against my ear as he leans in.

"I'd be more than happy to remind you right against this wall who your quick fix was." His leg moves between mine and instinctively, I widen my stance. "I know if my fingers slip into your shorts"—his fingers trail down my arm—"you'd be soaked and ready for me to slide right in." My breath hitches as his finger ghosts above the waistband of my shorts.

"I came here for a workout." My voice comes out in a whisper as I hear my heart thumping through my ears.

"Don't worry, Blondie. I'll make sure you burn a lot of calories." His hot breath hits the side of my neck. "I promise you will be breathless and sore tomorrow." With all my willpower, I duck under his arm and move away from him.

"I came here to alleviate stress. Not to rely on an orgasm from you." I grab my backpack and turn to walk out, but his hand pulls me back.

"I'm sorry." He means it. "It's been a shitty day, Lauren. I shouldn't take it out on anybody."

"Okay. Apology accepted." I sigh and look toward the door. "Can I go now?"

"How come you took the night off?" His brows push together with concern. "Are you alright? You're always hell-bent on taking extra shifts and working overtime."

Are you alright?

I despise that question. I've heard it so much throughout my life. Are you alright in this house? Are you alright with making new friends? Are you alright attending a new school? Are you alright at the new home? Why ask a child the question if nothing will be done if I say no? I've never had the choice if something was alright until I became an adult.

I'm not *alright.*

I'm tired.

I'm tired of trying to figure out people's emotions. I'm tired of caring why I should. I'm tired of wondering if my own emotions are valid or worth having. I'm tired of *not knowing* how to function in a relationship because I've never seen a normal one. I'm tired of having to explain why I don't want feelings to people who have no idea what I went through. I'm tired of saying *I'm alright.* I'm tired of being me.

But no one wants to hear that.

"I'm alright." I fake a smile, but by the look on his face, he knows I'm lying.

"Okay." He brings my hand to his lips and kisses it before letting it go. "I'm here if you want to talk, or not talk."

A tidal wave of emotion smacks me, bringing a sting to my nose. My tongue hits the roof of my mouth as I suppress unwanted tears. Why does his offering cease my lungs and make me want to break down? I turn the door to hide my face.

"I just want to go home." I walk out and take a strong dose of melatonin before bed.

Chapter 14

Lauren

I stare at myself for too long in the mirror as Rachel lets out a whistle on video chat.

"Stop worrying, Ren. You look classy but still totally fuckable," Rachel encourages, knowing I hate social events. "You look like a work of art."

Tonight is the art exhibit of the photographer who captured Adam and me on the mountain.

I smooth my silky dark-green dress and move my curls to the side. I look elegant and semiformal. I made a stop at Sephora to have professional help to create smoky eyes. Makeup beyond mascara and lip gloss has never been something I've put effort into learning. As a woman who lives in scrubs and casual outfits, I don't recognize the woman I see in the mirror. I brush a long blonde curl to the side and hold up two different earrings to the screen.

"Diamond studs or the dangly ones?" I take a shaky breath as the earrings jiggle.

"Dangly. Your necklace is really simple so the earrings will add a statement." Rachel shakes her head. "There is no need to be nervous, my nasty Nordic." I don't try to hide my cringe. "You look like every human's wet dream. Hell, I might burn this vision in my mind for later." Rachel does an exaggerated wink.

"Shut up. I've never been to an event like this. What if the photo looks terrible blown up and people hate it?"

"Then you still get free appetizers and I know Adam will be getting you out of that dress as soon as he can."

I smile and start to think about Adam's skillful mouth on my neck. I press my lips together feeling my lower stomach tingle. Rachel clears her throat, snapping me back to reality.

"Sorry, I can't get him out of my head sometimes." I feel my cheeks heat.

"How are you guys doing?" I haven't spoken to him since last night at the gym, but I have faith he will still pick me up.

"I have to get going." I glance at my phone, avoiding her question. "He will be here any minute. I'll call you again soon." I wave as she shakes her head, flipping me off.

I spritz on perfume when Adam shoots a text saying he is on his way up. I slip on my short heels and debate changing into flats. My height already draws enough attention as it is. I open the door and grab my clutch. Adam stops at the doorway in his tailored suit and my core responds, desperate for him to bend me over in front of the mirror as he hikes up my dress and fucks me. His eyes travel up my body and back to my three-inch heels. My self-conscious side is rare, but I'm still human.

"Are the heels too much?" I tilt my head toward the flats. "I can change into those if you want." This wouldn't be the first time a guy has asked me not to wear heels so he feels superior in height.

Adam steps closer and his hand trails up the exposed skin on my leg from the slit of my dress. His fingers stop at the top of the slit and then travel up my arm to give my shoulder a gentle squeeze.

"You are the most beautiful woman I've ever shared the same breath of air with." He steals my breath with a soft kiss. "Keep the heels on until you're screaming my name."

Annnd now I want to skip to the screaming his name part.

"Do we have to go to this event?" I poke my bottom lip out and let myself whine.

He takes a step back, clearing his throat as his hand reaches down to adjust his obvious need for me. "We do. We don't have to stay long. But we are the main attraction to this event."

"Main attraction?" My insides turn and I feel my heart rate pick up.

"That photo with the rolling fog is a gem itself. Add in a cute couple kissing on top of the mountain, and you've got a star piece." He holds out his hand, but my ears are still processing his reference to us as a couple. "Are you alright? What's really going on, Lauren?"

"Let's go." I straighten my shoulders and bypass his hand as we head out.

I keep a full glass of champagne close to me as if it's a comfort item. For the past twenty minutes, we have been talking to people Adam knows and I'm going to need a notebook if I plan to remember everyone I've been introduced to. I swear the entire city knows this man. I guess when you're attractive, tall and a Wheaton, it's hard not to stand out.

I force a smile at a woman who has the confidence to place a hand on Adam's arm while batting her flirty eyelashes while I stand by his side. I wish I could say she's the first to do this tonight. These women have some damn nerve. Adam lets her hand rest on him as she continues to make small talk, ignoring that I am right *beside* him. His charming smile stays in perfect place as he keeps the conversation flowing. She tells stories to keep the focus on her, so Adam's attempt to introduce me gets overruled. Her eyes meet mine with the fakest smile I've ever seen.

"Give me a call sometime." Her hand slides down his arm instead of pulling it off before she walks away.

Adam's hand rests on the small of my back but I arch out of his touch. It's enough to let him know I'm annoyed, but I also shouldn't care if another woman is interested. We aren't dating and I don't want to cause a scene. As he leans in again, I let him.

His lips brush against my ear. "I didn't peg you as the jealous type." His breath sends need through my veins, pebbling my skin with goose bumps.

"I'm not." Until now, when him flirting with another woman is threatening our arrangement rules.

"The glare you shot her way when her hand landed on me was fucking hot as hell." His hand moves to my hip and he gives it a squeeze. "Other women touching me don't light up my body the way your touch does, Lauren."

You seem to smile an awful lot when women do touch you.

"I'm sure they could get you off." I step to the side. "Unless you're viewing us as a couple." I cross one arm under my breasts and hold my champagne flute close to my face.

He moves in front of me, eyeing my full glass. "I never said you and I were a *couple*. You're *exclusive* to me until one of us decides otherwise."

"You said we were a couple at my place earlier." I keep my tone sharp but my voice low enough so no one hears us argue.

"I haven't seen you take a single sip of champagne, yet I'm still questioning your sobriety." I take a long sip out of spite and wince as the sour taste ignites my tongue.

"You said a cute couple on the mountain," I throw back.

"For fuck's sake, Lauren." I've never seen a man roll his eyes, but Adam rolls his and tilts his head back. "It was easier to describe the photo that way than to go on about two people casually hooking up with no strings attached while they climb the mountain together promising to stay friends and not fall for each other." He says the entire thing in one breath before tipping back the last half of his drink. "Is that what's really bothering you? Using the term *couple* for convenience?"

Is it?

Or was it picturing another woman conjuring explicit thoughts about the man next to me?

He continues as I have no words. "How about last night at the gym?"

I glance around to make sure no one is looking so I can unhinge my jaw and chug a flute of alcohol in the least elegant way. Immediately, I feel it cloud my head. My stomach turns as the bubbles settle. Adam takes the hint that now is not the time or place to talk this over. His arm links with mine as we round the corner to our photo.

The main attraction is an understatement. Everyone gathers around the panoramic photo of us. The length is probably one Adam long and a half of me in height. This is by far a jaw-dropping sight. The orange tint in the far background peeks just above the rolling fog clouds. Front and center of the photo are the silhouettes of us. My arms are locked around his neck as we kiss. Adam's arms wrapped tightly around my waist, tipping me slightly back. The sun casts a radiating glow from our figures and contrasts beautifully with the white fog. The photo leaves me breathless.

The photographer, Grayson, spots us and makes an announcement to single us out. I blush out of embarrassment as he makes his way over. "I'm glad you guys made it." He shakes Adam's hand then leans forward, touching my upper arm while placing a kiss to the side of my cheek.

Adam stiffens as his jaw tics.

Good. I smile inwardly.

"This size is a bit large for my wall." I giggle, already feeling the champagne kick in. "Have you had any interest in this piece yet?"

"Oh yes." He smiles. "I've had a few magazines reach out and this big baby." He points to our photo. "Has already sold."

"Already sold?" Adam chokes out. "I'd love to make you a higher offer."

"Sorry, this went to an anonymous buyer." Grayson shakes his head.

"I understand." Adam clears his throat, straightening his posture. "It's just odd to think of me and Lauren in a stranger's house."

"Well, Adam, you did approve for the image to be sold," I say through a tight smile. "A businessman like yourself should be aware of what that means."

While Adam's eyes roam around the crowd, he forces a snarky smirk and gives my hand a slight squeeze.

Grayson keeps his eyes locked on mine and smiles softly. "I'd love to shoot more of you, Lauren, around the city if you're up for it."

"Maybe one day. I'm still adjusting to seeing *this*." I giggle, feeling my cheeks tingle. The downside of drinking for the second time in my life is that it hits quick. "I hope this photo inspires others to go for a hike up there."

"Or find love." Grayson smiles as someone calls his name.

"Whatever they're into." I extend my hand and let Grayson kiss my cheek once more. "It was nice to see you, and thanks for inviting us."

He walks off and I make my way out of the building. Adam is trailing my back without a word. I know his eyes are burning holes through me. I don't know what made me attempt to make him jealous. It was innocent, just like his flirting was earlier. It was also a quick self-reminder that I'm not serious about a guy the way Lloyd wants me to experience.

The cool breeze pebbles my skin and I shimmy with the chill in an attempt to get warm. Adam's large hand grabs my upper arm to spin me around. My back pushes up against the building and I move my arm out of his grasp. Irritation with society's view of needing to find love is getting the best of me.

"What the hell is going on?" Desperation laces his voice catching me off guard.

"I'm leaving. I saw all of his work and thanked him." He doesn't stop me as I continue walking.

"Did I do something?"

I turn around and take a deep breath. "No." I hear my voice waver as new emotion takes over. "You flirting with those girls didn't bug me." I'm *not* feeling hurt over this, am I?

"Okay, let's say I believe that." I know he doesn't. "Why were you so hostile at the gym?" Adam runs a hand through his hair.

"I don't have to give you an explanation."

"Fair enough. But I don't play games or do drama." His face turns serious. "I like whatever it is we have going on. But if you have something to say, then say it. I'm not going to keep prying and guessing why you're all of a sudden pissed."

"I'm just tired." Which isn't a lie. "We all have something that keeps us up." I am sick of my internal five a.m. wake-up call.

"I know you don't want to get personal, but know that I'm here to listen if you ever need to talk." His hands cup my face and he places a small kiss on my lips. "Ready to head back?"

I nod and my head starts to pound from the alcohol taking over.

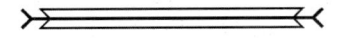

I spend the next two days curled up by my large window with a tub of ice cream. Cramps are in full swing and I write off why I was an emotional mess. My menstrual cycle has never been consistent, but I refuse to take a pill that alters my emotions even more than I already know how to deal with them. The heat of the sun is calling my name through the window. My skin beckons to absorb its vitamins and feel the sea breeze on my face. I should go for a walk and talk to someone other than my houseplants and fictional TV characters. Adam has left me alone since the night of the gallery.

Me: Care to go for a walk if you're not busy?
Charmer: I can head out in thirty minutes.
Me: I'll see you soon ☺

That gives me enough time to pop an Advil and have a shower. When I don't see him in front of my place, I make my way to his. Adam stands next to his dad in what seems to be a serious conversation. I turn around to exit the lobby, planning to wait outside unnoticed, when George calls my name. I freeze, scrunching up my face as if I've been caught doing something I shouldn't.

"Adam is free to go." His father nods curtly and disappears down the hall.

"You sure you're free to go?" My voice goes an octave higher than I wanted.

"Yeah, we don't normally have a Saturday afternoon meeting." He clears his throat and starts to roll up the sleeves of his dress shirt. "Let's head out."

"Breathe." I place my hand on his strong forearm admiring the width. "As sexy as you look in this suit, I'm sure you'd rather walk downtown in something else. I'm in no rush."

"I'll be upstairs for a few minutes. Want to come with me?" He reaches for my hand and walks me to the elevator.

We step into the elevator and Adam catches me off guard with his lips. His kiss is slow after entering his elevator code and we start to move. His arms snake around my waist, pulling me flush against him. I moan, wanting more than I can take, and he picks me up. One hand grips the back of my neck as his other hand holds me gently. It's a contrast to his tender kiss with the possessive grab of my neck. It's been too long since we've had sex and my body is melting against his with the need for him to touch my bare skin.

His hand tangles through my damp hair as we enter his place. Adam carries me directly to his bathroom without the kiss breaking. Dark-charcoal slate encompasses us as we enter the walk-in shower. A large two-foot rectangular showerhead hangs in the center. I'm speechless, counting the side jets on the wall. This bathroom screams masculinity and luxury. A wooden bench the length of the shower catches me off guard. Why does someone need this big of a shower? A small window lets a stream of light through.

My feet hit the floor as his hands begin to unbutton his shirt.

"I just had a shower." I point at my wet hair.

"So?" He drops his pants and his throbbing dick begs to be released from his boxers.

"It's that time of the month." I sigh, breathless and sexually agitated.

"Again?" He turns the shower on and the giant showerhead rains down beautifully. "How?"

I point with both hands to my stomach. "Because you didn't put a baby in me!" His eyes linger on my stomach for an uncomfortable amount of time.

"Stop picturing me with a balloon belly, jerk face."

"I'm not, Lauren." His eyes remain on my stomach, and I don't want him to think about whatever is going through his mind. "Maybe I was for a second, but you put the thought in my mind." I snap my fingers, bringing his eyes up to mine. "I don't want to put a baby in you. I swear."

"Do you want your dick in my mouth or not?"

His eyes heat and drop to my mouth. Irritation boils through me with his silence.

"I feel bad that you don't get to come just because Mother Nature is a bitch." He runs his hand over his face. "Get in the shower. It's been way too fucking long since I've felt your naked body against mine."

"Adam, I appreciate—" I protest as his hand grabs the hem of my tank top and lifts it above my head.

"It's a dark floor anyway." He tugs at my skirt. "Take care of what you need to and meet me back in here. Don't be shy."

If I wasn't this desperate to feel him inside me, I would have put up a fight like I had in the past hookups.

Adam looks like a freaking dream when I walk back into the shower. He faces forward as his naked muscular body glistens on full display. Water rains down as he lifts his hands over his face and tilts his head up, smoothing his wet hair back. A devilish grin tugs at his mouth as I step into the water. His hands cup my face as his erection pushes against my stomach. The lust I felt minutes ago vanishes because I can't believe I agreed to period sex. His lips meet mine for a moment before pulling back.

"Lauren, look at me." Adam slightly bends his knees so his dick rubs between my folds. "Relax. I want you to feel good." I nod and he spins me around, guiding me forward to the wall of jets.

His hand slides over my hip as the jets spray the front of my body. His lips graze my neck as his fingers brush over my clit. He repeats soft circles until I sigh, finally relaxing into his chest. I bite my lip and moan, feeling my pulse increase. Instead of him adding more pressure like I need, his hand slips under my thigh.

"Lift your foot on the bench." He nips my ear and widens my leg as the stream of water patters against my clit. "That's a good girl."

I gasp at the sensation and arch my back, finding the right angle to continue the pleasure. I lean into Adam and reach my arm up to wrap around the back of his neck. My hips buck as I ride the needed rhythm to continue the sparks coursing through my lower body. His hand reaches around to squeeze my breast and my stomach rolls with pleasure.

"You're so fucking sexy letting the shower fuck your pussy," he growls in my ear. "I'm getting jealous." Adam lets me go for a second to rip open a condom and comes back behind me. "That jet stream and I are gonna make you come, Blondie. Hard." He grips my raised thigh, opening me more to push all the way in.

I can't form a sentence with his punishing pace and breathless pants in my ear. His tongue occasionally runs along the side of it, swirling euphoria in my stomach. The jets build tension within as I try to let go. My mind flashes to what his dick might look like if I do let go and cover him with everything in my lower region. He senses I'm no longer in the moment and slows his pace.

"Stop overthinking." He spins me around and picks me up, pinning me to the opposite wall. "I need to feel your pussy tighten around me and your nails claw at my shoulders." His lips lock with mine as he continues to thrust.

I lean forward, draping myself over his shoulder so his dick brushes my clit the way I need it to. My body tightens and I bite down on his shoulder, crying out as my orgasm shakes through me. He stills in me a few strokes later but doesn't put me down. Instead, he carries us to the bench and I straddle his lap as he remains inside me. He doesn't speak. Adam brushes wet hair out of my face with a soft smile. His arms weave around my waist as one intertwines in the back of my hair. Our eyes never waver as I sit on him and watch the way he slows his breathing down. My hands cup the stubble on his jaw as I bring my forehead to rest on his. I attempt to steady my own breathing. His cock twitches inside, reminding me he still hasn't finished.

I want to break this moment because it feels too intimate. We are too close for too long, but I never want it to end. I surprise myself as I lean forward and start a gentle kiss. Our swollen plump lips move tenderly, and I wrap my arms around his neck to pull my body tight against his. I can't get enough of this man. Everything inside and out of my body wants to devour him. To relish in every rough and tender touch we let consume us. My center lights up with tingles and even though he's still inside of me, I physically ache for more of him. His hand travels along my body as he swallows my soft moans.

His hands grip my waist as he grinds deeper. Adam begins moving my hips slowly and I follow his lead. Our labored breathing syncs as I start to ride him. I'm so close to another orgasm and I already feel this one will be even more intense.

"God, Adam!" I shout in a whispered tone, his fingers ghosting over my thigh to circle my clit.

My legs stiffen as my body shakes around him. He grunts, lifting his hips up to pound harder into me, reaching his own orgasm. I take a moment and rest my head on his shoulder as the warm water rains on my sensitive skin. His hands feather up and down my spine before I finally gather the strength to stand. My head spins as my ears ring. I have never been more sated in my life. And fuck me if I'll ever find another guy with his capabilities again.

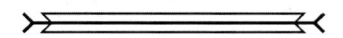

We wait for the light to signal us to cross as Adam gives my hand a squeeze. "We are a block away from every woman's heaven." He laughs.

"I'm pretty sure you just took me there in the shower." I had no idea how heightened my senses would be during that time of the month.

"This is second best, then." We make our way down the road as the large letters over a brick structure become clear.

"Ghirardelli?" My smile widens.

"First thing you should know; There is always a large crowd. Second, you can watch how the chocolate is made *and* there is ice cream."

My legs pick up the pace. "Just when I thought today couldn't get better."

Warm, fresh chocolate greets my nose as we make our way into the shop. I order my ice cream and we head out to the steps in the courtyard square.

"Are you happy with your puddle cream?" Adam shakes his head as he watches my vigorous stirring to achieve the perfect consistency.

"I am. Thank you very much." I flip the spoon upside down on my tongue and slowly drag it out of my mouth. His eyes track my movement.

"If you keep doing that, I'll take you up on the offer you gave me before our shower."

"Adam, there's people around." I dramatically raise my eyebrows. "I'm not one for putting on *that* type of show."

"Come on." He stands. "We still have more things to put in your mouth."

I wear a smile like a child as I hold Adam's hand and clutch a small turtle-shaped loaf of bread in my other. Up ahead, the large iconic Fisherman's Wharf boat wheel comes into view across the street. We push through the busy crowd and see a few street performers. The steel drums create the false tropical ambience while other entertainers stand on milk crates dressed as silver-and-gold statues. I squint and look up at the Wharf sign, wishing I had brought sunglasses. Crowds of people gather at the corner waiting to cross the street to the fish market that's too strong for my liking. Adam gives my hand a small squeeze as I smile faintly.

"Is it too crowded today for you?" he asks.

"I can handle it." My voice is soft.

"Well, I'll be." A Southern accent cuts through the music, sending chills down my spine. "Is that really you, Lauren?"

That voice, on the other hand, is one I don't think I can handle. Pretend you don't know the haunting voice, Lauren. Walk away and let Adam make you forget.

"Mabel?" I say her name, losing control of myself.

She has aged in the past fifteen years and it hasn't been kind to her. Good. Her hand shoots over her heart and she looks up, giving me a feigned expression. *If only I was this tall when I needed to be.* Adam remains quiet thankfully. My death grip on his hand probably sends a direct message.

"I knew it had to be you." Her smile churns the bile turning in my stomach. "You've grown, but your looks have not. I always wondered if you'd remain the ugly duckling. At least you're slim."

Because I was lucky to get two meals a day under your roof.

"Why are you talking to me?" I feel Adam's grip tighten against my hand and watch his jaw tic out of my peripheral. I know he's boiling.

"Your homely duck pout is easy to spot, even at this age. I saw you across the street as what I pictured you to look like as an adult and was curious to know if you made it this far in life. I stopped getting updates on you once my Stuart was taken away." Her tone drops with disgusted accusation. "You and that Ella girl ruined my Stuart. Destroyed my marriage and the foster side income." She shakes her head in disgust.

The stale brand of cigarettes on her breath transported me back to the mornings I'd lain in bed and been forced to smell it off Stuart's.

"He rots in prison while you flaunt around the city, living your best life like a selfish bitch." Her boldness has grown over the years.

Adam goes to open his mouth, but my thumb pushes against his index finger hard, begging him to keep silent. This is my battle to fight.

Mabel continues, pointing her finger an inch away from my chest. "If you little skanks hadn't been so tempting, Stuart would have kept interested in me at home." Her wrinkled lips roll inward as she takes a deep breath. "I knew we should have only fostered little boys."

I stand paralyzed. With the mention of his name, I feel his skin on mine, his words passing through my ears, and my eyes dart around to look for the poster they stayed glued to in mine and Ella's room. My teeth grit the way they used to when I'd bite the stuffed bear to keep quiet. Everything comes crashing back as she continues.

"You probably curse Ella every day that she ruined things by getting pregnant. You were still young enough to not have to worry about that happening to you." Her head vigorously shakes with rage. "Lauren, the selfish bitch who would have kept that daily secret to herself. Stealing my Stuart's love in hopes of staying at one foster home longer than a few months."

Adam and I are likely to have bruised hands by the end of this conversation. I feel his rage radiating off him as my childhood truths spill out. He takes a small step forward, and I sense he is ready to say something. I force a swallow and I beat him to it.

"Mabel, I wake every morning and wish I understood back then why Ella and I *should* have testified against you so you could rot in prison with him."

"Bold coming from the person who broke up my family. Your arm candy doesn't talk much." Her smiles turn my veins to ice as she lifts her purse higher. "I figured you'd end up with someone sporting more muscles than brain cells." She brushes past us, and before I can blink, she blends in with the passing crowd.

Was that even real? I feel Adam move in front of me as his black shirt blocks off everything else around. Broken clips of flashbacks dance before my eyes. The pain, Stuart's weight, and his threats rush through me and I feel my lungs closing in. My shoulders weigh a hundred pounds heavier and my head spins. Nausea filters through my gut and up to my throat. I gasp in an attempt to fight the gag that's forcing itself up. My eyes lock on the nearest garbage can, and for the second time in this city, I empty my stomach. I only wish it was due to the strong smell of the fish market beside us.

Chapter 15

ADAM

We don't say a word heading back to her place. My brain racking through every possibility, hoping that I heard wrong and there is no way that what I am assuming is what actually was implied. This is a situation I actually *need* details on. Lauren stares ahead as I go through the motions of setting her on the couch and handing her some water, which she refuses. I take it as a win when she allows me to put a blanket over her. She sits wide eyed in a shell-shocked trance for who knows how long. The sun starts to set, casting a golden glow on her blonde hair, making her look like an angel. One who seems to have gone through hell. My stomach knots, threatening its own contents to rise. With a deep breath, I somehow manage to keep it at bay.

I reach out and rub her foot. Her expression holds nothing but emptiness with the truth behind her haunting look. My heart tugs with desperation to take the pain away. But how the hell do I go about helping her in this situation? What the hell can I even do if I'm right about the sickening thoughts I imagine are passing through her mind? I feel my own eyes sting. Her heavy breath cuts through the silence and her shoulders give a small shrug. I nod and doubt it's fucking helpful, but it's all I can manage. Lauren crawls to my end of the couch and curls in my lap. My arms wrap around her as I place a kiss in her hair.

"I know you have questions." Her voice is a broken whisper.

"I haven't pressed about your past, but I can't leave without some type of explanation." My hand runs through her hair, trying to soothe her. "We don't have to talk tonight."

We stay silent until the city lights are the only thing left lighting up her place. Her breathing becomes more even, and I peek my head to the side to see if she is asleep.

"Ask me." Her voice cracks and she clear's her throat.

It shreds me to know I'm about to hear a painstaking answer. "How old were you?"

"Ten." She swallows. "Ella had just turned twelve. She and I shared a room."

Ten? That's three fucking years older than my niece. If anyone tried anything with Mal, they wouldn't live to see their prosecution. I hold Lauren tighter and rest my chin on the top of her head.

"That bitch. You have no idea how bad I want to go find her in that downtown crowd." As if it's the foster children's fault her husband is locked away.

I'm now the one completely speechless. I flash back to the night we lay in front of my large windows and how Lauren tensed when I made a joke about virginity, making my round more eventful than her first time.

"She didn't do what *he* did. Ella and I were too young and scared to speak up when she acted clueless to the authorities."

"She's just as fucking guilty."

"Probably. I'm sure she was aware that he'd sneak into our room, but Stuart had a way to make sure we didn't dare make a sound." Her voice trails off at the end. "It only went on for a few months until he was caught."

I run a hand through my hair, knowing we can't go back from this. This friendship thing has dug another foot into my heart. I know that no matter how we end, there are things you can't forget.

"I take it you shut down for the next few years."

"Until university, actually." She pulls the blanket up higher and tucks her arms under. "Rachel got me drunk one night and, for some reason, I gave her a briefing of Stuart. She knew how to fix it. Once I learned the power of controlled pleasure…" She pauses and forces a small laugh. "Here you and I are."

"Did you go to therapy?" It's not my place to ask, but I can't help it.

"I had a couple sessions, but I moved to another place, and I think someone stopped driving me."

"Did you keep in contact with Ella?"

"No. I was ten and traumatized. We got rehomed again and I can't remember her last name."

The way she throws out the word *rehomed* bottoms out my lungs. *Rehomed* is a word someone uses for a puppy, not a child. She relaxes into me, twisting her ring.

"Where'd you get the ring?" I change the subject, hoping she'll lighten up a tad.

She sighs. "There were two." *Okay, maybe this wasn't a good topic switch.* "They were the first gifts I had ever received from a foster home. Before the trauma house, I had a small birthday party at the church my foster people attended." I notice how she says foster *people*. "I never grew up celebrating my birthday, so I was excited. Anyway, I don't want to rant, but I received two gold bands from an elderly lady at the church." She smiles and looks down at the ring.

"The other one had a small pink stone on it. The rings used to fit on my index finger, but I've grown since I was nine." She laughs softly to herself. "I was in the shower without the rings and when I came out, the social worker was there to take me." She shudders and I place a kiss on the top of her head. "For an unknown reason, a few of us kids were put into another home. That's when I was placed at Mabel's. I could only find one ring on my dresser, and I knew some other kid had taken it. We didn't have time to look for the other ring and the foster lady said she'd let me know if she found it."

The weight of the world this woman carries is beyond compare. To turn out as a productive member of society at such a young age gives me no reason to ever complain or give her an excuse about my life. My instinct is to apologize for everything she's been through. But I know her too well. I know saying that will cause her to throw her guard up because it's not my place to say sorry. Or she'd run scared that I now pity her and will try to *fix* her. At least that's the brief rundown she projected after the first time we hooked up.

"I'm proud that you stood up to Mabel today. Hell, she deserved that wicked punch I know you are capable of throwing, Lauren."

"I wouldn't call that standing up for myself." Lauren's body shakes against mine as she laughs. "I was in too much shock to do anything."

"I'm sorry you lost that ring." My voice is barely a whisper as I rub her arm.

"I'm glad I did." She shifts in my lap to face me. Her demeanor alters into the well-rehearsed, guarded Lauren.

"Why is that?" I ask the question I'm not sure I want the answer to.

"It was during that moment when I realized wanting things is too much. If I never wanted the ring so bad, then I wouldn't have been upset to lose it." Her shoulders straighten as she looks me straight in the eye. "I had let my feelings become attached to objects and friends at school. I had given them so much power over my emotions and ended up disappointed." She reaches for her water, and I stay silent. "I allowed myself to be hurt over things that can be taken away. I felt angry with myself for wanting anything."

Annnd, there it is.

Whether she realizes it or not, that was the therapy she needed to say out loud. A child who had never felt love. A child who lost their innocence. A child whose needs were never met beyond food, water, and a bed. Hopefully she always had a bed. I wonder if she will ever want again. If I need anything in life, it's for her to feel okay to want something. Anything. I know the relationship status has always been an issue for me, too. If our arrangement is what brings her happiness, I'm all for it.

"I try to pay close attention to every child who enters where I work. Sometimes the signs of abuse are too easy to hide." She yawns before standing from the couch. "Do you mind sleeping here tonight?"

"You'd have a hard time kicking me out if you tried." I follow her across the room.

I open my arm, inviting her to lie on it and expect her to throw out a sarcastic remark or push it away. She hesitates for a second before closing the distance between us. Her head fits perfectly in the crook of my shoulder and her arm rests across my chest. Lauren takes a deep breath and holds it for a worrisome amount of time. I peek down just as she releases it, melting into me as if she's one with my soul. Her body molds perfectly into mine. Her soft lips make a trail along the edge of my jaw before she settles back down.

"Thank you." Her voice is strained, and it doesn't take long before her breaths become light and even.

By some miracle, she sleeps through the night.

I watch the sunrise glow behind the buildings through her window. It's six a.m. and my arm and Lauren are the only ones that have slept. Lauren stirs as painful tingles shoot through my arm. I clench my abs and hold my breath in hopes the pain will stop. I hope she can sleep in a bit longer. Waking up from trauma at the break of dawn every day isn't how someone's day should start. I look down at the loose bun of blonde waves starting to unravel. Her lips are plump and slightly parted with gentle exhales. There's a soft innocence about her.

The sick people in the world cause bile to churn in my empty stomach as I recall the truths of her past. How can someone be so evil to an innocent child who needed decent parents? Then to be blamed and told it was her and Ella's fault that the fucking rapist got locked up. My fists tighten with rage. Lauren's beautiful soul stood strong and made something for herself, but will she ever be comfortable enough to rely on anyone else? I take pride in being capable, but I know my family has my back if I fall.

My eyes finally feel heavy as I start to drift to sleep. Her body stirs as she starts to wake. Lauren's head tilts up on my chest and I let out a loud fake snore, causing her to jump. My eyes open as I stifle a laugh.

"That was not funny." She props herself up on her elbows.

"I can't have you thinking I'm perfect and never snore. You'd end up falling in love with me."

"Ha. You couldn't pay me to do that." She shakes with a half smirk. "I guess I'll never get one morning with a peaceful wake up."

"Sorry, I should have said *'good morning, beautiful'* and then ate *you* for breakfast." I tighten my arms around her waist and pull her closer.

"You don't need to lie about the beautiful part." I wasn't. "I look like a mess, Adam, and I'm still wearing yesterday's clothes."

"How about you go shower and I'll have breakfast ready when you're finished."

"I need to leave by nine because I'm meeting Tessa for a workout."

"I'm sure I can whip something up in your three-hour time frame." She nods and crawls out of bed.

We don't talk about yesterday or how she woke up in my arms as we eat breakfast. I'd like to ask more questions, but the last thing I want to do is trigger more if she's trying to move on. I walk home under the clear sky and long to sleep for the next few hours. Stepping into the shared elevator to mine and my sister's suite, Max steps out. He's in his usual bar attire from the night before.

"Bro, it's barely nine." I place a hand on his shoulder. "Did you crash at my place and realize I wasn't there?" Max is one of the few people who know my key code to unlock my place.

"Nah, Kelsie sent me a text last night and was pretty drunk." His face twists in concern. "She's not handling everything well this past week." This shit always has to happen when I'm out with Lauren. "I had a few hours of sleep before dropping Mallory off at camp. James is fed and situated with a show."

"Fuck, why didn't she tell me that it's bugging her this much?"

"Tell *you* that a man is causing her this much stress?" Max tugs his lip in a smirk. "Remember how that went in the past?" Kelsie hated how any guy who went near her in high school would have to answer to Max and me if shit went wrong.

"That asshole was spreading lies through the school about her." No guy showed her interest after I broke the nose of her tenth-grade boyfriend.

Am I the reason she's in this mess right now?

"Kels tried to kick me out when I arrived. Seconds later, I held her hair back as she puked."

"Fucking Benson. She should have gone to the same university as us." She clung to the first guy who showed an interest in her during her freshman year of university. "We could have fucking saved her from that asshole."

"Where were you last night?" Max clearly senses my rage building and diverts my attention. "You normally play the piano in the quiet wee hours."

"Lauren was..." I trail off, not wanting to reveal anything. "Something came up and she needed me to stay."

He narrows his blue eyes and carefully assesses me. "Something's off about you." Probably because I just discovered true childhood trauma, and there is nothing I can do to go back in time to stop it. "You care about her."

"Why didn't my sister call me? Or our mom?" Guilt and annoyance prick through my veins as my teeth press together.

"She didn't want your mother to know. You know how she is with her image." He raises his eyebrows and rubs the back of his neck. "Stubborn as hell to not taint her elite mother's perfect expectations of her."

"You're sure that's it, bro?"

"I need to run home and change. I have a class to teach." *How bad is my sister handling this if Max won't even make eye contact with me?*

"Thanks for loving her as much as I do." I hold the sincerity in my voice as his eyes go wide.

"Dude, she's like a sister," he spits out in a nanosecond, shaking his head as he walks backward. "She'll always be that tiny kid we'd beat in swim races." She used to get so pissed that she was a year older, and that much slower. "You and I are just as protective as much as we enjoyed teasing her."

Chapter 16

Adam

Four days later, I'm in my office as my phone buzzes.

Cherries: What?! At my work? How did you know?

Me: I asked Rachel when she was in town that night. Happy Birthday!

Bubbled dots appear but nothing comes through for over an hour. I bite my cheek, hoping she's not pissed I sent flowers and catered Thai food for the entire emergency room staff.

Cherries: Sorry, got paged for trauma. Thank you. Everyone lovesss the food too.

Me: Can I take the birthday girl out for dinner tonight?

Cherries: Don't feel you need to do more than you already have. You're probably tired from all your overtime at work.

After pulling a few fourteen-hour days, I am exhausted. Katherine barely came through with the marketing. My father loved Lauren's idea so much that Katherine had to incorporate it with her idea. She wasn't pleased. Nor was I, being tasked to put the final approval and oversee every damn step of Katherine's ad. With my workload here and helping with the new Aspen location, my CFO position was starting to feel more like my father's CEO role. Work aside, exhaustion isn't going to stop me from celebrating life.

Me: Trust me, I need a break from work. Good food, laughs and if you're a good girl, an orgasm.

Cherries: Oh, I've been a very good girl. ;) I'll be ready by 7:45 if I get out of here on time.

Me: I'll meet you at your place ;)

Instead of spending the next few hours at the gym, my fingers get lost on the ivory keys as the weight of life evaporates. I open with a few jazz scales and blend them into a '90s pop melody. The lyrics sing through my mind and I realize how powerful some of them are. When you strip out the busy production, the lyrics really hit home. Is this how Lauren feels when she listens to them? I continue to play, but the presence of someone lingering grows each moment. Before I lead into my next piece, I glance down and notice the pair of leather shoes I've walked beside every day of my life. My stomach jumps to my throat and my fingers fumble the keys and make an ear-piercing sound. I bring my eyes up to the face of my father.

He leans against a post and pulls his hands out of his pockets to clap. I feel the blood drain from my face and lose all words. The person who told me not to worry about anything other than appearance, family and business, has now witnessed the one secret I've been great at hiding my entire life.

"I had to see for myself. Our hotel went viral from a video, and I knew that wasn't our usual piano guy." His jaw doesn't harbor the tense structure it normally does. "How long have you been playing like that?"

"Since you caught me falling asleep in the back booths. I snuck every opportunity to play when I knew you were in your office." I stand back up. "Viral?"

"I didn't realize your talent." He nodded. "I thought you were being a foolish child wanting to bang on the expensive piano keys." He looks down at the foot pedals, avoiding my eyes. "A few teens posted a clip of a *'Superhot giant turns club songs into masterpieces.'*" He opens the video.

"I knew I should have asked if they'd recorded me." I wish I could read his body language better.

"I'm glad she did," he grunts. "You should play more. Sales have increased with written requests to hear you play."

"I don't play for the public, Dad." I shake my head, feeling the nerves in my stomach flip. "They caught me during the off-hours in the lounge."

"Nonsense. Play whenever. Especially when guests are in." His hand reaches up and rests on my shoulder. "Where did you come up with shitty pops songs slowed down? I would have pegged you as a jazz player."

"Lauren mentioned she likes to listen to piano covers." I shrug and step past him. "Speaking of. I need to get ready to pick her up for her birthday dinner."

"Ah yes, it *is* today." Of course, he'd know. "Don't break her heart, son."

"I don't *have* her heart. She's been through enough to rationally not give it away." I make an implying face that I'm aware something happened, but walk away before he attempts to talk about it.

My phone buzzes.

Cherries: One of the nurses arrived early and asked if I wanted to leave. I had one more patient left, but he said he would attend to her so I can get ready.

Cherries: I will be ready before 8.

Cherries: Heading home. I know how much you love irrelevant detail that us women give. :p

Me: See you soon. And don't give me that tongue unless you plan to use it.

Cherries: Maybe if you're a good boy, I will. Lol

One way or another, this woman is going to be the death of me.

Lauren finishes her last bite of dessert at my favorite Michelin-star restaurant in the city.

"What?" Her cheeks turn a hint of pink when she catches me staring.

"I'm remembering your face when you took your first bite of the parmesan and lavender tortellini appetizer."

"Everything I have put in my mouth today has been nothing short of phenomenal, thanks to you." Her hooded eyes drop down my body. "I can't wait to taste the final course."

My dick twitches which probably isn't allowed in a restaurant of this stature. "It's your birthday. It should be about you."

"And *I* want my final *treat*." She takes a sip of water, and a smile reaches her eyes.

The check, please.

The crisp wind seeping through my clothes sends a chill to my bones as we walk to the limo. I used one of our drivers today to make her birthday extra special. I duck into the limo after her and her hand immediately rests on my thigh. She shivers in her black silk dress, and I turn the heat higher.

"Thank you for tonight." She leans back against the seat and turns her head to me. "This was the best birthday I've ever had."

"I'm glad you enjoyed your day." My eyes flick to her lips, and she brings herself forward, taking my lips with hers.

My hands snake around her waist, pulling her on top to straddle me. Her dress hikes up to her hips as her hands run through my hair, stealing my breath to fuel her need. We snap. Her teeth clash mine in a hard kiss as her hips grind forward against my dick. I tangle my hand in the back of her hair and tug as my arm tightens around her waist. A moan fills the limo as my lips softly suction down her neck to her shoulder. I pay my driver well enough to pretend he doesn't hear what I damn well know he can through the thin plastic divider. Lauren's nails rake down the front of my shirt and land on the button of my pants. I reach down to stop her and brush my knuckles down the outside of her panties. The lace material is soaked through as I continue the ghostly pressure of slow circles around her clit.

Her delicate wrists drape around my neck as she pulls me down to lean over her.

"I need you now. No foreplay." Her voice is breathy, and it takes everything in me to not comply.

"We have enough time." I capture her lips as the limo heads to a lookout point. "You deserve every type of orgasm."

She whimpers and opens her legs wider as I slip a finger through her soft folds. My two fingers pump in and out as I kneel beside her with a devilish grin. I grab an ice cube from the drink bin and pop it into my mouth. Leaning down, I curl my fingers and feel the internal textured spot, and at the same time, I run the ice cube along her low stomach.

She squirms as a soft high-pitch squeak leaves her mouth. I continue with my finger as the cube melts in my mouth. I run my tongue down her hip until I hover just above her swollen clit. My cool breaths tickle her sensitive spot. Lauren pants as I watch her breasts rise and fall. With her head thrown back and anticipation radiating off her, I still my fingers.

"Ms. McAllister?" I keep my tone assertive, like how I conduct my business meetings. "Watch me." Her head tilts as her jaw hangs loosely. "Good girl." Her breathing is so heavy, I feel it hit me down her body.

"Do something!" she rasps with need. "I'm going to come at the thought of coming."

"Relax, Blondie," I purr, running my fingertips up her leg, through the crease of her pussy lips and stop on her hip. "Relish every second. Feel your body ache and tingle. Each breath bringing you closer to the edge." I gently blow across her clit and her back arches, desperate for contact. "There's no rush."

"Do that again." My dick pulses as I blow on her again. Her glistening pussy throbs and contracts. "God, that feels amazing."

My thumbs press on each side of her folds and I lightly massage them in a circular motion, pulling farther out to the sides when I reach the top by her clit. A sigh releases from her as she tries to relax. I continue up one more time and let my thumbs slowly press in toward her clit until I feel it pop up. I have no doubt I could come at the sight of getting her off. The movements are delicate with intention. I've never been so desperate to hear her breathy moans and witness the control she's managing. Her teeth clench her bottom lip as she fights off finishing in order to build her orgasm.

Lauren's body is something I can't help but savor. Licking my lips, I flatten my tongue and lock onto her eyes with mine. With one stroke from her opening to her clit, her hips buck as she cries out. Her hand grabs a fistful of my hair as her hips push forward, taking the exact pressure she needs from me. I keep my pace slow and suck her into my mouth as she fucks my face, coming undone. Her body palpitates as my palm puts pressure on her lower abs and I enter two fingers. As they curl, her tight core soaks them along with the leather seat.

I slide down my pants and search for a condom. "Fuck, you're kidding me."

Her sated eyes meet mine as she reaches out to me, hovering on top. "I trust you." Her hands lace with mine and she brings our hands over her head, pinning her own self down. "Don't finish in me."

My hands tighten around hers and inch by inch, I slowly thrust until I'm buried balls deep. The slick sound from pumping in and out is intoxicating. She feels incredible and I know I won't last much longer. "Lauren, I'm not."

She pushes me up to sit so she is straddling me again. The dominant side of this woman keeps getting hotter. Lauren pushes her forehead to mine and slides back down, grinding her hips. My hands trail over her hip with a tight squeeze, holding her in place as I push in deeper. Her teeth nip my shoulder to stifle a high pitch moan as my thumb rapidly circles her clit. Her breath becomes ragged. I feel her tighten around me, but then she eases up and tries to fight it.

"That's a good girl. Take all the pleasure you need from my cock." I grip a fistful of her hair and tilt her head back. "Show me how good I make your soaking pussy feel." I lick the spot behind her ear and her orgasm takes over.

My lap is full of her as she comes, but she continues to slowly ride me. "Lauren, I need your hand on my cock." My hands grip her waist in an attempt to lift her off.

"Mmm." She continues to move. "It feels too good." Her raspy voice tells me she's desperate for more. "I'm gonna come again." Her walls tighten like the grip she has on my hair and her body stills along with her open mouth.

I collect her silent scream in a kiss as her body starts to tremor. I think of every fucking turnoff so she can bask in this moment and save it to memory. She's beautiful.

"Lauren, if you don't want me to come in you, you have to get off." My voice is strained.

She gets off my lap and before I can reach for my dick, it's in her mouth. Holy shit, this is the most erotic moment of my life. My hand meets the back of her head, and her hands tighten on my thighs, signaling me that she'll take my load. Euphoria washes over me and I coat the back of her throat. She backs away, wiping her mouth with a smile.

"That was an interesting flavor combination." She giggles and I can't form a fucking sentence. "Best birthday ever."

It's then I realize the car has stopped and I can't remember when we stopped moving. I look out the window and see we have reached our spot on the hill. We were too busy seeing our own stars than paying attention to the ones shining above on top of the hill. I open the sunroof and poke my head out.

"I know it's chilly out, but come see this."

"Wow." Lauren looks over the city skyline and her eyes go wide like a light bulb went off in her head. "Oh, my goodness!" It's dark but I see the flush in her face. "The driver. Do you think he knew what we were doing?"

"My driver, Mason, is paid enough to not disclose or comment on anything."

"I should be more mortified at what he heard, but I'm too satiated to care."

"Happy birthday, Lauren."

Chapter 17

Lauren

I flop down on my bed in a towel and let out a huff. My energy has felt depleted lately. I reach for my phone, unsurprised how it's void of notifications. I'm not active on social media, nor am I one to shoot out the first text most of the time. I'm perfectly content whaling in this spot, with a book that has taken me way too long to finish. Due to a crazy workweek, and Adam, I'm completely exhausted-especially after the other night.

Not that I'm complaining.

The man is clearly skilled in everything. Except for remembering to bring a damn condom along, but I don't feel like our limo escapade had been on his itinerary. I debate about texting him to come over, but I need "me" time. I wish I was lazy enough to stay in bed for the next three days that I have off. It could be doable if Adam was here to keep my body occupied.

My thumb and middle finger twist the ring on my pinkie. Perplexity flows through my brain as I recall how he hasn't treated me any different since our encounter with my past foster person. *Parent* is an overrated word since the majority of the ones I had been placed with were far from what parents should be. Lloyd and Marsha were as close enough to parents as I could get. Marsha was overly sweet until her passing, but Lloyd had remained detached.

Adam didn't throw a pity party or ask me to go get help. Which is why I really hope our arrangement can obtain longevity. My gut twists, flashing back to his face as I uncovered my dark truth. He hadn't asked much about my past with respect to our deal, but I could see the worry in his eyes. The question of whether I'd call us off if he pressed for more details. I may be guarded, but I can rationalize a person having questions after our encounter with Mabel. I would have been weirded out if he didn't ask anything. He would have "sociopath" written all over him.

The giant bouquet of flowers from Adam holds a golden glow through the sun in the window. I wonder if our bright colors will die in time like the flowers. I shake my head to push the thought aside when my eyes land on the gift beside the bouquet. I can't fight my smile. Rachel had sent a large balloon cluster along with, nonetheless, a new dildo. I have no interest in a tall, curled sea monster tentacle. Its texture seems appealing, but the thickness of a beer can is a bit too intimidating for me. The bright-blue color is a pretty contrast to the vase of flowers, so I've left it placed beside them. A work of art, to say the least.

My phone buzzes but I decline Tessa's invite to join her in a fitness class. I feel myself getting skinnier than I'd like.

I've been too busy to eat the proper number of calories that I should in my active life.

My phone goes off again and I accept the call.

"Hey, Rach." I kick my feet back and forth. "I was just admiring my new table centerpiece."

"Bitch, you should be using it." Her laugh filters through the phone.

"Hard pass, but thanks."

"I hope you spent your birthday balls deep with Mr. Tall, Built, and Handsome."

I sigh, filling her in with the restaurant and limo details.

"Sounds like your arrangement is going well." There's a long pause before she continues. "Have you guys taken your relationship to a personal level?"

"Personal might be an understatement." Not only did I wake up today from my nightmare, but I also filled Rachel in for the next ten minutes about the breakdown that surfaced from seeing Mabel at Fisherman's Wharf.

"Flipping fucks, Lauren. I'm glad you didn't leave him hanging without some sort of answer." Her voice drops to a pained whisper. "And he just let you be? No telling you to lean on him or get help?"

"Unfortunately, he's becoming everything I want him to be."

"That doesn't seem unfortunate, girly."

"I can't believe I'm saying this, but I hope our arrangement works forever." I mean that with every ounce of my being. "What we have is amazing. He doesn't push me or shy away when I think I'm too damaged or decline when I only need him for a quick bang."

"Are you saying you think you're ready for a real relationship?" Hope fills her voice. "There's nothing wrong with a boyfriend."

"He doesn't want a relationship. You also know my heart won't reach out for love." I sigh. "We have been over this."

"I am just saying that there is nothing wrong with a label. You two act like a couple, and I could see the sparks in his eyes whenever he looked at you. If he's checking everything off your dream list and fictional character chart, what's so wrong with having a lasting deathbed memory?" I bite my lip hearing her use my own words against me.

"Rachel."

"Don't Rachel me. You and I have fucked-up pasts, but that doesn't stop me from enjoying a boyfriend, or three." This time I laugh. "If you and daddy Viking don't work out, you should consider a real-life version of a reverse harem."

"He's not my boyfriend. He just *gets* me the same way I get him."

"Okay, whatever. Enjoy your forever arrangement. But sometimes it's worth risking the heart."

After we hang up, I order Chinese and consume a tub of ice cream.

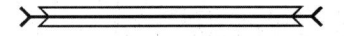

>=======<

The next morning, I walk down to my favorite coffee shop. The foggy mist is still lying low and the chill in the air calls for a hazelnut latte. My phone starts to buzz as I round the corner.

"Good morning, Charmer." I answer in front of the coffee shop.

"How is my beautiful Blondie?" His voice is a groggy rasp shooting right to my lady region.

"I'm not yours. I'm out grabbing a latte."

"Can we meet up at some point today? My dumbass brother is in town later tonight."

"I can stop by now. I'll bring you a coffee."

"I'll stay in bed and wait for the pick-me-up." His voice was laced with hope.

"Hmm, that thought of yours will have to wait until I am well caffeinated."

"See you soon."

I'm grateful he sent me his elevator code so I could let myself up. I make my way through his ridiculously fancy palace, I mean *place*, and see him lying in bed. He's shirtless with both arms tucked behind his head, displaying his mouth-watering muscles. I nearly set down both lattes and take up his suggestion to ride him as a pick-me-up.

"You purposely pulled the sheet that low, didn't you?" I narrow my eyes and mentally trace his *V* lines with my tongue.

"I figured you could use some sunshine on this gloomy morning." His eyes roam my body as I see his dick spring to life. "Love your attire."

"I should probably give you this hoodie back now. For some damn reason, it's much comfier than all the ones I own."

"You can keep it if you come over here." He licks his lips.

"No, I said I need to be well caffeinated." I place his coffee on the nightstand with an extended arm in order to not get too close. "I know you will take up a good hour of my morning and I'll end up with an iced latte."

"You can drink it off my body." He winks and slips his hand under the covers.

"Is this really why you called me over? For a booty call at eight in the morning?"

He sits up and reaches for his coffee. "No. I just wanted a better start to the conversation I plan to have with you." He clears his throat and looks down.

My throat jumps as anxiety swirls in my stomach. *Don't ask for more and make me want to call off our relationship.* He's the first guy to know my past truths and not run. Is my past too dark for him to handle and I'm a constant downer when he sees me? I don't want to say goodbye to his dick this soon.

Sensing my nerves, Adam pats the spot on the bed beside him. My legs halt. As if the paper cup is capable of masking the fear running across my face, I take a long sip of my latte as an attempt to hide behind it. If he's calling it off, I don't think I can emotionally go through the probability that no man will ever be able to live up to his skill set.

"Hey," he calls out in a soft voice. "I didn't mean anything that will scare you. I just wanted to talk about why my brother is in town."

"Oh." I drop my shoulders and feel more relaxed. "He's close to my age, right? The one who is still in school but travels?" I sink into the mattress beside Adam.

"He's twenty-six," Adam replies with slight irritation. "Emmett is trying to be well rounded, as some would say."

"How is your relationship with him?" I realize that might be too personal. "Never mind, that's probably irrelevant."

"He's the youngest, so getting his way has always been easy for him. It doesn't help that he's many years younger than Kelsie and me. My mother really milked the baby stage with him." Adam takes a long drink of his coffee. "Emmett brought a chick home this time, so my mom is completely distracted with her and their love life. I'm sure he paid this chick to pretend to be his, so my parents focus on her instead of caring about his position in the family business. He mentioned he's interested in my role."

"Which means what for you? They wouldn't give it to him, would they?"

"No, but it could mean that I get promoted." He doesn't sound too thrilled.

"Or you could come clean and tell your family how you really feel and what you desire to achieve in the next chapter in your life." I let hope spew out of my voice for encouragement.

"I can't let them down." He shakes his head. "My father asked me to head out of town for a few days to make sure the Aspen location is going well. He and my mother want to start passing more responsibilities on to me."

Could that mean moving out of town? I don't bring myself to ask.

"Well, that's cool. A little getaway could be good for you. Aspen seems like a cozy place."

"I fly out tomorrow for three days."

"How does that make you feel?" I don't know why I'm taking a page out of my psychology class, but the words filter out before I stop them.

"Tired, I guess." He shrugs. "I'll be a couple days behind work here, so that'll mean extra hours when I fly back." He gives me a smug grin. "I'm more frustrated that I won't be able to explore your sexy little body while I'm gone."

"I'm sure you'll survive." I laugh and lean into him.

My hands rest on his chest as I take in his intoxicating, manly cologne. His scent is enough to get my lower stomach swirling with desire. The muscles and sharp jawline help too. His hand slips under my—*his*—hoodie and grips my hips to pull me on top as if I'm weightless. I straddle his waist and grind against his growing erection. I lean down to meet his lips, but I can't connect with the moment. As much as I want to, the pit of my stomach can't shake the fact that I'll never find another man as skilled as him. He breaks our kiss and looks up at me.

"Come to Aspen with me."

"What?" I was not expecting that.

"I'll have to work, but we can have meals and evenings together."

"Adam, I have work relying on me *here*." I search his brown eyes for disappointment, but he's good at hiding it. "I can't ask for time off to go have orgasms in another city."

"That seems like a very justifiable reason." He gives me a smug grin as I place my hands on his chest.

"Booking a last-minute plane ticket is pricey." *I also want to save the money for my heartfelt project.* I watch his cheeks suck in like he's fighting back words. "You have your own jet, don't you?" His eyes dart around the room because he doesn't want to admit how bougie his life truly is. "Of course, you do. I can't leave the hospital on short notice. Again, they rely on me."

"I know. I admire your work ethic and heart to help others."

"Thank you." I smirk and feel his dick twitch under me. "Now, you better make this orgasm good enough to last for three days."

I yelp as he flips me on my back, making the cold latte worth it.

"Okay, so I dip the chicken in the egg before the flour?" I ask, staring at the multiple food stations laid out on Adam's kitchen island.

"*Eggsactly*." Adam shoots me a cheesy grin and I roll my eyes. "I promise, this fried sesame chicken bowl will be the best you have ever had."

"You're the best I've ever had." I should have asked for another orgasm instead of how to make my own takeout.

"Who's the cheeseball now?" He winks as I continue to dredge the chicken chunks.

I'm mesmerized watching the veins in his forearm as he chops the vegetables in perfect even chunks. He hums along to the music, and I appreciate the flex of his abs when he lifts the giant wooden cutting board to scrape food into a bowl. My hands are covered in flour and egg as I try to brush a strand of hair out of my mouth using the top of my wrist. My messy bun flops about, gathering Adam's attention.

"Look at you, my little sous-chef." Adam's fingers brush behind my ear as he fixes the loose strand. "You'll want to use a little less egg." His hands slide down my arms, turning me to face the counter. "Keep the batter thin so it doesn't clump." My breath hitches, feeling his hit my neck as his hands hold mine, helping get the right amount.

This basic task should not be as much of a turn-on as my body makes it out to be. There is something intimate about his actions that makes my stomach flutter. For once, I don't mind. I *like* how close he is to me. I *like* that he's having this effect on me. There is nothing sexual about raw chicken and eggs, yet my body ignites as he holds my hands to complete the task.

The music shifts to an upbeat rhythm. Adam shakes the batter off his hands and rests them on my hips as we start to sway. I can't fight the giggle at how corny this all is. He moves his hand to my stomach as the other extends my arm out.

"Ah! Batter is dripping everywhere." I laugh and shake my head.

"Who cares." He laughs and spins me around to face him, keeping our dance flowing. "We can't let a good song go to waste, Blondie." I fall back into a dip, wrapping my battered hands around his neck.

"Well, Charmer, you're a spectacular dancer." I feel light and a wave of elation washes over me as I determine to remember this moment.

His finger boops my nose as I scrunch my face, feeling the batter cling to it. "My mother made us take dance lessons for one year in high school. This is as good as it gets." He laughs, then bends to grab my hips and extends his arms, lifting me in the air.

My hands reach out to his shoulders for support as I let out a squeal. His arms are fully extended as he holds me above his head and spins. "Adam," I manage to say between laughs. "Put me down!"

"I want a turn!" A little voice comes from the side and startles us.

Adam lowers me down and both our faces flush. Mallory and James stand by the kitchen island, anticipating their turns as Kelsie and Max share a look I can't quite read. Knowing I look too exposed in panties and Adam's T-shirt, I want to run. His shirt thankfully covers my bum, but my height is all legs. I open my mouth and lift my hands to explain as if caught like red-handed teenagers. The batter flakes off my hand and falls to the floor as my eyes follow. Adam ignores his niece and nephew and turns to his sister.

"Why didn't you knock?" Adam's face flushes for the first time.

"Sorry, you said you'd be around all day and to stop by later." Kelsie shrugs. "The kids wanted to say goodbye to you before we take them to the activity festival in Golden Gate Park."

"I'm going to go—" In need of leggings and a hand wash, I point to Adam's room without finishing my sentence.

The weight of Adam's hoodie comforts me like a warm hug. I slip into my leggings and take a few deep breaths. What his family had walked into was too personal. That moment alone made me feel more exposed than my bare legs. I grab a shirt for Adam on the way out of his room and toss it to him as I walk back into the kitchen. Adam and Max both have their arms crossed in deep conversation by the window. Kelsie hands her kids a few fresh-cut veggies from our bowl.

"Sorry again for just showing up." Her brown eyes are apologetic. "We knocked but Mallory barged through the unlocked door when she heard music."

"You're his family. No apologies needed." I shrug. "We didn't hear the knock."

"Well, I have to keep in mind that Adam has you over sometimes." Her eyes glance toward her children within earshot. "The last thing I need is for Mallory, or myself, to walk into you guys *forking*."

"That is not a conversation I'd want to have with a child." I laugh, feeling a jitter through my hands.

"Relax." She places a hand on mine and for once, the contact doesn't make me flinch. "If I was young, hot and could take advantage of the single life again, I'd be living it up too." I don't miss how her eyes sway to Max as she speaks. "But I'm now a single parent who has two little minions relying on me."

"They're cute though." I smile.

"I wouldn't change a thing." Kelsie looks at Mallory who fails to secretly eavesdrop. "My kids are the best thing in my world." Mallory's eyes soften with contentment before running over to Adam. "Their father hasn't always been present, so I think that's why the kids are handling his absence well."

"At least they have your family giving them plenty of attention and love."

Mallory's laugh fills the room as Adam picks her up above his head like he spun me. Max bends down and lifts James. Part of my ice wall melts when I didn't think it was possible. Watching them warms my body, but it aches with the absence of my inner child, never experiencing that type of love. Their family love presents itself as something you lean into. Their love presents itself from the day of conception to be nourished and taken care of. Their love presents itself in a way that would gut you completely and torture you to lose. Except in death, your pain ends. With love, it gnaws at you internally until your life on earth expires.

To me, a glimpse of love presented itself in the form of an adult finally cleaning your clothes that started to smell. A glimpse of love was an adult letting you stay at their house in return for money from the state. A glimpse of love was being thankful I wasn't out on the street. I never knew what *being* loved was.

Love presented itself as a task and trade.
Manipulation.
Pain.
Love exposed itself to a monster. The word *love* came in a low grunt when Stuart would come into my room each morning. I'd bite the stuffed bear I loved to muffle my screams. Love taught me to stay quiet so the younger kids wouldn't experience what I went through each morning. Finally, love presented itself as a house that didn't hurt me, but still, I wasn't loved enough to be adopted.

Thanks to Rachel, I channeled love into a power where others could pleasure me.

"Lauren." I shake my head, coming out of my trance as embarrassment washes over me. Everyone's eyes focus on me. "Where did your mind go?" Max scrunches his forehead with confusion. "You look distraught."

My eyes lock with Adam's and he sees me. I feel anxiety spike through my blood and my neck grows tight. Adam doesn't say a word but keeps eye contact. There's comfort in him understanding my demons without having to speak. I look down at James and focus on the attention he is trying to get from me. He is now barefoot with an accomplished smile on his face.

"Doo-doo-dooo," he sings, waving his new sock puppet hand around. I hope he never knows the cruelty of the world.

I have no idea how long I'd been staring in a trance, reliving horrors, but it was long enough to cause concern. I don't need people worrying about me, so I smile down at him and clap my hands.

"Good job. I love your sock puppet." I can handle things on my own and I don't need to gather a group of people to join the pity party.

"Lauren and I should get back to cooking," Adam speaks up. "You kids have fun at the park." He bends down to say goodbye.

"Daddy's coming in the morning." Mallory's words make my stomach internally churn bile, but no one needs to know that trigger.

Adam's head shoots up as his jaw tightens. His glare toward Kelsie is chilling, but she shrugs her shoulders with a half smile.

"Enjoy your trip to Aspen," Kelsie sings out. "I think Max should join you."

"Not a chance in hell." Max places his hand on Kelsie's lower back as they walk out.

Adam's eyes burn through them with a darkness I've never seen. "Do you think they're—" I change the subject with my implication, trying to break the tension.

"That's my best friend and sister," he cuts me off and looks to the kitchen. "Max goes for every chick that *doesn't* look like my sister. I'm surprised he didn't try to pick you up the first night." He tosses a pepper chunk at my left shoulder playfully.

No, not that shoulder.

"Okay, then." I turn on the stove and feel a phantom wiggle on my left shoulder.

Sometimes I can't pinpoint what triggers the feeling, but when it starts, it's hard to ignore. The press of ghosted lips that woke me every morning resurfaces and my nails rake over the spot. My breathing creates a shallow staccato rhythm as I battle to satiate my lungs with a full breath. I rub my shoulder harder as a chill breaks through my body. I turn away, hoping to go unnoticed as my head fogs with the start of a flashback. Large hands cup my face, and Adam towers over me.

"Lauren." Adam holds my face in place as his head lowers to level our eye contact. "Do you smell the burning oil? How about the orange sesame sauce on my fingers?"

My eyes squeeze shut with desperation to focus on Adam's voice and the smell, but staggered breaths continue as my shoulder feels the haunting lips.

"Focus on my thumbs brushing over your cheekbones and breathe in for four seconds." I do as he says. "Good, now hold it for four and release it on a four count." He nods as I comply. "Good girl. Do it a few more times."

My nerves settle, but my heartbeat thumps loudly through my ears. Embarrassment fills me. "I'm sorry."

"For what, being human?" Adam shakes his head. "I don't know what was going through your mind, but I hope it wasn't me who set you off."

"Don't worry about me."

"Lauren." His voice drops with concern.

"Don't, Adam. We have a good thing going between us." I hear my voice break at the end and want to run out of the building.

"If it was me, how can I avoid setting you off next time? Was it my family walking in unannounced?"

"No." I've fought these battles alone my entire life. I don't need Adam trying to be my charming white knight.

"Your eyes went blank. Like the other day at the—"

"STOP TALKING!" I throw my hands up. "I don't need you to pretend to care. You don't know *half* the shit I've been conditioned for in this life." My lungs deflate as I wrap my arms around myself. As much as I want to spill my life story out and feel understood, he doesn't need the burden with the weight of everything he has already found out.

"I won't judge you." His voice doesn't waver. "I won't tell you to get help or sympathize with your past. I'll be strictly whatever you *want*." His eyes are pleading, making it hard to say no. "I don't want to set you off."

He's cracked the code to my vault and each time we are together, I can't help but let myself become a bit more vulnerable. I'm finding safety in him. It should make me run like hell, but I can't. He hasn't done anything to breach our arrangement. I've been strong all my life, and Adam has managed to break through my armor in a short couple of months.

My eyes fall shut and I copy his long breath in.

One, two, three, four.

The four second breath expands my lungs, but they feel like they're going to burst as I hold the four counts in. His proximity temps me to let go and relish in his therapeutic touch, but I hold myself together.

One, two...

Dammit, fight it, Lauren.

I breathe out early and I lose it. I feel my lips pull down as my jaw tightens. My eyebrows pull together as tears blur my vision. My shoulders jolt up with a silent sob as I clasp my hands together to bring them under my chin. Tears stream down my face, dripping off my chin. I open my mouth to gasp a steady breath, but before I can hold it in, it rushes out with a deep foreign cry. I try to pull myself together, but I fall deeper into my pain.

Adam opens his arms and I melt into his invitation. My shoulders shake and my nose burns while he holds me against his chest. His arm locks around my body, stabilizing me as the other weaves through my hair. He remains silent without a single *shh,* or an *it's okay.* Every time I try to take a breath and regain composure, years of trauma and suppressed tears export themselves. His shirt is soaked as I turn my head to find a dry area. His hand rests on my head as his thumb brushes back and forth. He's giving me the floor to break the silence.

Through unattractive sniffs, I stare at the fridge handle and recall my past. "Stuart would kiss my shoulder every morning. That's how I'd wake. He said I needed to be thankful that he loved *me* more than the others. If I didn't accept his *love* and keep quiet, my punishment would be watching him love Zora the way he loved me. I didn't understand why love hurt, but I knew Zora didn't need his love at age seven." I place my hand on the cool counter and take another breath.

"I'd bite my stuffed bear's leg to muffle the sound. He'd always call himself daddy when he was coming. Then Stuart would kiss my shoulder once more and tell me that one day when I'm a teenager and too old, I'll be begging him to wake me up the way he used to." My tears slow but my words pick up fuel. "Love isn't something I've ever known and by what I see, it's painful to lose. I can't help but think back to my past and how mistreated I was. I wonder what I did to deserve to have that happen to me."

What karmic wheel did I put myself on? Am I paying off my mother's sins?

I take a step back, but he won't look at me. "Maybe I was a terrible person in my past life." My chest pinches again as the anxiety pounds in my chest. "What if *I* was a Mabel to a Stuart?"

Shame hits me as my damaged past sits heavily in this room. I've said too much. I'm too damaged for even a casual hookup now. My tainted body is probably more repulsive to him now than the current state of my messy, tearful face. I've shown my vulnerable, scared little girl card too soon and I wish I could go back in time. His body faces the counter as his arms rest on the edge of the granite. Adam's head is turned away as his chin rests on his shoulder. Each second he stays silent, aggravation within me starts to build. The least he can do is look at me before he tells me we are over.

"Adam." My voice is strong as I move closer to catch a glimpse of eye contact. "You can't even look at me, can you?" I huff, wiping my blotched face before I turn to leave. "I told you I'm too damaged."

He turns to me and his arm reaches out, pulling me into him. His damp shirt is cold from my tears. I cringe and place my hand as a barrier between my cheek and his shirt. His chest expands as he takes a deep breath and clears his throat.

Did he just sniffle?

His eyes are glassy as he peers down at me. "You still don't have any idea how proud this world is of you. I don't believe you were terrible in a past life." My teeth tug at my lip and I shrug, unsure. "I know this life gave you a shitty hand, but look what you've done with it? Did you end up on the streets like the people you resuscitate? No, you graduated early and are kicking ass in life."

"Some call it a trauma survival mode. You learn to tune it out as best as you can and stay busy." I shrug again because it's true.

"I know you're well aware of the professional medical help that's available to you, but I know it's your choice how you choose to heal." Adam blinks back a tear and I still can't figure out how I feel about his reaction. "I will be here to tell you how amazing you are, and will do whatever it takes to keep your demons at bay."

I nod and look over at our mess on the counter. I really don't have the energy to cook. I can still feel the dried batter on my body. I could use a shower and a pint of ice cream. As if Adam wasn't helpful enough, he knew just what to say next.

"Screw cooking. Let's order room service and I will have them send up melted ice cream." And just like that, a smile reaches my eyes. "And if you need another memorable shower moment, I'd be happy to help."

Chapter 18

Adam

I catch a quick work break and hop on a sky gondola through the mountains. The past two days have been draining as hell. The tall trees call out my name and I'm tempted to build a cabin down below and live the simple life. No more numbers and paperwork or the luxury bullshit society makes us think we need to work toward. Accepting what nature has provided us with to get through life seems easy enough for me. To chop wood instead of numbers. I keep my pity party to myself since my family needs me. I allow my thoughts to wander while I'm flying sky-high through the Colorado mountains.

It would be nice to take Lauren here during the burst of fall colors if our arrangement can hang on that long. I haven't heard from her since I flew out, but she seemed in better spirits after she let her guard down. I've never had to bite my tongue so hard to not tell her to go to therapy or let me be the one she leans on. My breath hitches with the thought that I've never cared enough to want someone else to want me.

Has she crept into my life, making it more enjoyable? Yes. Has she managed to make me think about her beyond the sheets and crave to know what goes on in her mind? Also, yes. Have I thought about her every free second and wonder what she's up to? Maybe. Would I do anything she asked to make her demons dissipate? Fuck yes. I'd wake up next to her every morning if that's what she needed. She makes my life brighter.

I swallow the lump in my throat and ignore the obvious feeling my heart and gut are telling me. My brain has worked hard over the years to develop rules like Lauren has. What we agreed upon works and there is no point in furthering our relationship status beyond what it is. We have lasted this long because of our solid rules. Things have been blurry lines at times, but we can enjoy those moments knowing that it was just *the moment*.

A deathbed memory, as she likes to call it.

I spend the next lap around this gondola sending out texts to family. I check up on Kelsie to see if Max has seen any jail walls yet, and Lauren to wish her a smooth work shift. Benson is still in town for a final goodbye, and my family wants to keep me a plane ride away.

I only see red with this divorce, because the fucking dick still gets a small percentage of our fortune. Yes, part of that is my sister's fault for not doing an in-depth prenup with her own money. My ex filters through my mind, causing more anger with people trying to loot our family. At least Lauren seems to not give a damn about our lifestyle. I take a deep breath of fresh mountain air and remind myself how lucky I am to find someone like her. The gondola ride ends and I'm right back to work mode.

I finish out the next day strong, getting everything in order and present a few different ways to help the staff run a smoother shift. I lie in bed wide awake as the clock turns to midnight. I hate that I've been counting the hours of how much sleep I will get if I am able to fall asleep at *said second*. My flight leaves early in order to make it back so I can finish out my workday in San Francisco. I need to give proper attention to the financials of our company, but with my mental exhaustion, it'll be hard to achieve. A couple days to recuperate seems warranted, but the chances of that happening are far fetched. How my father managed to work this many hours his entire life beats me. I pull out my phone, knowing it's still early enough for Lauren to possibly be awake.

Me: Are you awake? My dick is so hard right now.

Cherries: Hard to find? ;p

Me: I said no tongue unless you plan to use it.

Cherries: Hey if women could do *that* to ourselves, we'd be set.

Me: I want you in my office at ten tomorrow morning.

Cherries: Bossy! I have an appointment. You swing by my place after work.

Me: Deal. Now what is your stance on sending me another photo? ;)

Cherries: I got myself off earlier. Hope this helps your problem. Nighty Night.

Video delivered

Me: If there was a jaw dropping emoji, I'd send it. Night.

I click open the video and it more than helps. She's smart to not show her face, but goddamn, those little moans she makes are distinct and have me busting my load as quick as my preteen self. Yeah, she's going to ruin me if this doesn't work out.

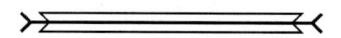

>=====<

I give a full rundown of the past four days to my father and grandfather about Aspen and answer more questions than I thought possible.

"Thank you, son." My father nods, standing up from his desk. "Your grandfather and I will fly out this weekend to make sure everything is running smoothly."

"Why did I need to fly out there?"

"Because, Adam George Wheaton..." My grandfather smiles with pride and stands next to my father. "One day, you will be in our shoes running this place."

I hope their vision has weakened with age and they don't see the fake plastered smile I put on. I nod and hope my father can't see my slight disappointment. He knows how much I enjoy simplicity and quiet, but he has chosen to ignore it.

"I look forward to it." I stand with them, growing a larger set of balls to test out their reaction to putting my need first. "I will be taking two days off this week to head up to our cabin. I need a clear head to return to business. This past week has been overwhelming."

My grandfather grunts. "I never needed time off. I still only take one day off as a senior."

"Does Lauren have those days off too?" my father asks, grabbing the attention of my grandfather.

"What does she have to do with me wanting to relax *alone*?" My eyebrows shoot up.

"You haven't seen her in a few days, and she works long hours, right?" I keep quiet and see where this is going. "Mallory said you two were dancing in the kitchen."

"So?"

"Lauren has an admirable work ethic, that's all." He smiles but I know that's not *all*. "Enjoy your cabin trip. I don't want you slacking anymore. You'll be pulling long days for the next week until you're caught up. Are we clear?"

"Yes, Father." We head out of the boardroom and I work through my lunch hour.

>=======<

"It's open!" Lauren calls when I knock.

I open the door as the sun is setting, casting a golden glow on the bed. I look over as she sets her ice cream on the nightstand. My dick springs to life within seconds. My hand reaches the back of my shirt as my eyes remain transfixed on her body. Lauren lies on display like a fucking goddess. She props on her side with one leg bent. The green La Perla set hugs her body the way I want to. A coy smile plays on her lips as her eyes roam my bare chest. I pull down my shorts and fight the urge to rip down my boxers as I stalk toward her.

Her tongue darts out to lick her lips as she pushes to her knees. Her arms wrap around my neck and I capture her lips in mine. A soft moan fills my mouth, testing my restraint as the video she sent flashes through my mind. I'm desperate to savor this moment, but at the same time, my hands grab the back of her knees as I lay her down.

My cock slides between her legs and I feel her slick slit through my boxers. It's a huge ego stroke to know how much I affect this woman. I bury my face in her neck, breathing in her sweet scent as her hands grip my hair. Snaking my hand underneath the lace, I cup her breast and pinch her hardened nipple. Her breath hitches and her hips buck up.

"I need you inside me," she pants. "Now."

"What if I want to savor you?" I taunt. My hand rests on the side of her face and my thumb traces her plump bottom lip.

"Savor me in round two." She arches her back to shimmy out of her panties.

I reach for the condom already on hand by her nightstand and slip it on. "You sure you don't want foreplay?" I line myself up at her entrance. "Your video plays in my mind rent-free."

"I'm about to explode with just your scent." Her heels dig into my ass. "It's pathetic how bad I need your dick right now."

I enter her in one move. Her wet center easily accepts me, so I keep a hard, constant rhythm. I pull one of her legs over my shoulder, lifting her back off the bed. I'm hitting the right spot by the look on her face. Her mouth hangs open and her eyes are wide. Her chest heaves for air and I notice a small vibrator from last night's video by her light. I reach for it, holding eye contact and place it between her folds, directly against her clit. Her hips move to angle the exact position needed as I continue to pound deep. Her arms rest above her head, taking as much pleasure as she can. In seconds, she tightens around me as I pull out and hold the vibrator against her clit. When a stream of fluid gushes out, I push back in and finish with a grin.

"That was fucking hot." I pull out as she looks at me in disbelief.

"I've never squirted before."

"Glad to be of service." I lie beside her to catch my breath. "I missed your body the past few days, and maybe even you."

"I may have missed you bringing me ice cream." She nudges me. "And orgasms. How was Aspen?"

"Full of mountains, paperwork and lack of a pretty girl." I wink, kissing the top of her head. "How were your shifts?"

"I worked as much as I could to try and rid you from my mind." She shakes her head. "What has your body done to me?"

"Likewise." I notice a large binder on the floor covered with sticky notes. "Homework?"

"No. It's something I've been working on for years." She gets out of bed. "You'll find out one day. This binder is why I sold my car and the real reason I work so much."

I hide my suspicion with a brief nod and give her the benefit of the doubt. She wouldn't use me for whatever is inside that binder, right?

It didn't take much convincing this time around for Lauren to agree to spend a couple of nights with me. I even offered to steer clear of her if she needed time alone to just enjoy the quiet outside of the city.

A chill follows us through the door stealing the coziness from inside. The rustle of trees is the only sound for miles. We both sigh after our busy week as I set our bags down.

"I'll start the woodstove and we can cook steaks on top later." I head farther into the cabin. "You can choose whatever room you want, or we can share." A shudder courses through me as I push a past memory away. "Just please don't choose the main master bedroom at the end of the hall. I learned the importance of knocking the hard way as a teenager."

"Did you assume parents stop having sex once their kids are born?" Her laugh fills the cabin.

"I wanted to pour bleach in my eyes after."

"So, if you become a father, you'd give up sex?" *Is she changing her mind about children now?*

"I wouldn't risk my kids witnessing me in action." I keep my face straight to catch her reaction. "As soon as the woman tested positive, I'd cut my dick off."

"Well, it's a good thing you won't ever have to worry about that then." Lauren, yet again, passed another test. "I'm going to go change."

The woodstove is crackling with warmth as Lauren walks past me in a dainty bikini. I should focus on the jiggle of her ass when she walks to the back door, but I zone in on her hand gripping a book with a shirtless guy on the cover. Kelsie had given me the rundown back in university when she'd do freelance PR for some authors. I never understood the craze of *reading* sex, but then again, I *watched* a fair amount of it online through my teen years. I never picture Lauren to be one to read those books, especially when her own bedroom life is as eventful as it is. Lauren's hand rests on her hip as her teeth pull her bottom lip back and forth. Is she thinking about pulling one of those hip strings and giving me a tease?

"I probably should have asked before changing, but is the hot tub on the deck working?"

"That bikini is working." I glance down at my pants.

She rolls her eyes and shakes her head, flopping her messy bun side to side. "Later. I want to relax and finish my book."

"The hot tub should be heated, or it won't take long to warm up."

"Cool. Feel free to join me when you're done."

I nod and add another log to the fire. I prep the steak and potatoes with a side of broccoli before I head outside. I take her in for a moment before she notices me. She sits in the corner with her blonde hair thrown up and elbows resting on the sides of the hot tub. Her book is closer to her face than most people I've seen reading. Judging by her cute, squinted eyes, I imagine she should be wearing glasses. Slowly, I round the hot tub at a distance and walk up behind her to catch a glimpse of what she's reading. Clearly, women are into these books. Her hands move the book closer to me as a smirk plays on her lips.

"If you want to read, all you have to do is ask."

"I don't." I place a kiss on her cheek and climb in the warm bubbly water. "I just don't get what the big deal about these books is. Do they all end up happy?"

"Most of the time, yes."

"And you know the people will end up together despite hating each other or the universe throwing them curveballs to wreck their love?" I take a sip of my beer and keep my eyes on her blushing cheeks.

"It's more about how they overcome their problems because they are fated to be together."

"Ha!" I feel the burn of the beer hit my nose to stifle my laugh. "This is coming from the woman who won't have a boyfriend. What is so enticing with these books?"

"It's fiction. I know my reality is different. These are an escape for me." She shrugs and closes the book. "Some people have celebrity crushes and I have book boyfriends."

"Book boyfriends?" There's no way. "Please tell me that's not a thing."

"I'm not the only one." She laughs and I wonder what makes book boyfriends more appealing.

"What if you found a real book guy though, would you still ignore him in reality?"

"There's a lot of boxes to check off with that question. They're one in a million." She sets her book down and lies back, popping her toes out of the water. "A book boyfriend has their downfalls and will screw up at some point. But they know the girl better than she knows herself. The chemistry between them is next level no matter how hard they fight it."

Well, hell. This is sounding too familiar.

"Why the shirtless muscle guy? That's pretty cheesy."

"That is usually the dead giveaway for spicy scenes." She clears her throat and takes a sip from my beer. "You give these men a good run for their money. We have had hotter sex than *this* book." She taps the front cover.

"Good." I puff out my chest dramatically, earning a giggle from her. "I can't be outdone by a fictional man on a page."

"It's so peaceful out here." She changes the subject and tilts her head back, closing her eyes.

"I would give up everything to move out here tomorrow." I sigh and stare out at the tall redwoods surrounding us.

"I don't blame you. Why did I apply downtown to a city again?"

"Because takeout doesn't deliver here, and you'd starve."

"Hey." She splashes me. "I can cook eggs and oatmeal pretty damn well."

"Aspen is beautiful if you ever want to transfer." I watch a quick flash of fear pass through her eyes.

"Why Aspen, Adam?" Her voice wavers in question and her eyebrows scrunch for a reason she won't admit out loud.

"There's a hospital. It's more peaceful, and you can have food delivered." She relaxes back into the water, but her eyes search mine. "I don't want you to go. I was just keeping the conversation going."

"I was born here. I guess I'm trying to find out why my womb supplier chose this city to live in." She bites her lip and starts her nervous habit of twisting her pinkie ring. "Or maybe she was stuck here. I see what goes on through certain streets of the city. I doubt my mother is even alive."

"Did you move here in hopes of finding her?"

"I don't know." She goes quiet as her eyes fixate on the trees. "I thought maybe I'd run into her, or save her if she was brought in. But being an addict twenty-five years ago doesn't give much hope for now."

"Hey." I wrap my arm around her. "She could have gotten clean over the years."

"I didn't leave the hospital with her. Her own *daughter* wasn't enough to give up the addiction. She chose *fun* over me."

How do I respond to that? "I'm proud you didn't choose the same path as her."

"Did *she* choose that path or was she groomed into it at such a young age?" Lauren's shoulders shrug and her half smile pangs my heart.

I stay quiet and let her thoughts process. An apology for something I have no control over will just make her mad.

"Adam." Her green eyes scan my face. "You've been great with no pity, but an *'I'm sorry you have all these unanswered questions.'* would be acceptable in this moment." She climbs onto my lap resting her hands on my shoulders.

"Dammit, woman. I can never win with you, can I?" My fingers wiggle as I hold her hips, tickling her sides. That's when I catch the two round scars under her arm. I'd always been too entranced with sex to pay attention to what the marks really are.

"Yeah." She pauses and her eyes follow my discovery. "I don't really remember the pain of that."

"Do you remember how you got them?" I swallow, only seeing cigarette burns on a movie.

"I think I was throwing a fit around three or four years old and the foster person picked me up by the arm. I tried to go back down, and in his anger, he burned me into listening." Her arm moves flush with her side to hide the marks. "Apparently I didn't learn the first time, so it happened again." She lets a light laugh escape, though nothing about this is funny.

It's then our eyes lock. It's then I want to kiss away every ounce of pain and trauma she's gone through. It's then she solidified how she has never asked anyone to love and cherish her strength. It's then I know I want to be the only one to protect her at all costs. I know she's taken hold of my heart.

I reach up and brush a loose strand of hair out of her face. Her heartbeat sounds loud through her slow, heavy breaths. The shift in our air isn't from the cool breeze surrounding us.

My hands reach under her bum as I stand and carry her out of the hot tub. The heat inside comforts us with the fire burning in our eyes. Our lips still haven't touched as I carry her up to a bedroom. Her arms stay locked around my neck as I lay her down on the duvet, pulling me to hover over her. I stare through her emeralds, looking for the answer I already know. She feels this too, but for the sake of keeping our arrangement, we can't say the words out loud.

I place a kiss on her lips and make a trail down her collarbone to her breasts, purposely avoiding her shoulder. I push up her bikini triangle and flick my tongue over the hard nipple. My hands reach for her arms as I guide them above her head. I continue my trail of kisses near her two small scars. Her body tenses underneath mine so I let go of her arms, expecting her to push me away. Instead, her eyes glass over and her hand runs through my hair.

"Do it again." Her voice cracks in a whisper. "Kiss away every scar you know my body never asked for."

"Every?" I hover above, resting my forehead against hers.

I watch her mind run through what she's told me in the past, but I'm a century ahead of what she's expecting.

"Every, Adam. Your lips are my therapy." Although I don't feel qualified to heal her, I give it my all.

I kiss her deeply, pulling her lips to mine with a long, slow kiss. A whimper releases from her lips as vulnerable, trusting eyes meet mine. I slide down her body, catching her off guard. My lips meet the top of her foot. "You've stood strong your entire life, even when it tried to knock you down." My lips ghost along her skin up to her knees. "For all the times you spent begging to be in another world." I run my tongue up her thigh and stop before her entrance.

Her thighs automatically open. "The strength it took to keep quiet when these were forced open against your will." I manage to keep my voice from wavering as a sting in my nose fights against my eyes watering. I continue to kiss up her hip. "This kiss is for every time you've needed someone to worship at your hips, hoping it will numb your past pain." She inhales sharply as I watch her stomach clench.

My truths are more than she expected but everything I know she needs to hear. A line of kisses feather up her stomach. "For the times your stomach knew hunger over nutrition." I kiss from her ribs to her scars. "The determination to keep your lungs breathing in times you wished they'd stop. For the child trying to understand and express her feelings." I kiss the second scar. "For the child who acted out in need of a hug and stability instead of a burn."

I hesitate over her shoulder, but she nods. "For every morning you woke to trauma." I kiss her forehead, eyes, and cheeks. "Your integrity and drive to do good for the world is inspiring. To the child whose eyes saw more homes than one should. To your cheeks for holding a smile through threatening tears."

I watch a single tear slide to her ear.

"This kiss is for your ears, never hearing how much a family loved you. How much they'd be there for you." I swallow the thick lump in my throat, brushing my lips against hers. "For these lips that have gone a lifetime unable to tell someone 'I love you.' To the child who bit the stuffed animal leg to protect another child."

Her lips purse together as a few more tears fall.

I move back down, hovering over her chest, placing a single kiss on her heart. "To the child that never had her heart feel overwhelmed with love and joy. For all the times you've never been able to open it up and feel what it's truly like to be loved by a parent, a friend, a significant other."

She wipes her cheeks and releases a shaky breath. "Lauren," I continue. "I can't tell you enough how much your strength amazes me. I am sorry your life has been that hard on you. I want you to know that anytime you need a reminder of how far you've come, I'm here for you."

"You truly mean that," she states without a question.

"You know I do." Her hands pull my head down to connect our lips.

Everything is slow. I follow her lead as she places her hands on my chest and pushes us up. Her fingers pull the string at the back of her neck, removing her top and my hands pull the two strings at her hips. She leans down to kiss me again and my hands trail down her spine. She's still not close enough. Her legs straighten so she is flush against me. My cock grinds against her fold and she brings one leg up to the side. I arch my back, sliding my swim trunks down and feel her wet warmth glide against my length. Her eyes hold mine as she angles herself to the tip of my dick and slowly pushes herself deeper onto me.

Air abandons my lungs as she continues the gentle rhythm. I let her set the pace and take control over what she needs. My hands trail up and down her sides, relishing every thrust and breath. I don't want this moment to end. I flip us over and bury my face in the crook of her neck, committing this moment to memory. Her skin is painted with goose bumps as my tongue traces over her ear and down her neck. Her breathing picks up as I quicken my hip pace. She's close, but I want her orgasm to build slowly.

"Take your time, baby." I grind my hips up for the next few strokes to hit her clit. "Let it keep building. I'm in no rush." I pinch her nipples and slow my pace again, pulling out to the tip and driving back in.

"Mmm, my entire body feels you." She moans and spreads her legs wider for more access to her clit.

I pull out and run my tongue over her drenched slit and lightly circle her with my tongue. "You're gonna come on my tongue and then on my dick." I continue to suck, bringing her to the edge and backing off until she can't take it anymore.

"Please," she pants. "I want you inside me when I let go. I want to feel you."

I realize she's never wanted anything from me until now.

I thrust in hard and give her what she wants. Her body trembles underneath mine and it's the most beautiful sight. No one else gets to see her head thrown back and lips parted. Her pupils dilate as a breathy cry escapes her mouth. Her hands grip the sheets as I let myself go, holding myself in place deep inside her. I don't know if I'll get hell for doing this, but in this moment, I'm too wrapped up in the way she's imprinting on my heart. I know she has the power to ruin me, I just hope she doesn't use it.

I slide out and lie beside her, fixated on the large wooden ceiling fan above. Several minutes of silence go by as our breathing calms, but I feel an unknown tension build around us. Lauren's head turns toward me with questioning eyes laced with fear.

"What—what just happened, Adam?" Her voice is quiet and thick with emotion I wish I could easily decipher.

This is about to go one way or another.

Chapter 19

Lauren

"What—what just happened, Adam?" I turn my head to Adam, unsure where these emotions are surfacing from.

Emotions I've only read about or witnessed on a screen. My hands tingle and my throat feels heavy, sinking deep in my chest. I'm light and heavy at the same time and I don't know why I feel my eyes pricking with damn tears again. I'm not sad.

"That was..." He clears his throat and rolls his lips in as if he's worried about saying his thoughts out loud. "That was us breaking a level of friendship."

I stay silent, turning my attention back to the ceiling fan. My ears ring in the silence as my mind runs wild. The only thing I hate about what just happened is that I didn't hate it. I didn't hate how he made me feel important.

Seen.

Wanted.

He saw my truths and accepted every part of my being. Adam kissed away my heavy burdens, as if he took on the weight I carry, for himself. Can you even make love with someone you don't love? Vulnerability crashes through my fearful soul, but I ache for the way he takes away my pain. I'm torn between my petrified heart and the antidote.

"We broke a level meaning...?" I feel my heart race every millisecond he doesn't finish my sentence. "Adam!"

"I don't know, Lauren." He places both arms under his head. "I'm waiting for my brain to tell me this is all wrong."

"But it's not?" I'm confused and terrified.

"No. No, this is nothing I have ever experienced." He rolls on his side to face me. "Did it feel like more than you wanted?"

"It *was* more than I wanted." I roll to face him and feel tears threatening once again. "I don't know how to accept these emotions." I'm taking a chance with the recent advice someone gave me to speak about my emotions.

"Let me show you." His face softens as his hand wipes a tear from the corner of my eye.

"I'm scared, Adam." I surprise myself with honesty.

"Me too, Lauren." I bring my hand up to hold his wrist on my face. "Whatever came over me, it feels right."

"Shouldn't this be a deathbed memory?" I want him to say this was a mistake so I can build another wall and leave before I let my heart be susceptible to possible pain.

"Is it so wrong to make this memory last a while?"

"We have rules for a reason, remember?" I toy with my bottom lip. "You've experienced love and heartbreak." The feeling of losing love is foreign when you've never had it, but my experience with abandonment runs deep. "I don't want to go through it."

"I'd go through past heartbreaks a hundred times more if I knew it would lead me to you. Until this very moment, I never thought I'd feel again."

"What do you feel?" I can't commit to anything further than what I just experienced, but what just happened healed wounds I never knew possible.

"Honestly." His eyebrows draw together in concern. "I feel you're about to call this arrangement off. You'll be the only woman who is the entire package, but I was only granted a sample."

"Entire package?" I laugh. "I'm pretty emotionally damaged, Adam. Even my therapist says I don't know how to accept emotion." I let the last part slip and put my fingers over my mouth.

"When did you start therapy?" A faint smile dresses his mouth. "I'm proud of you."

"I didn't do it so you'd be proud. When you were in Aspen, I had a terrible day at work but couldn't bug you." I close my eyes, recalling the young teen girl who managed to escape her traffickers. "I decided to talk to a therapist and things snowballed into my past and how I want to be normal." I shake my head, feeling ridiculous. "Normal in the sense of understanding how others can handle their *feelings* better than I can. Rachel is kookie, but still can rationalize love."

He swallows but it sounds more like a gulp. "So you want to love?"

"I want to feel like it's okay to feel. That I can trust others with my emotions." If he leaves me now, at least I was honest with him and myself. "The only person I know how to emotionally keep safe is myself. I feel like I'm hindering the parts of her that deserve to be happy on a different level."

"I feel something between us." He licks his lips before pressing them together. "Something I want to continue and grow, but if you can't handle that, I understand."

"You're all or nothing now?" *Is he giving me an out?*

Do I want this to end?

"I didn't say that."

I close my eyes and try to picture myself drowning in extra work shifts and finding random men to scratch the bedroom itch. Do I continue my numb trance in life? I breathe in for four counts and hold it as long as I can before exhaling. I speak my first gut instinct.

"I want to hate what just happened. You exposed all my dark truths and still made me feel like I was needed." I look into his brown eyes, searching for anything conniving. "I want to curl into the disturbed triggers and push you away as a painful liability."

"But?" Adam asks softly.

"But every time I break down or my past is exposed, you don't judge me. You build me up. I like how you treat my truths."

"I'm worried you'll close up the second we hit a small bump and I won't be able to go back to my old ways." His honesty hits me in the gut, but I mimic his fear.

"I don't want that to happen to you." My stomach turns with the fear of being the cause of someone's deep pain. "I like what happened earlier, but I can't leap into a relationship. I can't trust myself to fully feel right now."

"You do exactly what you said. You trust whatever feels right."

"How will I know?" *God, I feel dumb right now.*

"Lauren, you were the one that told me to kiss your traumas away. Did that feel wrong?"

"What if you're the reason I'll receive more?" My heart twists with the thought of us not working out, but the thought of us furthering our friendship scares me too.

"Ditto. We take things slow. One kiss at a time. One label at a time. I'm not asking to be your boyfriend."

"I can't forget about the moment we just had."

He kisses my cheek. "I can't forget it either."

Neither of us mention the conversation about our first night at the cabin until the ride home. Adam's hand encompasses mine as we enter the city limits and hit traffic. Already, I miss the serene music of the birds and how irrelevant time was.

"So." I break the silence. "Will we take us day by day?" I'm actually looking forward to my next therapy session tomorrow.

"If you're not comfortable with something or have any questions, please speak up." He gives my hand a squeeze. "I don't play games. So, if you say you're fine, I won't ask what's wrong a hundred times."

"I can't slack on my job because you take up brain space. My patients need me."

"Noted. I'll slack off on the bedroom skills so you don't think of all the ways I can use my talented tongue."

His words hit me like kryptonite and my legs clench together with sudden need. "Dammit, Adam. All I can think about is your tongue now."

His hand reaches over and unbuttons my jeans. I look around at the cars surrounding us and I'm thankful for his dark tinted windows. His fingers slip inside my panties as I open my legs wider. Gently, he slides his middle finger down to my center and back up to circle my clit. His pressure is heavy, and I angle my hips forward, desperate for more. I moan, reaching down to move his finger faster. He continues the pace and then slows down, causing me to whimper.

"Fuck, I want to eat you out right now." He brings his finger to his mouth.

"You should have taken the limo," I tease.

"I'll taste you against my hotel window soon enough." A smile creeps across his face. "San Francisco will be able to see how you come undone for me."

A call comes through the car, breaking our moment.

"Adam speaking," he answers.

"Hey, where are you?" Kelsie's voice echoes through the car. "Are you driving?"

"Yeah, sorry I haven't talked to you since Aspen."

"That's fine." Her voice is pained. "So, Benson came to say goodbye,"

Silence rings through my ears and my gut turns. My eyes meet Adam's as his fills with hate. His hand clenches the wheel, turning his knuckles white.

"How did that go?" His voice is dry and an octave lower.

"Mallory has been in her room for the past two days. She doesn't want to come out and will only eat if I drop the plate by her door." Kelsie's voice cracks and a sniffle fills the speaker. "Adam, I don't know what to do or say. *Everyone* in this family has tried to talk to her but she says we don't know what it's like to be given up."

"Dammit, Kels. Fuck, what do I even say?" Adam starts to ride the ass of the car in front of us but it's pointless with the traffic. "Did you tell her she's loved?"

"Duh, numbnuts! She doesn't think I understand because both *my* parents stayed and love me."

"I've got this." The pang in my stomach digs deeper.

"Oh, sorry, Lauren I—" Kelsie starts.

"We will be there in ten minutes. I know I can help," I say as Adam ends the call.

"Are you sure this isn't something too personal to share with my family?" Adam begins and squeezes my hand. "I don't want to pull you into family drama."

"A child needs help, Adam." Agitation rises within me from his comment. "I don't give a fuck who she is related to. I want to try to help her."

I enter the hotel ahead of Adam while he parks the car and takes a minute to cool off. The rage going through Adam after the phone call spoke loud enough about how he feels toward Benson. I understand why they sent him away while Kelsie's ex was in town. That man wouldn't have been able to walk out of the building if Adam had been within city limits. Awkwardness creeps over me as the elevator dings. They're expecting us, but I've never been to Kelsie's place. I step off the elevator to an open door on the opposite side of Adam's. I step through the foyer and see Max against the kitchen counter with Kelsie buried in his chest. Both arms are wrapped around her body as he leans forward, placing a kiss on top of her head.

Just friends, they say?

The elevator opens again, and I clear my throat, giving them a moment to break apart before Adam sees her in Max's arms. They jump and look my way, but Kelsie keeps her head pressed between Max's pecs. It's then I really observe how short she is compared to him. Somehow, the Wheaton height skipped out when giving her their signature genes.

"Shit, dude, go home and fucking rest," Adam says, shaking his head at Max. "I can take over now. Kelsie looks like she's drained you."

"Bro, don't be a fucking dick." Max brings his hands to cup Kelsie's face and wipes her tears with his thumbs. "What the fuck?" He shoots Adam a glare.

"Sorry." Adam shakes his head. "I've always fucking hated Benson."

"Stop the swearing." Kelsie steps back, wiping her own eyes. "James doesn't need to repeat that. Now, how can you guys help?"

After an extremely vague summary of my life, Kelsie brings me to Mallory's door. I don't want to open this can of worms again, but I also know what she's going through. I knock, but of course, no reply.

"It's Lauren, Mallory. You don't have to open the door, but I wanted to talk to someone who knows how poopy it feels when you feel unwanted by someone." I wait and take a seat against the door. "Mallory, your heart feels like it's hit the floor, doesn't it? I didn't know my parents. I've never met them." I pause again, trying to think of how to not downplay her feelings or as if I'm looking for pity for having one up on her.

I'm no therapist, that's for sure.

The door opens as she stands behind it and I enter a legitimate palace. *And she thinks I'm the princess?* I ignore the canopy double bed and castle playhouse built into the length of her entire wall. She closes the door, looking up at me with a tearstained face. Her brown curls are a matted mess, and I don't think she's slept.

"You're not good enough to love either?" The monotone in her voice tightens my ribs inward. "I should change the sign on my door to the Island of Misfits."

"That's my favorite Christmas special." I stifle a laugh but appreciate her wittiness.

"Well, maybe Santa will bring us new daddies." She's hurt, but there's a hint of sarcasm that cuts through.

I bend down to her level and open my arms to offer a hug. Her bottom lip quivers and I feel my own eyes start to sting. She sniffles and shakes her head, trying to gain the composure that no seven-year-old should need. She fights her tears and refuses my hug as I witness new walls forming around her innocent heart.

"It's okay to cry, Mallory. It's okay to be mad at the world. What happened to you isn't fair." I take a seat at the bottom of her bed, needing to balance myself. "You, my little princess, are loved by many."

"How come you never met your dad?" She walks over and takes a seat next to me.

Because the chances are my mother slept with him for drugs or she was raped.

"I don't even know his name." How age appropriate can I keep this? "My mom must have forgotten it when she gave birth."

"Where is your mom now?" Her little hand rests on top of mine as my emotions make my tongue swell.

"I don't know." I swallow the lump in my throat, forcing my tears to not fall. "But I know your father *does* love you. Sometimes, life just gets complicated."

"I know that he chose his other life over me." Her tiny hand tightens around mine as her jaw hardens with anger. "Is that what your mom and dad did?"

"They did." I nod. "But that led me to where I am today, and in this moment, I can tell you how special you are. One day, your father is going to realize he missed out on the amazing things you will be doing in this world. You are so intelligent and joyful, Mallory. Don't let *anyone*, no matter who it is, steal your light." I fight my own tears and fill my lungs to stabilize my voice.

"Sometimes life is better off without the people who don't appreciate basking in your light." I smile down at her. "You did absolutely nothing wrong, Mal. Your father chose a different path and doesn't deserve your tears."

She falls back on her bed and sighs. "You're right. I shouldn't have to beg someone to love me. I need to focus on everyone who does and ask them for *more* hugs since I'm down one person."

"I'm sure you'll get plenty of hugs anytime you need one."

"Let's go." She bounces right back to her seminormal self, and I assume my conversation with her was helpful.

I follow her down the polished marble floor back into the kitchen as she moves from her mother to Max and Adam, giving them hugs while saying how much she loves them. Her bouncy curls and smiling face turn to me and she skips over. Her tiny arms wrap tight around my waist as I feel the joy radiating off her. I've never encountered this radiating joy directed at me.

"Princess Lauren, I love you." Her arms tighten and I freeze.

My hands pause in midair before I rest them on her back. This child loves me, and I know it's pure. My breath vanishes as I watch three pairs of eyes on me in the distance. Only one of them knows what's going through my mind. My brain screams at me to repeat the words back to

Mallory, but my mouth can't. My heart rips in sheer pain, knowing she's waiting for the response. Guilt washes over me as Mallory repeats the words again and all I want to do is curl inward and run. I know she'd never cause me pain, but my tongue is tied.

"I need another hug, Mal." Adam waves her over. "Your last hug was too quick. I didn't get to pick you up and spin you."

She releases my waist and runs to jump into his arms. The anxiety eases, but this room is suffocating me.

"Thank you." Kelsie locks eyes with me and whispers. It's obvious she and Max are trying to hide their questioning faces.

"I don't know if I helped much. Keep an eye out if things start to not become a big deal to her anymore." I tuck my hands in the back of my pockets, feeling like my walls are coming down too quickly. "I need to head home."

"Your bag is still in the car." Adam sets Mallory down.

"I can grab it another day."

"Lauren." Adam's eyes are wide, pleading for me to not take off.

"The weekend was fun, but I need to get ready for work." I don't have work until tomorrow, but Kelsie and Max nod, believing my lie.

Adam tightens his jaw and doesn't look thrilled. I'm able to see a hundred questions pour through his eyes, but he respectfully nods and watches me head out.

I swear my lungs are going to burst as I hold my breath as long as possible until I get back to my place. The joy radiating off Mallory speaking those three words so freely to me, physically squeezes my heart. My ears have never heard those words unless it was from Stuart or Rachel, and hers was usually followed by the word *bitch*. I place my hands over my chest and breathe. This tactic is what my therapist suggested when feeling overwhelmed. I close my eyes to center myself. This is another learning moment. What hurts most is that I should have told Mallory those words back. That's what a child needs to hear. They need the security and comfort from those around them. I couldn't bring myself to say the words I've never felt.

I expect Adam to send me a text or swing by with my bag, but he doesn't.

I pace my condo and wonder if I've completely been written off now. How fucked up can I be to lack humanity? A simple smile letting a child know they're loved should be natural. I won't be surprised if I don't hear from Adam again. Tears burn my eyes, but I blink them away and try to distract myself by staring at the city life through my window. I've made it this far on my own and keep succeeding. The only love I truly need is the way I treat myself.

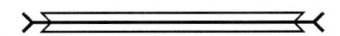

Due to a fatal apartment building fire, I end up with a twenty-four-hour trauma shift my first day back. Once everyone had been triaged, I pull out my phone and see a message.

Charmer: Hey...

Charmer: Damn, 238 is next level. *Fire emoji*

Was that the apartment that caught fire? Lacking the brainpower to decipher what he is talking about, I slip the phone back into my bag to reply later. I finish my patient rounds and head home to crash. Staying busy is what I thrive on.

Today, therapy caused tears but rationalizations. Abandonment is an obvious diagnosis in my world. How to deal with it is another thing. I'm proud of myself for being able to talk bluntly to my therapist about my issues. I have Rachel to thank for that. No shame in asking for what you want, because in recent experiences, it has helped. Letting someone into my mind doesn't mean I have to open my heart right away. I need someone to prove that they want to be around me even though things can be an unstable mess. If *I'm* not what Adam needs in his life, then that's on him. Not me.

I walk through my door and head to the kitchen to pour a glass of water. I have high hopes to grab an hour or two of sleep before I head into my night shift. Depending on traumas, your schedule can be changed around short notice. A knock taps on my door. I peek through the peephole and debate if I have enough energy to open up.

"You're here." I don't know where to start.

"I thought you'd want to finish your spicy shirtless guy book." Adam gives me a wink and a charming smile. "I'm down to try the kink on page two hundred and thirty-eight if you are." My mouth opens with surprise. "Spoiler alert, they end up together."

"That's usually how these fictional worlds end, Charmer." I make a mental note to pay close attention on the suggested page and step out of the way for him to enter. "I want to apologize for the other day."

"You have nothing to be sorry about."

"Right. Still learning." I chug my water and refill it. "How is Mallory doing?"

"You helped her a lot. Whatever you said made a difference." He reaches out, pulling me against him. "How are you? I wanted to give you some space after you took off, but at the same time, I wanted to see you." I don't miss the pain in his voice. "I'm still learning what to do in situations like this."

Did I really want that space? I have crawled back into my guarded self the past two days.

"The hug moment with Mallory was unpredictable. I get it if you had doubts about seeing me again." My voice is light and airy.

"Lauren." His hand reaches under my chin and tips my head up. "I gave you space because that's what I thought you wanted. You left in a blink and didn't return any of my texts."

"I like my space." I look off to the side.

"There's a *but* to your sentence." He moves his head to regain eye contact. "Please tell me if you don't want space. I know you're on a different path than the previous women I've known. But I need you to be direct with me."

"I didn't know if you thought I was too fucked up after what happened with Mallory." I sigh and try to avert my eyes away from the hold his have on mine.

"You know I don't think that."

"I didn't respond because I had a twenty-four-hour trauma shift from a fire. I honestly was too exhausted and forgot to reply." I sigh. "I was scared if I reached out that you'd tell me we are done with whatever we are." I'd rather us end quietly so I could sink back into my routine and avoid a problem head-on.

"We"—his finger waves back and forth between us—"are in these moments together. I want to be there for you. I need you to be honest. If you didn't want to see me, that's okay too. I just want your truths."

"And it's okay if you don't always like them?" I reconfirm the coping skill that I learned earlier.

"How you feel is more important than anything else. You need to address what you want." He places a kiss on my forehead.

"Only truths. Got it." I step away as emotional exhaustion kicks into high gear and I stare at the clock. "One more shift." I yawn and try to widen my eyes as if that will help.

"You're going into work?"

"Yeah, I came home this morning and went to therapy. I need a couple of hours to recuperate before heading in tonight."

"Your helping heart is beautiful." His hands cup my face as I feel my cheeks blush. "Also, your scrubs fit you so well that I'm considering getting admitted so I can stare at you all night."

I giggle. "Maroon scrubs do it for you, huh?"

"They do when I know what the body under them is capable of." He winks and pulls me in for a hug. "Enjoy your shift and give me a call when you're rested." He walks to the door. "Or if you want to rest together."

Chapter 20

Adam

I can't fight my smile watching Lauren board the company jet. Finally, she shows some astonishment walking past the cream leather seats. Her eyes light up as her cheeks beam with excitement. We make our way to the back of the jet and fall into the chairs. Joe, another colleague, boards after us and I internally groan. I guess making Lauren a part of the mile-high club is on hold this time around. The door seals as our pilot prepares for takeoff.

"I've never been on a plane before." Lauren bites her lip, unable to contain her smile.

"Well, this is going to be one hell of an initiation." Her hand laces through mine and I lift the back of her soft hand to my lips. "Are you nervous?"

"Not at all." The plane ascends as she looks out the window. "I'm glad I said yes."

I picked her up from her last work shift when I found out I was needed in Aspen for a meeting this afternoon.

Our five hotels across the country keep us busy and it's becoming clear that my generation isn't as passionate as our grandparents or parents. Kelsie is finally putting more hours in, but our cousins in Las Vegas and Miami have been struggling to show interest in the business side. By their social media and our brief conversations during business meetings, they'd rather reap the money benefits than put in hard work. Our New York location, on the other hand, loves this world. With a family business relying on the next generation, it's not that simple to leave them high and dry.

Lauren's head rests on my shoulder as her breathing becomes even. I lean forward and realize she's passed out before we hit thirty thousand feet. I'm dumbfounded with how much things have changed in the past two months of her moving here. How much she's changed me without trying to. I never wanted a relationship until I met a woman who is still not sure she'll be able to give me her heart.

Go fucking figure, universe.

We land and Lauren walks into the hotel half-asleep. Her messy bun and oversized sweater are definitely out of place at our luxury hotel, but her authenticity warms my heart. I've seen her done up and dressed for lux, but her natural, true self is the most breathtaking.

I preordered room service to be delivered for our arrival. Our large room overlooks the mountains and for the first time since the plane, Lauren speaks.

"Wow, this is really nice." Her voice cracks as she looks out at the large trees surrounding us. "I need coffee."

"I have a meeting after lunch." I kiss her forehead because if my lips touch any other part of her skin, I'll miss my meeting. "Why don't we eat, shower and then you can grab another couple hours of sleep?"

"I'm really exhausted. Usually I'm fine working constantly."

"Your therapy and emotional traumas probably haven't surfaced this high in a while though."

"Emotionally drained is a real thing, I guess." She gives me a half-hearted smile. "It seems I am human after all."

"I'll give you a nice massage in the shower." I wink and only then remember I forgot fucking condoms. But does that matter anymore?

Three hours later, I'm back in our room and Lauren is passed out with her arms wrapped around a pillow. She looks like a peaceful angel that shouldn't be disturbed. It's late afternoon and my meeting was brutal. Going over accounts, merges and meeting with the mayor has fried my brain. I strip out of my suit and crawl up beside Lauren's soft, bare frame. Turning on my side, I wrap my arm around her and the pillow. Her normal scent is replaced with hotel shampoo and I'm thankful to find someone so low maintenance that she doesn't need a large suitcase for an overnight trip. I glance at the clock and tell myself to wake her in twenty minutes, if I can hold off that long.

Tonight, I have a date night planned out for us. I figure since we agreed to see where this was going, she deserves a proper night out *with* a label on it. One date isn't too scary to start with. It has been a long time since I've felt giddy about taking a woman out. Lauren and I have been on mimic dates, but it isn't the same as knowing a person is letting their guard down and putting their heart on the line.

My fingers dance on her bare skin and I lower them down her body slowly. My hand slips beneath her panties, brushing lightly over her pussy and I feel my dick start to perk up. Screw waiting twenty minutes. I bring her out of dreamland in my favorite way.

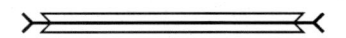

"That restaurant was amazing!" Lauren's hand laces with mine as she wears a content smile. "I'd say that was a perfect start to a first date." She playfully bumps my shoulder as we walk. "Minus my orgasmic wake-up call. Your fingers are magical."

"I had to start off on a good note because I wasn't completely sure you'd be on board with a *date*."

"I feel our previous outings were dates too. My birthday segment in the limo constantly plays through my head." She looks ahead but her cheeks hold a tinge of pink.

We follow the sound of instruments and find a group of music students practicing their compositions. Music buskers are quite common in this area with the university. Lauren and I stop as the melody changes to a familiar artist I have heard too much growing up through the years.

"No way!" Lauren grins, dropping my hand to move closer to the mini orchestra. "This is even cooler than a piano cover."

"*He's so tall, and handsome as hell,*" I start to sing along. "*He's so bad, but he does it so well.*" Her jaw drops, but I know it's not from being impressed by my off-key voice. "I think they chose this song on purpose."

"Are you a closet Taylor fan?" Lauren raises her eyebrows as her mouth parts in surprise.

"Kelsie is a Taylor fan. I had to hear that damn music from the other side of her door every day as a teenager."

"You really love your sister." The yellow glow of the streetlights brings out the softness in her features. "You act annoyed, but I know you'd break down and sing along with her if you knew it would make her smile."

Damn, Blondie is right again.

"Maybe." I smirk. "Come on." We walk with our hands intertwined along the small downtown strip. The chill of mountain air revives my soul and I pull Lauren in against me. A smile spreads across my face as I capture her lips with mine. It's soft and short and we carry on walking.

"What was that for?" she asks as our hands swing.

"It felt right. I'm glad you said yes to joining me in Aspen at the last minute."

"It felt right." She gives me a side smirk as her hand squeezes mine.

I lead her toward the gondolas. "How about a night ride overlooking the city lights?"

"Well, aren't you just checking off all the book boyfriend boxes." Her eyes bug out as her face drops, mortified by what she admitted out loud. "I mean—"

"I'll pretend I didn't hear that." I chuckle as we head to the gondola.

"It's a long list, so don't bother getting any joy from my comment."

We board the gondola in silence, both of us running through our thoughts. Watching Lauren experience new things has become addicting. Her face holds a subtle smile as she peers out the window, staring at the city lights shrinking from our ascend. My heart picks up its pace, confirming I am undoubtedly falling too fast for this woman. Falling for a woman that holds too much uncertainty for me to predict what the next three months will look like.

Lauren leans in closer and rests her head on my shoulder. "Thank you for today. This is the best date I have ever been on."

"It's the only date you've been on," I respond playfully.

"I'm glad I waited till now." She looks up and gives me a soft kiss.

"Wow, she kisses on the first date." I fake a shocked look, leaning away.

"Hey, Adam?" I nod. "Is there a camera in the pod?"

"No," I reply, wondering where she's going with this.

"Adam?" There is nothing but the moon lighting up her sultry eyes.

"Yes, Blondie?" I think I know where this is going.

"I'm not against fucking on the first date, either." Lauren licks her lips as her eyes travel down my body, painting a devilish grin across her face.

"Hop aboard the gondola express, baby." I reach to unbutton my pants and push them down to my knees as she straddles me.

"Let's stop talking and take advantage of the next seven minutes back down the hill." I shut her up with my lips and rip a hole in the center of the tights she wore under her skirt.

No trip to Aspen will ever be the same without flashes of her running through my mind.

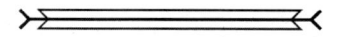

I kiss Lauren goodbye and promise she will join the mile-high club next time around before I head straight to my office. My father does his signature five knocks on my door before poking his head in.

"How was Aspen? Joe said you brought a very *leggy friend* along." He points at me. "His words, not mine." I can't fault anyone. Lauren's long legs alone could land her a modeling career if she wasn't content with her current lifestyle.

But I'm content with those legs wrapped around my waist or neck anytime she's available.

"Adam. Aspen. Focus." He snaps his fingers in between his words.

"I know. I was just taking a moment to appreciate the business meeting in Aspen." I don't even try to hide where my mind went a few seconds ago. "Aspen seems to be running great. I helped work on a few things, so we shouldn't have to worry."

"How are you and Lauren?" He leans forward, using the edge of my desk to steady himself. Clearly, more interested in the answer to *this* question.

"We are taking it day by day. I wouldn't call us acquaintances or only her *tour guide* now." I don't blush but I swear I can feel my goddamn cheeks heat. "I wouldn't put a label on us just yet."

But she makes me feel like we are fated. Fuck, I sound like a damn chick now.

"She's not the same as the other women you've been *friends* with."

"I'm well aware, Dad. She doesn't care about profiting from our family name."

"I'm surprised you didn't ask to transfer to Aspen when the location opened months ago." Where the hell is he going with this?

"I do love the mountains, but leaving Mallory and James held me back. Kelsie needs me too." I had thought about transferring to Aspen when we opened at the beginning of the year. Before the shitstorm blew up with my sister and her now ex.

"I think your mother and Max have her well taken care of." I don't miss how his eyebrows rise when he mentions Max's name. "I know how much those kids adore you." He taps his pen on his lip before pushing off the desk and straightening his spine. "Stop by tonight for dinner. Your mother misses you."

I nod and lose myself in numbers until the day is finished.

I head down to the lounge to relieve some stress on the piano when I spot Kelsie and Lauren at a table. Papers sprawl out as they huddle over them in deep analytics. They both know I play, but I can't get lost the way I want to if I know people are actually focusing on me. Lauren glances my way and her smile falters. Her eyes grow with a questionable panic. *Huh.* She mutters something to my sister and starts to clean the table, putting the papers back into a folder. I quicken my pace as curiosity gets the best of me.

"When did you two become besties?" *Is this a bit awkward or concerning?*

"Since you were a jerk to both of us at the gym and we bonded by talking shit about you." Lauren slips the folder into her bag and stands. "Kidding. Sort of." She kisses my cheek and looks down at my sister. "Thanks again, Kelsie. I will send you a text in a few days and let you know how this week goes."

"Looking forward to it, girly." My sister's eyes light up for the first time in months.

I take Lauren's seat and wait for my sister to choose where this conversation goes. Lately we haven't had much time together and I am at complete fault for that. Thankfully our best friend has been there for her, pulling most of the weight, but guilt fills my soul knowing I should be putting more effort in. Kelsie twists in the chair to crack her back, making me cringe. She relaxes into the chair, crossing her arms around her frame. Starting a conversation closed off already tells me I'm not on her best side.

"Kels, I'm sorry."

"Don't be. You've been carrying the weight of this hotel far more than I have." She sighs. "I know I've let everyone down lately. I'm trying to get back into the routine for work. The plus side is how James is loving preschool."

"You're a mother giving attention to her kids and going through a shitty situation. Don't apologize for that." I stare down at the table. "I've just missed working with you."

"You have me part time through the week." She smiles. "Max was right. I do feel better when I get up and get ready for the day."

"He's been helping a lot, it seems."

"Max has always had my back. I don't know what I would do without him." She smiles but it falters. "I swear he loves my kids more than their own father."

"Who is with the kids right now?" I redirect the conversation, hoping to change to a lighter topic and make her laugh.

"Mom is. I'm headed there for dinner and to pick them up." She glances at her watch. "Hopefully they'll be tired enough for an early bedtime."

"I'll help you put them to bed." Max's previous words come to mind. "I know that can be a tiring situation."

"It's not a situation I will complain about. They're my kids. I chose to have them."

"You didn't choose this situation. I *want* to help you tonight, Kels." She nods and a small smile of relief filters over her face. "What were you and Lauren looking at?"

"She didn't tell you?" Her puzzled brown eyes widen in surprise but she's excited about something. "She wanted marketing advice to launch a business-type idea thing." Well that's a lot of words and fucking vague.

"Sorry, a what?" Naivety washes over me as Kelsie speaks those triggering words.

"It's not my place to say much. I know she will tell you when she's ready, but it's a brilliant idea. I'm happy to offer my time." She smiles as my gut drops.

I force a tight smile and rise from the table. "Cool. I'm going to change before dinner."

My head spins as I step into my penthouse. I can't pinpoint if it's anger, distrust, or hurt that spews through my clenched stomach first.

Lauren has a business plan? Am I the only one smart enough to catch on to what's happening? Kelsie sure as hell isn't aware of what's going on. You would think Kelsie's wound from being used was still bleeding. Yet, she was manipulated all over again. We all were. My father couldn't even see through the fucking witchcraft of this woman.

I know I'm experiencing firsthand foolishness in thinking Lauren was different from the rest. She's not different, just craftier. Using people is a mode of survival and probably how she most likely coped through life. Is she really a practitioner because she studied her ass off or just slept with the right people? I remember how she threw herself at me when she officially moved to this city. Is she playing hot and cold to test how far I'll give in? Her secret agenda is easy to accomplish when you haven't been taught how to morally use your damn heart.

I turn on the shower and lean over the toilet, emptying my stomach. The distaste in my mouth matches the one my heart feels. I should have known this was too good to last more than a couple months. I wonder how she will go about using our family name or what ploy will be used to con a *donation* from one of us.

I need her to say it to my face. To at least have the dignity to admit this was her plan all along. Only, I wish I didn't feel this fucking sting in my heart from it. I decide to play it cool and play her at her own game. I want to give her the benefit of the doubt, considering she has never shown interest in my family's money. Part of me feels uneasy because her attitude might be quickly shifting to profits as our relationship grows. *If I let it grow.*

I quickly change, down a scotch, and head to my parents' for dinner.

Chapter 21

Lauren

I walk through my door and melt into my couch. I should change before resting, but exhaustion gets the best of me. This week has been the busiest week of my life in the best way. I smile at the pile of items in the corner of the room, feeling accomplished. This project is something I've been itching to accomplish since I was sent to an emergency overnight placement. I respond to Rachel and Lloyd and let them know I am alive and well. I haven't heard from Adam in three days since my meeting with Kelsie.

My phone buzzes. "I was just about to shoot you a text." I smile and sit up. "I hate to admit it, but I've missed you the past few days."

"Yeah." His voice is strained. "Mind if I stop by to talk about something?"

"I'd love to see you. I'm going to have a quick shower, but I'll leave the door unlocked."

"See you in a few." His voice clips short and the line cuts off.

I've let myself open up to the feeling of being his. I remember how tentative he was in Aspen and how he has responded to every breakdown I've failed to keep hidden. Life has been more enjoyable since opening up to him. He can handle me. He didn't run when I broke down after consoling Mallory. A far-fetched thought, but maybe my guard will eventually drop and I can have it all one day.

I step out of the shower and change into workout shorts and a loose tank top. The sun is setting behind the skyscrapers, giving the building a beautiful glow. I look forward to this time of day. The prettiest hour there is. I hear the kitchen tap turn on as I walk out and drink in the strong forearm holding the glass of water. His tailored shirt is rolled up at the sleeves and his lips make me wish I was the rim of the damn cup. I don't think I'll ever get over how my stomach flips at the sight of him. I feel like I should have put more effort into my outfit, but he's made me feel confident and beautiful no matter what I wear. He glances my way, giving me a brief once-over unamused.

His eyes don't darken and devour me like they normally do. My arms wrap around my waist as an odd insecurity washes over me. I follow his gaze to the mound of supplies. Adam's brows furrow and I understand why he finds the corner more interesting than me.

"I've been busy." I smile, making my way over to the contents.

"I see." He clears his throat, keeping the distance.

What's with the hostility?

"Okay, I'll tell you even though you haven't asked."

He motions his hand toward the piles with a nod.

"When I was younger, I had an emergency overnight placement. I had no time to pack what minimal things I owned. I, like many others, had a trash bag which hosted a handful of clothes and if I was lucky a few hygiene products." I pick up a duffel bag and start adding some contents to it.

"The emergency placement lady I stayed with took one look at my garbage bag and shook her head. Stacy, the lady, said no one deserves to live out of a trash bag. I was given a proper bag, and it was filled with everything I had been lacking." I throw in a pack of underwear, socks, pads, and other necessities. "My clothes were a size too small. She took me out that night and bought a few new clothing items. The feeling of owning something *new* and having a bag that was *mine*." I pause, feeling my nose sting, but I blink back tears. "It gave me hope that someone actually cared about my well-being, if only for a night. Stacy helped me find a new self-worth after Stuart and Mabel's. She took me out for pizza that night and gave me a reason to live for another day."

I add a rolled blanket, journal, and pack of gummy worms into the bag, then set it down. My dining area hosts stacks of boxers and panties in various sizes covering the table. Adam keeps his eyes fixed on the piles avoiding my eyes. He swallows thickly and crosses his arms. I can't quite read his body language, so I carry on because he hasn't stopped my rant yet.

"Now that I am able to support myself, I've been saving every dollar I don't need to invest in this charity. That's why I don't own a car anymore. I'd love to be able to hand out these bags to as many children as I can. I need to work on marketing with hopes of gaining sponsors, because my funding alone can't reach as many children as I'd like." I shrug, still confused by his closed-off frequency. "Kelsie has been an angel and offered her time to share marketing secrets and pointers. She also proofread my professional speech to pitch for sponsorships."

"Has she *donated?*" His voice strains as his eyes lock with mine.

Ah, I know where this is going.

A light bulb goes off and I see through the mist.

The fear.

His long list of past burns creeping up on him.

"The only thing I felt comfortable taking was her time." I step into him. "This is my project and I've worked hard on it. Your money and name on this would take away what I have worked for."

His lips roll in as his eyes remain skeptical. "How do I know for sure that you are not just toying with me until I completely fall for you and your plan works?"

"Plan?" Rage begins to pulse through me as my jaw tightens from his accusation. "*Completely fall for me?*" I take a step back, feeling anxiety kick in at the thought of him wanting me forever this soon.

"You said it yourself." His voice wavers and I sense he is more guarded than he lets on. "You've been in trauma survival mode your entire life. You do what you have to get what you want." He bites his cheek with a slight attitude and I know he is faced with the dark truth of his past. Have the tables turned and now I am supposed to be his support?

His words hurt but I walk up to him to stand my ground. Our chests are one deep breath away from touching as I look him straight in the eyes.

"Keeping my dignity is worth more than any world record orgasm you can give me. If you are questioning my authenticity at this point, then you can leave and delete my number." My heart thumps to my ears as I hold our gaze, awaiting his next move.

"God, I'm an asshole." His hands cup my face as his lips press gently on mine, and I deflate with relief.

"I will never use you for your name." My arms wrap around his neck and I pull back. "But you have every right to doubt me, given your past."

"You're mine, Lauren." He drops his voice an octave, but it's his words that cause distress.

The fear of the unknown.

The fear of feeling something more.

The fear of my own walls crashing down.

The power shift he's given me to potentially break *him*.

"These lips, mine." He kisses them. "This beautiful, intelligent head." He fists my damp hair, tilting my head back. "Mine."

My breath hitches as his possessiveness continues.

"Your giving heart. Give me a piece of it." He kisses down my throat, over my shoulder and down my arm. "Your gentle donating hands? I don't want to forget how they feel on my body." He kneels, places his hands on my hips, and looks up at me. "The path you've walked to get to this point in life takes true strength. I want all of you."

"You want me?" My heart pounds through my ears and I feel I can't hear what he's saying correctly.

"No." Adam shakes his head and tosses one of my legs over his shoulder. "I *need* you. And I have no doubt about that."

"But we said—" I choke out, reaching the chair for support as his nose brushes against my pussy over the fabric on my shorts.

"I said that before I knew someone like you truly existed. With you, Lauren, I'm all in."

His fingers move the fabric to the side as he presses soft kisses on my clit. My legs buckle as desire builds. Everything in me wants to give in to this moment. To let go and bask in the glory of being needed, wanted, worshipped. But I'm hit with flashbacks of those saying goodbye to loved ones at work. Lloyd was a mess for years after losing Marsha. A phantom fist clenches my heart and I pull my leg back down to step away. Tears sting my eyes as I look down at the man who is willing to endure all my pain and past. Instead of fear or hurt flashing across his face, I see empathy.

"I don't know if I can *want* you that much just yet." My voice breaks as the lump in my constricted throat grows.

Adam stands and picks me up, carrying me over to the bed. My back gently meets the mattress as he hovers over me. His forearms cage in my head as one hand delicately massages my scalp. His brown eyes are soft and understanding. His lips brush against mine, fluttering my stomach, shooting pleasure down to my toes. Adam's hands cup my jaw, turning my head to expose my neck. His mouth feathers open kisses little by little down my throat.

"Please," he whispers. His warm breath hits my ear as his lips meet that spot, leaving me surrendered at his mercy. "Let me show you how much I *need* you."

The world stops. The sun officially sets behind the buildings, leaving nothing but the city lights reflecting in Adam's eyes. Even in my darkest hours, he shines through, igniting hope.

My hands cup his face as I look from his eyes to his lips. With reluctance like my heart, I bring my head forward to capture his lips with mine. I anticipate the moment where he snaps, flipping me over to fuck me senseless like every time. Each kiss trails down my body like a wrecking ball, smashing down years of doubt, self-worth and neglect. It's the most beautiful thing I've allowed myself to feel. Helpless to free myself of past darkness, I transfer my demons over to him. He is in full control over my body, mind, and dare I admit, my damn heart.

His fingers pump pleasure through me as they curl deep inside. It doesn't take much for this man to make me come undone and fall to his mercy. A ragged breath leaves my lungs and I can no longer wrestle with lifelong suppressed emotions. He kisses his way up my body, bringing his thumbs under my eyes to wipe away my silent tears. His lips pepper my jaw with kisses. Needing to feel the weight of him as a blanket of security, I wrap my arms tight around him. His hard length pushes against me but he doesn't try to enter. Our tongues collide in perfect sync and savor the moment.

"God, your soul is beyond beautiful, Lauren. I don't deserve what the universe has granted me."

"Make me believe it." My need for him aches as I move to position him in front of my core.

Adam's eyes hold my gaze as he eases into me. Each stroke is intentional, delivering the overwhelming thoughts we can't bring ourselves to speak. I don't know what this is I'm feeling. The feeling of safety. The feeling that if I die tomorrow, I'd lived knowing the feeling of being *wanted*. Want on a level my heart could burst from. I wrap my legs around him, trying to bring him closer than he physically can get. I want him to sear through my soul, possessing my mind and body with the bliss that's always been foreign. I open my mouth to express my thoughts, but no words form.

"Adam, I..." My voice trails as more tears pool in my eyes. I should feel embarrassed or pathetic, yet with him, I feel safe.

"I know, Lauren." He brushes a strand of hair stuck to my teary face. "I feel it too."

"What is this?" I feel ashamed to ask again, but my life has been devoid of the emotions that Adam clearly recognizes.

He pauses as if he doesn't want to break the moment or say something to scare me off. "This... this is a level of intimacy I've never shared with anyone else." He picks up his pace, thrusting into me as a predatorial gaze takes over. "This is me devoting myself to you and only you."

"That sounds intense." I feel my orgasm building as I push down the feelings of fear.

"We are intense, Lauren McAllister. Embrace whatever feels right in this moment." His hand circles my clit and his lips silence my mouth and mind.

I let go leisurely. Taking my time to relish in his touch and each thrust. Feeling my high build until I can no longer hold off and dig my nails into his back, filling the room with a pleasured cry. He finishes deep inside me with a throaty grunt. Adam pulls out and warm liquid seeps down my ass onto the sheets.

With a kiss on my forehead, he walks over to the bathroom and returns with a warm towel to clean me up. I cock a brow and reach to take the cloth. This is one task I've never had anyone do.

"Just let me take care of you for once." Adam holds the cloth back out of my reach. "I made this mess."

I lie back and let him clean me. I can't push away the uneasy feeling of giving up control for a simple task I can easily complete myself. Aside from the time I was given that supply bag, no one has ever shown interest they wanted to take care of me. I feel a strong connection as I look down at the man tending to me. This is probably the damn oxytocin from bareback sex. Do I want him? Yes, who wouldn't want to spend their days like this with a man so giving? Can I let the fear that this could be ripped away and I'll be left tending to myself, for everything, again? That, I can't face.

"I don't think I can do this." The words rush out of my mouth, but I immediately wish they didn't.

"Hey." Adam leans in closer. "I know this is a lot to take in. All I'm asking is if you'll let me need you until you are ready to give your heart to me."

"And if I can't?"

"Then..." His eyes roam my body before meeting with mine again. "Then, this will be one hell of a deathbed memory to look back on. I hope you try to give us a chance to see where this goes."

I nod. "I want to try."

"I'm scared too, you know. You may shatter me, but it's worth the moment we just shared."

"I should sleep. I have my last twelve-hour shift tomorrow." I clear my throat as he stands, gathering his clothes.

"Sweet dreams, Lauren." Adam kisses my forehead and heads home.

My feet ache from constant running and the grumble in my stomach is getting embarrassing. Another crazy day has flown by and I still haven't gotten around to lunch by late afternoon. I grab the chart outside the door to a patient's room. The lump in my throat drops to my gut, but I push a smile forward. I know this system too well. A lot of children get let down, and others eventually rise up for a fighting chance. I waver back and forth as to what scenario mine was.

I wrote a previous report and the social worker had been notified about the recurring visits. The pendulum in my mind sways since the adult is stepping up to bring this child here, but why does the child keep needing this place? The nursing student who gathered the information earlier warned me she felt something was off.

If this is a sick game, I need a clever angle to reach the untold truths.

"Ava Rose, this is not an ice cream store, but I feel like I owe you an ice cream after our last interaction." She gives me the same weak smile I wore for too many years.

"It hurts to use the bathroom again."

Her guardian rolls her eyes. "I told her to wipe front to back so this wouldn't happen again. A nine-year-old should know this by now, right?"

"Some people can be more prone to bladder infections than others. Allergies or dehydration can play a part as well." The guardian crosses her arms with a huff. "We can run multiple tests to get to the bottom of this." I look over Ava's file and know this can't be a lingering infection from the last time. "You guys might be here for a while."

"Is there any way I can get a coffee? I came home from work a few hours ago and my son said she had been complaining since she arrived home from school." She stands, adjusting the designer purse over her arm.

"If you go to the nurses' station, they'll be happy to get you one." I smile, feeling bile rise to my throat.

"Maybe talk to that one about basic hygiene." The woman nods in Ava's direction and takes off.

Ava's eyes dart around the room as she twists her fingers. My heart picks up speed as I steady my breath. I push the door closed and take a seat next to her.

"Ava." I keep my voice soft. "I was in foster care too, growing up. We don't have much time, but I think you know proper hygiene."

Her face pales as she slowly nods, bringing her eyes up to mine. "Are you alone with that lady's son after school?" She stiffens and sucks in a breath, still unable to speak. "Does he put his hands on places you don't want him to?" Terror reaches her eyes telling me everything I need to know. "I promise I can help you, but you have to talk to me and a few others. I can help you get out of this, Ava Rose."

"I can't go back home with her." Her voice breaks and her body shakes.

"When was the last time he touched you?"

"After school." Ava's lips purse together as her little face holds back tears.

"You'll be okay." I give her a quick hug and stand to gain composure. "I'm going to tell your guardian we need to rule everything out. When you're asked questions by us, I need you to be honest. Can you do that?"

She nods, rolling her lips, and I watch a layer of armor build around her. Armor that no child should ever feel the need to build.

I switch to autopilot, going through the necessary steps and tests to keep Ava safe. Her confession was made to the right people, but not without protest and doubt from her guardian. You can't argue or lie with lab results. Ava had indeed been sexually abused, assaulted and mistreated beyond what her hospital visits brought her here for.

"He won't hurt you anymore." I fight to keep my voice strong and wrap Ava in a hug.

"Thank you." Her arms lightly wrap around me, but she can't relax into the hug. "Can I go home with you?"

I glance up at the social worker, knowing the answer. "I wish you could, honey." I never thought about fostering, but in this moment, I wish I could bring her home with me. "I gave your caseworker my phone number and we can arrange a time to go out." I pull back and bend down to her level. "We can plan a girls' day. Shopping, manicures, ice cream and whatever you want to do."

"Promise?" Her eyes light up for the first time I've seen.

"I never make a promise I can't keep."

"Because you were like me." Her voice fades out.

"We are more alike than you think." I squeeze her hands. "That is how I *know* you're a strong fighter, like I am. I'm proud of you. Today wasn't easy." I pull her in for another hug. "You're going to do great things for this world, Ava Rose."

"I bet you're the best mom in the world." Ava smiles and steps toward her caseworker. "Or you will be one day."

"Have a good night, Lauren." The caseworker gives me a nod before placing her hand on Ava's shoulder to guide her down the hall.

I exhale, letting my shoulders deflate and turn around to a bunch of staff who start applauding. I force a smile and head to my spot to gather my belongings. The applause feels unnecessary. I'm just doing my job. The real person who deserves the claps is the little girl who just walked out of here with her head held high and cheeks void of tears. I head out of the hospital, knowing I need to blow off steam before I completely lose it.

I make it to my fitness class just in time tonight. I change and head straight into the circuit room, only to find Max setting up the class instead of Adam. My lungs seize as my ribs cave in. I want to retreat back out the door and find the one person who can handle or prevent my oncoming spiral.

"Lauren!" Kelsie calls out and waves me over.

I guess tonight, it's up to me to fight the weight of my emotional control. I twist my pinkie ring and walk to the space next to her.

"Hey, Kelsie. Is Adam not teaching?"

"No, he had a bad headache and offered to watch a movie with the kids if Max filled in." She shakes her head. "Men have no idea the pain we work through every month during our periods."

I laugh, pushing the past few hours to the back of my mind and follow Max as he warms up the class. My body is exhausted, but I throw as much power as I can into each circuit. I see Kelsie eyeing me then exchange glances with Max. It isn't until the last station when Kelsie speaks up.

"How was work today? You seem distant."

Most of this class had been spent detached from everything except the energy put forth to the fitness task at hand. Ava's trauma rings through my ears, taking me back to the life I once endured.

"Difficult." I decide not to lie but I make sure to avoid her eyes.

I continue to throw the medicine ball up and squat until my muscles burn with a silent, screaming plea. My jaw aches as I clench my teeth and inhale, pushing myself until I physically break. The sting throughout my body is the pain I'm choosing to cause. My reminder that I'm in charge of what my body can feel. Kelsie says something, but I'm too zoned in to listen or respond. I shut the world out around me and continue to throw the ball up until it doesn't come back down. My vision blurs as I stumble back. Small hands catch my waist and guide me to the floor. I blink, waiting for the dizziness to subside and my vision to focus. I feel a drop on my chest and it's then I realize my vision is blurred from tears.

I wipe my eyes and see the class clearing out. I sniffle to pull myself together and go to stand.

"Just sit for a moment, Laur." The gentle touch from Kelsie rubbing my back *should* feel comforting, but I tense the same way Ava had when I embraced her. "Take a deep breath." I take the water bottle she holds out with a shaky hand.

"Thank you." I chug half the bottle, feeling even more sick to my stomach. "I'm fine. I should get going." With all my willpower, I stand up, gather my bag and make it halfway down the empty hallway before turning to the nearby garbage can.

My stomach contents flow into the trash, burning my throat.

My body shakes as I grip the round metal rim, silently cursing my involuntary reaction to trauma. Tears fill my eyes and I'm thankful this hallway is empty. Guilt seeps through me for vomiting inside a building. Let alone one that Max's parents own. I feel Kelsie's hand rub circles on my back. I look up to blink the dizziness away as Adam rounds the corner with a look of concern. I straighten but keep a hand on the garbage for support.

"I heard you were quite the energizer bunny tonight." Adam pulls me to his chest, and I find comfort leaning into his touch.

"Who is watching the kids?" My voice kicks up an octave, remembering Kelsie's words.

Adam holds me tighter, and I feel his chin brush back and forth on top of my head.

"They are with my mom. They should be the least of your worries." He kisses my head as I pull back. "Kelsie sent me a text saying you were working out hard after having a difficult day at work."

I glance her way and nod.

"What happened?" Max asks and Kelsie shoves him.

"You can't expect her to answer that right now, you moron," she replies with an eye roll.

"It's fine. He's just worried." I give a half-hearted smile to Max and lean into Adam's chest.

I give them a very brief recap of how I spent the last few hours of work and how proud I am that Ava was a warrior through the entire process. I'll be able to sleep knowing she's no longer near that family.

"Shit, if anyone ever came near Mallory, I'd rip their dick off." Max fumes as his fists tighten. "Do you think she'll be okay? I imagine you can't erase that sort of memory."

"No, you don't." My stomach turns again and I forget how to swallow. "It happens to kids a lot more than people think."

I zone into a poster on the wall and my lungs constrict. Its blue hue takes me back to a familiar one I spent countless mornings staring at. I'm brought back to an old bedroom, staring at a poster, clenching the stuffed bear's leg through my teeth while Stuart slaked his need. My temples ache as my teeth clench down harder. Instinctively, my hand goes up to my shoulder, rubbing at the haunting pair of lips. The air around me is stifling and the ripping of my nails against my skin isn't erasing his lips.

A firm grip on my chin pulls my head away from the poster. "Lauren." Adam's deep voice rings through my ears. "Lauren, he's in jail. You're safe now." He snaps his fingers but no matter how much I try to inhale, it's not enough. "Do you smell the pool chlorine? It's pretty strong."

I flinch, pushing my shoulders back and arch into him as cool water trickles down my back. "Do you feel the water?" I nod, centering my vision and mind on the man in front of me.

"What can you feel?" he asks.

My hands brush down his chest as my fingertips bump over each ab crevice like an attempt to read brail. "Jeez, your abs are unreal." I feel a smile tug at my lips, enabling me to take a slow breath in. "I'm okay."

"You're okay. You're in the gym with us." Adam rubs my back.

I'm in the gym.

I step out of his hold as my cheeks heat with embarrassment. I just vomited and had a breakdown in front of his best friend and sister. God, they're going to think I'm crazy. With reluctance, I turn toward them. Their eyes hold a damn good guess as to the cause of my panic attack. I don't have to explain anything out loud. Kelsie wears a sympathetic smile as Max's face is even redder and his fists remain clenched. His blue eyes are full of rage as opposed to his brooding, cool self. Pissed would be an understatement.

"I'm here if you ever want to talk." Kelsie blinks back a tear and takes Max's hand. "We're going to let you two carry on with your night."

Max walks down the hallway and punches the wall, hurting himself more than the cement. Kelsie rests her head against his arm and turns back to us with a faint smile before disappearing around the corner.

"Please stay with me tonight." My voice strains.

"Like hell I was going to leave you alone." He kisses the top of my head and picks up my bag. "Let's get you some ice cream and a hot bath."

"We don't have a bathtub." I laugh.

"Oh, my private rooftop has a hot tub," he slowly announces, as if he forgot he owned it. "That should do, right?"

"I guess it shall suffice." I nudge him with a sassy smirk.

Chapter 22

Lauren

"Ugh, just vanquish him already." I toss the blanket aside and close the lid on an empty ice cream tub.

"I thought you said he was a pretty hot demon?" Adam chuckles and the alarm on his phone goes off.

"No, it can't be time for you to go to work already." I turn the episode of *Charmed* off and feel ridiculous for pouting. "I mean, go make that money so you can keep buying me ice cream."

"Are you sure you're okay if I head to work?" Adam leans over, pressing a soft kiss to my temple before holding my gaze.

I took my therapist's advice to acknowledge the pain but do the things that take care of me. I've been learning it is okay to feel sad, to hurt, and let others help you when you feel the weight of the world. So, Adam and I spent most of the night watching *Charmed* and rolling around the sheets between episodes. Adam has been nothing short of helpful when it comes to dealing with my emotions. And, Lord, can he ever take my mind off the things I need him to.

"You've been by my side since the gym last night." I smile, accepting the feeling of happiness he brings me. "I have a therapy session in a few hours anyway." I stand up, stretching my arms above my head, catching his eyes drifting to the bite mark I know he left on my hip. "Thanks for the branding." I wink.

"Don't get me turned on before work, Blondie." He makes a tsking sound and shakes his head. "Are you staying here?"

"No!" I don't mean to shout, but I want to be clear that we aren't on the level of staying at each other's places while the other is gone.

"Okay." Adam backs off, holding his hands up as if he were surrendering.

"I want to make a few more duffel bags this morning." I switch my tone to my normal self.

"I'd be fine if you wanted to stay and wait for me too." He shoots me his charming grin, which instantly triggers a heartbeat in my pussy. "I'm not opposed to you surprising me in the shower when I come home from work."

"That seems too traditional for us." I fight the temptation.

"Blondie, nothing about our arrangement is traditional." He picks up my ice cream bowl on the nightstand.

"I'll wash that."

"Good girl." His voice holds grit as he winks, and I instantly want to make him late for work.

"I'm getting myself off before I leave your place though." I tease and before I can finish a breath, he's hovering over me.

"You better hold off until tonight." His minty breath halts mine. "If my meeting wasn't one of the most important ones this year, I'd be late."

***

The hum of this city vibrates through me, bringing me back to life. Today's session was heavy as I explained Ava's situation and my breakdown at the gym. The heavy weight I put on myself for not catching Ava's troubles sooner has been eating away at me since I confronted her. A large part of me wants to blame Adam for the possibility I had been too distracted with thoughts of joining him after work. My therapist confirmed I had done the best I could have. I filed the report prior to Ava's last visit. Learning to accept fates is still something I need to work on.

The sun beats down, leaving me breathless in front of Adam's hotel. His offer to stay at his place without him there feels more inviting than walking the extra three blocks uphill to my place. I head into the lobby and type in his code to the private floor. I can easily entertain myself in the penthouse for an hour until he returns.

I take the longest shower of my life under his gigantic raining showerhead, then head to the large windows to enjoy the view. Life has taken me by surprise the past couple of months. I pull out my phone and, for once, make the first call.

"Lauren, sweetheart." Lloyd's voice smiles through the phone screen. "It's nice to *see* you."

"I always forget these phones have a video option." I laugh, putting off what I actually called about.

"I hope the city is being kind to you."

"I met someone." My words rush out and I fight the urge to cover my mouth.

"I knew you would." He nods as his creased eyes light up. "When did you two meet?"

I pause for a moment reflecting on how much truth I want to share. "We met the night I flew in for my interview, actually." I smile as I'm taken back to the lobby and the high-maintenance woman slapping his cheek in front of everyone. "We aren't extremely serious yet, but I thought I would keep you informed."

"I'm happy for you, sweetheart." Lloyd takes a bite of pizza, and my stomach craves a slice. "I bet you'll have that *moment* soon enough." I smile and bite my tongue. Adam and I have had many, but I still can't fully commit to each moment.

"Your apartment looks like they gave you quite the raise." He leans closer, taking in the leather furniture and chandelier.

"I'm at his place. He makes a bit more than I do." I clear my throat and hear the door open. "I should get going. I will call again soon."

"Okay, take care, sweetheart." Lloyd ends the call as Adam closes the door with a happy, puzzled look.

"Um, hey." I stand and zone in on a box of pizza he's holding. "Is that the place we went to after I fainted in the gym?"

"It is." He sets the box on the counter. "I thought I was picking you up at your place later on."

"I hope you don't mind that I'm here. I know we are heading out tonight and figured, why not wait here?" My nerves spike as my rib cage tightens with unease. Maybe I have overstepped a boundary.

"I like coming home and seeing you." His smile warms me as he walks forward to give me a kiss. "Who was on the phone?" Not that it's his business to ask, but I was in his house.

"My previous foster guardian, actually." It's odd to admit it out loud. "I stayed with him and his wife through high school and they let me stay through university." I smile, appreciating how lucky I was in that aspect. "That is a rarity once you age out of the system."

"They must have known how much potential you had." He kisses my head before opening the box of pizza.

"I'm drained." I yawn as Adam and I take a seat against the tall windows.

"Well, this cheap pizza is going to make you sleepier." He shoots me a smug grin as I roll my eyes.

Mr. Healthy Pants and I stare at everyone down below walking the streets. Who'd have thought a man buying cheap takeout would make a girl smile more than him cooking. Not that I hate his cooking. I just appreciate him joining me in inhaling garbage for once.

"I'm glad you don't have to work tomorrow." I smile, taking a bite of pizza into my mouth.

"I still have a fitness class in the morning to teach."

"Why do you teach at the gym when you have a job that pays well?"

"Sense of normalcy." He shrugs. "Max and I used to take those classes, and honestly, I enjoy witnessing people feel a sense of achievement when they reach their fitness goal. I find more meaning in *that* than the work I do in my office."

"That's sweet." I set my empty plate on the table. "I have a fitness goal for myself right now." I pull my shirt over my head, walking to his bed.

He follows my lead and pushes me onto the mattress, crawling on top. "Oh, do you now? What type of fitness are we talking about?"

"A heavy mix of cardio and gymnastics." My arms lift around his neck, crossing my wrist to pull him in closer. "I need a trainer who knows how to work me just right."

"Hmm," he murmurs against my neck. "I may know a thing or two about how to help you reach your *goal*."

"Let me warm us up." I arch my back to remove my pants.

"We are meeting Max and the kids in thirty minutes."

I place my hands on his chest, pushing him off me. This man deserves a live show after everything he's dealt with this week. Adam's eyes track my every move as I walk toward my bag. I pull out a new toy I picked up in one of the shops I passed by today. Adam's jaw slightly opens with surprise as I walk back to the bed. Slowly, I remove my panties and get comfortable on the bed. Adam still hasn't spoken a word and I sit against his headboard and part my knees.

"I think you deserve the first showing of what this new toy can do to me. Enjoy the show. Feel free to show me what I do to you." I wink as his hand reaches into his pants.

"Fuck, I'm the luckiest guy on earth," he rasps as I select the vibrating speed of choice.

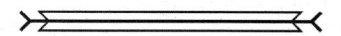

Golden Gate Park is a playground to appear in every child's dreams. The large green field holds multiple playgrounds and even a carousel. Mallory and James run to the swings, asking to be pushed. If it isn't Kelsie and Max together, it's Adam and Max. The one thing I have come to realize in these past couple of months is that Adam and Max will stop at nothing to meet the needs of Kelsie and her children.

My gut plummets, and my stomach feels woozy. My past childhood needs remind me how they were not checked off. I wonder what it feels like to have people so dedicated to take care of you. These children don't ask for love or blink an eye as to whether they are or not. There is always an adult there for them to meet every damn need.

We spend the next twenty minutes pushing the kids and chasing them around before retiring to a bench breathless. As fit as we are, there is no question as to how endless a child's battery life is.

"Push us on the swings again." Mallory bats her brown eyes at the three of us.

"No, we're done." Max shakes his head. "We are here to burn *your* energy."

"I'll join you on the swings in a few minutes," I speak up, sucked into the pout of disappointment on Mallory's face. "We can see who can fly the highest."

"You're the best, Aunt Lauren." Mallory runs toward the slide with James and Adam's finger moves under my chin to close my dropped jaw.

"I'm not..." I go to correct her, but she's no longer in earshot.

I'm not qualified for that title.

"I guess that's her blessing for me to get down on one knee." Adam's shoulders shake as he and Max chuckle.

"The only time you can take a knee for me is when my leg goes over your shoulder," I clip back. "The only *ring* I need is in my ears after an intense orgasm."

"Mm, your pussy is amazing." Adam turns to me with heat in his eyes.

"Fucking hell, guys!" Max stands, throwing his hands up in the air and takes off toward the kids.

"In all seriousness, you really don't want to get married? Ever?" Adam scans my face looking for answers.

"I thought I was clear about everything from the start." I roll my lips in, feeling my heart quicken. "I know I said I want to try to feel... *more* with you, but that doesn't mean I *will* or *can* in the long run."

I would have missed the flash of pain across his face if I hadn't directly looked through his eyes or known him as well as I do now. He pushes it down and shoots a cocky, charming grin my way.

"I get it. It's just a legal contract anyway." He shrugs.

"I'll be with you because I want to," I assure him. "That hasn't changed whether we have that contract or not."

"I just wanted to test how head over heels you are for me."

"I'll let you know depending on how many times you make my body shake tonight." I let a seductive crack lace my voice as it drops.

"Sounds cheaper than your three-carat oval diamond on a rose gold band." He says as I nudge him. "*Engraved.*" He laughs.

"Ugh, you're never going to let me live that down, are you?"

"Come on, we should chase the kids so they're tired for Kelsie." He taps my arm with a childish smile. "Tag! Lauren's it!" He runs toward Mallory.

Where normal people climb into minivans after leaving the park, we climb in a limo and head back to the hotel. James yawns, cuddling up to Adam and I fight the urge to let my heart beat in this strange melting way. Mallory whines, clearly tired but still doesn't want the night to end.

Adam and Max go over what the kids need to do when they get home and to listen to Kelsie when it's bedtime. It's a strange dichotomy seeing two tall alpha men gently tending to children with empathy.

"Princess Lauren, are you coming up with us?" Mallory bounces on the seat, clearly, she didn't burn as much energy as we did.

"I'm going to your uncle's. You don't have to keep calling me princess." I smile. "I'm far from one."

"I wish my mom was a princess."

"Hey!" Adam and Max speak at the same time.

"Your mom is a flipping *queen*." Max points a finger at Mallory. "You have no idea how much she deserves a pedestal."

"Exactly." Adam nods. "You kids are her first priority and her whole damn world."

"*Dang* world." Mallory tilts her head and sasses back.

Her arms cross as she falls back to the seat with a huff. I notice her smile falter as she fidgets. Something else is bugging her. I sense it.

"Mallory, you know, since your mom is a queen, that makes you a real princess." Her body perks up. "Yeah, you even get to live in a tall tower. That's pretty cool."

"It's just..." Her shoulders deflate. "Every queen has a king and her king left."

There it is.

"Emotions are hard to deal with, aren't they? Some things don't seem fair." I empathize as Adam and Max watch me, stunned. "How about next time when you feel upset, instead of being sassy and getting yourself in trouble, you tell people how you really feel?" I feel myself healing from past wounds as I tend to hers. "We are all here to listen and help you, babe."

"Hey, I know!" She smiles and looks at Max. "You're always the king when we play together. You could be mom's king to protect her. Maybe she'll stop crying at night."

"That would be awkward." Adam laughs as we climb out of the limo.

"Why would that be awkward?" I pry as we all head toward the elevator.

"Short brunette Kelsie is not his type." Adam raises his eyebrows. "This guy has never dated a brunette or any woman close to my sister's resemblance."

Maybe there's a reason for that. Also, why do I feel so invested in these two?

I watch Max's jaw tic. It's not my business anyway, so I keep my mouth shut.

"Aunt Lauren, you're going to be the best mom ever one day." We reach our floor and Adam and I walk to his door and Mallory runs for a hug. "Thanks for the park." She smiles and runs into her penthouse.

Again, I'm left speechless and dumbfounded with no time to correct this child of all her wrong assumptions. Adam opens his door, pushing me against it as his lips part to meet mine. He doesn't dare speak a word about what his niece threw into the universe. I moan, falling under his spell as his lips, hands, and cock work their magic for the rest of the night.

Chapter 23

Lauren

Adam has spent the last three days in Aspen. This past week gave me a glimpse of what things would have been like had I not met Adam the night of the interview, or the first few days moving to the city. This week has flown by with my extra shifts and meetings with charity donors. I think back to how I would have never seen Adam again, if not for him interrupting my burger. The hotel lounge was my last attempt in hopes that Max would show interest in me or someone worthy of my arrangement would come along. I'm thankful for Adam and his mindset.

If Adam hadn't been my crutch that night when I fainted at the gym after that newborn lost her fight on the streets, would I have been this strong and able to push through the other events he's helped me with? Would I cope with being swapped at work and still be able to get my side charity off the ground? Would therapy have even been on my mind? I shake my head, pushing back the what-ifs. It amazes me how far I've come with my own emotions and coping skills. I'm now able to start to embrace the feeling of being wanted.

Of being enough.

I've started to believe that when someone says they care, they do.

Because Adam's showed me. Time and time again.

"Enjoy your entire week off, Ren!" Tessa waves, pulling me out of thought. "Tell Adam he better make it worth it."

"See you next week, Tessa!" I call down the hall and pick up my workbag to head to Adam's.

The blender sounds through the penthouse as I enter. Adam stands in the kitchen, shirtless in a pair of basketball shorts. His hair is damp and his skin is glistening off the candlelight.

Wait, candlelight?

His fresh shower gel is extremely alluring and possesses my body to go kiss every inch of him. He glances my way as I watch his eyes light up with my arrival. A soft smile plays on his lips. My abs tighten as I internally rage at any past woman who has ever done him wrong. He cares deeply about people and most importantly, the light in his smile is how much he cares about me.

Because I've let him.

Realization smacks my consciousness, knowing I've lived in such darkness by my own doing. It's now that I don't want to think of myself in the arms of anyone but him. It's now that I want to be the only person he cherishes this way.

When I look at him, I see the sun burning through the mist, eliminating every ounce of fog clouding my vision.

He's every flicker in each flame surrounding us. The defibrillator bringing me to life with every beat of my wounded heart.

He's my *wants* I never knew I could attain.

Sensing my wandering mind settling, Adam walks over and wraps his arms around my waist. I lift my arms around his neck, pulling myself flush against him. His lips press to mine gently but emanate a groan of hunger. I part my mouth, deepening the kiss, feeling his need grow against my stomach. I slide my hands down his chest, resting them on his hips as I pull back with a playful smile.

"Hi." I look up into his eyes. "It's been a long three days."

"Hi." He pecks my lips and tightens his grip on my ass. "These fitted scrubs put filthy thoughts into my mind."

"Yeah?" I raise a brow. "Did you miss your naughty nurse while you were in Aspen?"

"I think you'll have to prescribe me something for wrist support." The thought of him getting off swirls even more pleasure between my legs.

"Hmm, I'll take good care of you tonight." My stomach grumbles and he drops his arms.

"Dinner will be ready in fifteen minutes." Adam heads to the stove, watching me poke out my bottom lip in a pout. "You need food before I put you in all the positions I've mentally put you in while holding my cock."

"I guess I'll have a quick shower. I love the mood lighting too, by the way." I walk toward his bathroom and strip off my clothes, turning back with a wink as his eyes stay glued to my body.

I never thought I'd feel comfortable using another man's shower without him in it. There's something domestic about the comfort I feel coming back to Adam's place after work and dinner is made for us. We now share intimate moments beyond an orgasm fix. I swallow my silent fear as tears prick my eyes. Maybe one day, the desire for each other will fade and we will end up a boring couple who go through the motions. The moment we are still together but become nothing more than roommates. Or worse, one of us no longer wants to continue this while it's going great.

I turn the water to cold before stepping out and changing into my thin tank top and his tight boxers.

"Hey, where's your mind?" Adam finishes his last bite breaking through our silent dinner.

I look down at my half-eaten chicken rigatoni.

"I don't want us to fall into a boring pattern. I like our heated moments of lust." I've gotten better at speaking my mind with each meeting with my therapist.

"You're scared I'll stop thinking about dominating your body?"

"I don't want work, dinner, sleep, repeat and you ending up bored of me." I push forward a half smile and shrug. "I enjoy the orgasms you give me."

Adam stands, pushing his chair back. "You want to know all I've thought about since you walked through the door?" He towers over me as I come face-to-face with his erection.

I swallow, unable to answer and glance into darkening eyes. His fingers grip my chin, pulling me up out of my seat. He bends slightly and brings his hands behind my thighs as he picks me up and carries me to his large window. My breath hitches as my back hits the cool glass through my thin tank top. My legs drop to the floor as his arms cage around my head. This dominant stance never fails to put me under his mercy.

"Your soul is beautiful, Lauren, but your body entices me to do wicked things to it." Adam holds my gaze as he slides down my frame, his fingertips feathering down my sides.

He drops to his knees and his thumbs delicately slip into the waistband of the boxers I chose to wear, and he pulls them down.

"I've taken a knee for you Lauren, now let me give you your favorite *ring*." I damn near lose all control with his words alone.

I lift my leg onto his shoulder as my hands press against the window.

My head tilts back, arching my body farther into his mouth as it connects with my center. He hums in approval of my gasp and the vibrations ricochets throughout my lower stomach. His tongue swirls my clit before penetrating inside then back up. I can't figure out if I am so responsive to his touch from our time apart, or how much power he possesses over every inch of my body. I don't have time to think as Adam quickens the pace and my breaths become heavy. Each breath brings me closer to the edge, building a higher intensity through my veins. He's only in contact with one spot, yet I feel him everywhere. Through my bones, the tingling in my hair and in the shaking of my body.

"Adam!" I call out, reaching down to grip his hair for more support on my palpitating body.

He presses a soft kiss to my sensitive bud before lightly scratching his nails up my body. His hand laces through my hair with a tight grip as my head yanks back. His nose traces from my jawline to my ear and his teeth sink into the crook of my neck. His hot breath quickens as my hands trail down to his throbbing dick. His workout shorts hit the ground as I lightly run the pads of my fingers from the base of him to the tip. My fingers wrap around him and give a firm squeeze, discovering him harder than I've ever thought was possible. He bites down harder on my neck and hisses. I start to lower, wanting to drop to my knees, but his hand encompasses my throat, halting me.

"Uh-uh, I'm owning your body tonight, Blondie. You said you have doubts that one day I'll get tired of you." His grip tightens around my throat as he licks his lips. "I'm reminding you just how bad I've got it for you, woman."

I'm guided to the bed as he grabs the hem of my tank top but doesn't fully remove it. Instead, it lifts just enough to cover my eyes and the extra fabric holds my arms above my head. Everything is heightened. I feel a finger press into my bottom lip and slide into my mouth.

"Suck." His voice is low and demanding and lights my body up again. "Good girl," he whispers as I wrap my lips around his finger.

His fingers trail down my neck, across my collarbone and down the valley of my breasts. A whimper escapes as his teeth graze my nipple the same time his finger runs from one hip to the other. My breath hitches as my stomach sucks in, rolling like a wave from the unexpected dual sensation.

"Yes," I sigh, and he does it again.

"I'll never get over how responsive you are to my touch," he growls, and I feel him hover above me.

My tank top is yanked off and his lips capture mine with greed. Deep kisses transfer between us, and I pull him closer to me, needing to feel his weight. His hips push into mine as his cock slides up and down my soaked folds. My core aches as the sensation on my clit gets more attention. Needing his deep penetration, my legs wrap around his hips to push him into me. Adam continues grinding against me, ignoring my plea.

"I won't push into you until I make your body shake one more time." He smirks and replaces the tip of his dick with his finger, circling me with the perfect amount of pressure. "Open your legs wider, baby, and take every bit of this."

Tension builds and just as I let go with his name on my lips, he pushes into me. My nails scratch down his back as he starts to thrust hard. He pushes to his knees, hiking both of my legs around his hips to arch my body off the bed. He is so deep I barely have time to recover from the last orgasm before this one takes over. The sound leaving my lips is unintelligible, like my mind.

He pulls out, kissing each of my inner thighs and gives me a second to catch a few breaths.

"On your side." He grabs my waist, flipping me as if I weigh nothing.

Yeah, there's the ring in my ears.

He finishes me off strong before letting himself go and heads down the hall. I could pass out from the exhaustion of orgasms, but I'm giddy.

"I may be offended if you absolutely hate this." Adam enters his room holding a bowl of what I assume to be ice cream

"Wait," I pause, looking at the color and remembering it matched whatever he had in the blender. "Did you make me ice cream?"

"I did." He wears a proud smile beautifully, taking a seat next to me. "I took your love of chocolate ice cream and mixed it with your love for hazelnut coffee."

I feel my cheeks tighten as they ball up in a wide smile. My heart skips a beat at his thoughtfulness.

"Adam, this is incredible. Seriously, you have every shop I've tried in this city beat." The smoothest consistency of flavor and perfection hit my tongue.

"You don't have to go that far with the compliment. I know Kelsie prefers it a little thicker."

"You make her ice cream too?" I shamelessly devour the bowl in front of him.

"I used to. This was all she craved during her pregnancies, so I also had a large tub stocked in her freezer at all times." He laughs.

I set the bowl down and look at him. The thoughtfulness of this man has exceeded my expectations for any human. He will go above and beyond for the ones he cares about, and I know he won't let me down either. I smile, pressing my lips to his and feel another layer of armor dismantle. I've finally found the point of simply being happy and comfortable with receiving someone's gestures.

It's then I want him to *need* me.

>=====<

A maraschino cherry rolls over the roof of my mouth. The smooth "plastic" coating expels juice as the pressure of my tongue increases upward. My Shirley Temple craving lands me thirty minutes early to the hotel lounge before I meet Adam. I swirl my drink watching the bubble float to the top as I think over how far I have come with healing. Another week with Adam has passed with him proving how he is much more than I could have asked for. He is my sense of what normalcy should feel like. I'm blossoming into someone who allows herself to enjoy her time with another person - beyond wrinkling the sheets.

I smile, remembering the past week of our cheesy tourist fun house museums, The concert in Golden Gate Park, soaking up the heat as we lay on a blanket. My head on his chest, listening to his heartbeat more than the live concert, sent a new signal to my brain of contentment. My heart flutters at my plan to admit I'm not opposed to a relationship title. Calling him my boyfriend doesn't seem as scary since he hasn't flaked off and prioritized my well-being. I embrace the warmth in my chest, knowing that he deserves a bit more of my soul. Maybe, commitment might not be as terrible as I've witnessed. I know I'm enjoying this new side of me. What I don't know, is what the limo driver's ears think of me after mine and Adam's multiple drives the past week.

Max gives me a nod and says something to the young guy behind the bar who only served me three cherries.

"It's been a while since you've come in here solo." Max smiles as the other employee looks me up and down. "Adam is in the back room with his father."

"I came a bit early. I told you I would stop by to hang out with you and the best cherries." I smile, finishing my drink.

"She'll take another Shirley Temple, no alcohol," he calls out, drawing his eyebrows together. "And, Eric, this pretty lady gets a complimentary side dish of cherries every single time she visits. Remember that."

"Thank you, Eric." I smile back. "Are you guys hiring more staff for the fall?"

Max looks down at the counter as if it has an answer before meeting my eyes. A customer takes a seat at the opposite end of the bar, calling him over. Max holds up a finger and heads over to the guy that clearly knows him. An aggravated groan echoes around the corner. Adam stops at the opening entrance behind the bar with his clenched jaw.

His eyes remain forward on the shelf and I take it he hasn't noticed me. Why he hasn't entered to grab himself a drink beats me. The veins on his arms rise as his closed fists rest on the sleek counter. I've never seen Adam this angry. This is nothing like the bit of attitude he threw at Kelsie and me a few weeks back at the gym. I remain silent to see how this plays out. Eric makes his way over with Max behind.

"I'll take a double bourbon," Adam clips, nodding to Eric. "Top shelf."

Eric turns to the shelf as Max shakes his head. "Hold off, Eric, he had a double before his meeting."

What the hell?

"Do you want me to fire you on your last shift?" Adam squares his shoulders as growing tension vibrates off him.

"Fuck off, bro," Max whispers though it's a muted yell.

A few heads turn, taking notice of the bickering scene. George struts around the corner with a grim look and meets my eyes. They're unreadable as he shakes his head and storms toward the lobby.

Was that disappointment?

"Max?" I make myself heard with high hopes of changing the tension if Adam notices me. "Is this really your last shift?"

"Yep. I decided to—" He goes to elaborate before Adam cuts him off.

"The guy down there keeps waving his glass." Max's glare burns through Adam before he takes off down the bar.

"Intense meeting?" I raise my eyebrows, hoping my confused expression stifles his attitude.

"What fucking gives?" His voice is sharp, like a knife to my gut and I curl inward.

"Okaaay," I drag out as I stand, pushing my chair back to walk up to him. "If you want to toss around that much dick energy, you can use it to go fuck yourself."

I'm close enough to know that nobody can hear me, and close enough to watch his temples dimple every time his jaw clenches.

"Weren't we meeting *later*?" The hostility in his voice is enough to start my own rage.

"I don't know why you're in a tantrum state, but I'm leaving. I respect your family too much to start a scene." I turn and head out of the lounge bar. Adam trails behind even though I know he could bypass me and beat me to my building.

My head remains forward as I power walk the few blocks to my place. I skip my elevator and walk up the many flights of stairs, trying to rid myself of unwanted tension. My gut burns with the aggravation I unwillingly acquired from the bar. He follows without a word. My foot trips up the steps and pain shoots through my shin as the sharp edge of the stair slams into it. Still, Adam remains mute as I stand back up and finish the last flight.

"What the hell was that about?" I set my keys on the counter and turn to face him.

"There's two things." His arms fold across his chest, shutting his body language down. "I have to go to Aspen." He pushes out a long breath and returns to his normal, collected self.

"Okay, so?" My back leans against the counter and I cross my arms. "That doesn't warrant the dramatic show you gave to the lounge earlier."

"My brother wants to take over the Aspen location after graduation in the spring." He pauses and steps toward me as silence lingers.

"Adam, I don't play games either." *Can we make up so I can finally tell you how much you mean to me?* "Is your business trip to get things ready for him?"

"The person running the place right now had a family incident and resigned starting next week." His dark eyes that held frustration moments before are now full of hurt. "I'm heading there to oversee everything for the next six to eight months until my brother gets his shit in order."

Blink.

Deep breath.

I will be alright.

Process nonattachment.

Blink.

My past armor internally clicks together as I manage to hold my unwavering expression. Some would call me a statue with a mechanical inside as the pieces click back together into the person I once was. The dejected drop in my gut travels up like a rocket to my thoughts. No one ever stays, no one is *entitled* to. Adam's words shouldn't take me by surprise when I've had a lifetime of disappointing preparation. Our arrangement was temporary at the start and I knew that. The nanosecond of my fleeting thoughts for us being *more,* was a hurtful mistake.

My cheeks act as a barrier between my clenching teeth, but I like focusing on this pain. It hurts less than what my heart might feel. Adam is another confirmation that no one has ever stayed true to their word, besides Lloyd.

"Lauren, did you hear me?" Adam takes a step forward, reaching his hand out to my arm and I flinch.

I don't mean to flinch, but his touch burns as much as his toxic words. I swallow, taking a calm, steady breath to hold my composure. A small smile rests on my lips before I meet the charming brown eyes that see me better than anyone else has. Or so I thought.

"Well, the past few months have been great deathbed memories." I nod curtly and swing my eyes to the door, expecting him to leave. "So, thank you."

"*The fuck...* wait, you're not..." His hands cup my face and I've never seen so many lines scrunch on his forehead. "Lauren, I didn't tell you that because I want us to end." His head crooks to the side as his eyes scan my face, but I don't know why he looks fearful.

"Then stay." My voice is pleading as I use every ounce of willpower to not let my tears fall. "Stay here and be happy with me." It should be that simple. "There are other people who can temporarily fill the position." This has to be my last attempt to allow my armor to crack before assembling all the pieces to never break again.

"I am happy with you, Lauren." His jaw is tight, fighting his own emotions. "I want us to work. But I have to move to Aspen for the time being. I will be back for good eventually." His head shakes. "Don't end this."

"What the hell am I supposed to do? I let you leave and wait until you come back for me?" *I've heard that one too many times in my life.* "You want me to spend every day waiting on standby for you to live your life until you decide it's convenient to give me the time of day again?" My fingers reach up, wrapping around his thick wrists and removing his hands from my face.

"You have days off. I have a jet so we can fly to see each other whenever." His voice pleads but I'm already half closed off to let myself care. "If you really love Aspen, you could take time off work or even transfer—"

"No." The deepness in my voice surprises me as I step to the side, creating more space. "No one will tell me how to live. I did that for eighteen years."

"Am I the only one trying to make this work, Lauren?" I know the waver in his tone shows how hurt he is, but he's not the *only* employee that can fill the Aspen position.

"Adam, you're the one choosing to move."

"Lauren, I lo—"

"Don't!" My voice drops an octave and jumps in volume. "Please, don't." My heart prickles as I feel myself begin to lose control of the version that I spent a lifetime curating.

"I know you don't want to hear it for many reasons. But for my sake, you need to know." Adam's hands cup my cheeks once again as his forehead touches mine. "I love you, Lauren. I love every piece of your soul."

"You said you wouldn't fall for me." My voice wavers as hopeless pain clamps around my lungs, stifling my breath.

"You said you wouldn't let me," he whispers against my lips, clutching my cheeks as if his hands are meant to stay molded there forever.

"Adam, I..." I falter backward before his lips capture mine, taunting me to fall under his spell of empty truths. "I won't. I shouldn't have even asked you to choose me over your family." How dare I summon up the nerve to ask someone to stay. It's easy to become desensitized by words when your entire life has been built around studying actions.

"I want to choose you. I need to choose my family as well." Adam growls with a frustrated sigh. "I want this to work. But not like this. If you can't accept my heart or realize how worthy *you* are of being loved, then I *need* this to be over."

His hand runs over his jaw as this giant man fights back tears. "At least until you figure yourself out."

"I'm not the one on the brink of tears," I bluntly lie in a casual tone. "I've got myself figured out."

"Lauren." He shakes his head as his eyes call my bluff.

"You won't have trouble finding another chick to stick your dick in." I try to break him before he fully breaks me. "I know I'll find a replacement in a city of millions."

"You own what's left of me, Lauren. You are the most monumental person I have ever been blessed to cross paths with. I have nothing to give to anyone else."

"Maybe we can have an occasional hookup whenever you're back in town." I shrug, keeping my gaze at the door I wish he'd walk through. "If I'm even still in this city." The last sentence stops my heart, knowing I meant to keep that to myself.

This vulnerable situation is messing with my damn head.

Little does Adam know, I applied to a few places around Tahoe after the first time I visited his family's cabin. Something about the tranquility and longing for a smaller community struck deep within. Little does he know he's been the reason I haven't reached out to *any* of the offers. Until now.

"What the fuck does that mean?" Adam steps closer, crowding my space once again and this time, I'm against the wall. "Fuck the casual hookup. We're more than that. Are you leaving?"

I swallow down the pain I know I'm causing him and myself, but it's for the best. It's easier to sever ties now and part than if we invested a year or more of our lives and ended up saying goodbye. This, without a doubt, *is* the right choice.

"If I want to. I'm not the one who is owned."

"You said you *wanted* to try with us." His breath hits my lips, stealing the air from my lungs once again.

"And look where that's gotten us." My vision hazes with little stars and I'm thankful to be against the wall so I don't faint in his arms.

"Do you not hear yourself?" Adam is too close as his scent pervades the air and awakens the spot between my thighs.

"Do you not hear yourself, Mr. I Will Only Do Casual." I move to the side, hating what his dominant stance is doing to my body, but he mirrors my step.

"I'm not sorry for having a fucking heart. For wanting it to beat for you." My god, this man must have memorized this from a stupid romance film.

"You mean that only *one of us* stayed true to our original agreement?" I throw his past words back at him and push my tongue to the roof of my mouth, hoping to not form tears. "Was I not clear about my terms from the start?"

I'm glad I put on a loose shirt because I swear he would see my heart beating out of my chest otherwise.

"People change, Lauren." *So, he does remember what he said to the lobby girl.* "Keep tossing money toward therapy. It seems to be working wonders." The sarcasm cutting through his voice has never been stronger.

"I didn't start therapy in order to fall in love with you," I bite back as I push past him.

"No. It just proves that you still don't love yourself enough to be loved."

"You don't respect yourself enough to tell your daddy how you truly feel about work. The type of life you want to live."

"That is completely different." His voice rises. "My work is complicated, and you know that."

"I'm complicated." I throw my hands up in defeat and meet his volume. "Yet, you have no problem leaving me."

"I don't want to."

"Stop doing that," I say through clenched teeth. "I don't care about what your mouth says." I glance around my condo, looking for a place to storm off to and wish it wasn't so damn small in this moment. "I get that your family trumps anything. Every. Damn. Time." I stand my ground and cross my arms. "I don't and won't put my life on hold for anyone, Adam."

"Lauren, they don't own me."

"Riiight." I hear my voice reach the brink of unstable humor. "I forgot how much you absolutely *love* your job, Adam."

"We can't all excel at a great paying job to fill past voids, Ms. Practitioner."

I can now confirm an emotional gut punch feels worse than the real thing.

"You can leave now." I motion to the door with squinted eyes, a tilted head and a tight smirk full of dramatic attitude that only a teenager is proud enough to use.

"Enjoy rebuilding those castle walls, Lauren." He holds my eyes one last time before opening the door. "I really thought I'd be the wrecking ball your heart needed." And then, he's gone.

Little did he know, he was the wrecking ball my guarded soul needed but vacated the job before the dust settled.

I don't make it to my bed. My hand grabs the couch for support as I fill my lungs with air, caving into the excruciating hurt that pulverizes my stomach. Tears sting, flooding over my eyes as a foreign, pained cry leaves my lips. My body tenses as if it's responding to a terrible past trauma, only a hand was never laid on me. Adam's words echo through my head, punishing me for standing by my choice.

    I fall to my couch, curling my legs to my chest. My head feels light and spiny as I watch the city lights blur through my vision. I say a silent prayer for sleep to bail me out of this conscious realm.

Chapter 24

Adam

My fists ball as I wait for the elevator and channel every ounce of self-control to not punch a hole or five through the drywall. Or jump through the center of eight flights of stairs because the pain will end at the concrete bottom.

Just a fleeting thought.

Get a fucking hold of yourself, Adam.

The blood pulses through my ears as my heart tries to process the last life-altering hour. My head spins. Anger spews toward myself most of all. I shouldn't have let myself fall for Lauren. I should have stuck to my rule and listened to that voice in my head telling me to not ask for our arrangement in the first place. She was willing to leave without asking for my name. That should have been the giant neon sign warning me that she had been through shit.

I hear a sob echo through the hallway as I wait for the elevator. My ears don't want to translate to my heart what they just heard. As tough as she has made herself, she's still human at her core. My heart pulls forward, drawing me with the need to run back and hug the woman who has been through so much that she can't bear to hear she is loved.

I'd spend every night next to her if it kept her nightmares at bay. As much as it pains me, if she can't fathom any time apart without taking offense, that's her problem to work through. If I love her, I don't want to beg her to let me.

The cool night air revives my lungs as I take off in a sprint. I don't care if I look like a crazy man running in a five-thousand-dollar suit down the road. Each stride attempts to melt away the buildup in my mind. The aggression with my job, my family, this situation, my heart plummeting to the depth of hell like it never has for anyone, but it's Lauren who fuels my need to burn everything off. My ribs are heaving as I reach the top of a vertical hill, still unable to find any relief. Tonight, I know only two things will be able to help fog my mind. I sprint back to my place, drowning in bourbon and the ivory keys.

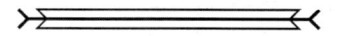

>=====<

I don't hear from Lauren the rest of the weekend. I've been in a chronological trance of meals, packing, paperwork and staring at the ceiling all night, cursing myself. In a shameful, hopeless manner, I half hoped Lauren would show up here. She'd knock on my door breathless, even though she would take the elevator up. I'd open my door, shocked, as Lauren explains the mistake she made. She'd rant in one breath, explaining that the time I am gone is still worth the weekend visits. How her schedule made it easy for us to work, and on her last breath, she would tell me she loves me.

I head to the hotel gym so I can punish myself for thinking such a stupid scenario.

Damn Kelsie for suckering me into watching those stupid romance movies with her as a teenager.

I grit my teeth and rip my gloves off as the punching bags sways slowly. The small downstairs gym is all I have time for today, plus Max hasn't spoken to me since his last shift at the bar. Not that I blame him. He is happy with his next career move and I took my anger out on him. I'm pissed about being uprooted to a new location without a choice in the matter. Having your life planned out for you seems great on paper, until you have a different outlook on the world around you. My grandfather can manage my position for the time being here, as most of his workload has been passed down to my father, who is now putting pressure on me.

Aspen *is* too far for my parents to leave their grandchildren and work affairs here. So, until someone else fills the Aspen location, it fucking falls into my damn hands. Being diverse in more than my CFO job title is great for a person who doesn't want to give up this lavish lifestyle.

As much as my heart dips to my stomach with the need for Lauren in my life, my family needs me more.

I've only spoken to my father once this weekend and it was to confirm my flight. His words were a knife to my gut as he preached about the way Lauren looks at me, saying she would be willing to make our relationship last. The only clear thing is that he and I both need our fucking eyes tested.

Like the morning fog in this city, my vision had been hazed. The clarity in her conviction scorched my fucking soul, burning away every single thing I thought we *would* be.

I turn my phone to silent in case my father tries to call. I can't deal with hearing his words of "encouragement." Especially since he constantly brings up how proud he is of Emmett for finally working hard to finish up his degree. *Emmett technically doesn't even need his fucking degree.* Who the fuck *minors* in business on and off for years when you are born to heir a luxury hotel chain with on-the-job training? My father is well aware of how aggravated I am with my brother pussyfooting his way through Europe, taking his sweet time with schooling.

Fucking pussyfooter Emmett. My fist crashes into the gym wall, leaving the dust of drywall fluttering to the floor. I storm up to my place, shower and grab my luggage.

My eyes scan over my pristine place once more to make sure everything is turned off, and I spot a hair tie by my floor-to-ceiling windows. The same window I had Lauren against, breathless at my mercy, not too long ago. My teeth clamp together, eliciting pain to my head instead of my heart. Pushing down the feelings of hurt and hate, I head across the hall to deal with more goodbyes and tears from my niece and nephew.

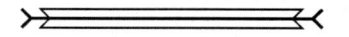

These first three weeks in Aspen have been jam-packed, but during every split second of silence, I'm lost in a fucking thought about Lauren. Jealousy and hurt meet the punching bag every night in the small hotel gym. Each punch to the bag reverberates with unhealthy thoughts. *Has she gone back to her old ways of bringing new guys home? Has she woken up from her traumatic past nightmare? Does she have a hair tie if she pukes or a person to help calm her down when she spirals from work?* She is so fucking strong to cope with her entire life up until I had been there for her. I can't fault her for wanting to be responsible for her own healing, but I can't shake the fact that I want to stand by her side.

I chug my water until I need to gasp for air. Sweat drips down my face as my gloves beat against the bag again. This round is for the possibility of remaining celibate since I can't even smile at an attractive woman without feeling guilt. Lauren is out of my life, building her walls back up as I mentally beg to be the mortar piecing her back together. Only I've failed because my brother, yet again, doesn't have his shit together. Emmett hasn't reached out once to see how things are going in Aspen, but I see how actively hard he's working on his studies while posting beach photos with a handful of influencers.

I swipe my phone open to answer Kelsie's video call and two youthful smiles greet me on the other end.

"Hey kiddos!" I wipe the sweat off my brow.

"Uncle Adam!" they cheer.

"I miss you guys. Mallory, how is school going?"

"Ugh, well, you know Julien Beaumont is in my class again." She rolls her eyes. "That boy seriously thinks he's better than me because of his last name." I smirk, knowing the Beaumont's prestigious snobbery from owning most nightclubs around the States. "I'll show him who is boss during our business week."

"Business week?" I miss the way Mallory talks on a professional level at times, though I never know if it's reality or the scenario she's made up in her mind.

"We have a class project to come up with a business plan and invent something. It sucks because my enemy is my PARTNER!" She exaggerates by throwing her hands in the air. "Can you believe the audacity of my teacher pairing me with him? She knows how much we bicker."

"Oh, Mallory. Sadly, you don't always have a choice when it comes to business." We talk for a few more minutes before Kelsie takes the phone.

"How are things going on your end?" she asks, biting her lip, wondering if I'll ask the same damn question I do every time.

"Busy." I shrug. "Have you seen her at all?" God, I feel fucking pathetic. "Does she smile?"

"Adam, if you want to know, call her." I know Kelsie has seen her for the charity project. "I'm not getting in the middle of you two."

"Has she at least asked about me?"

Her eyes move down the hall as the kids start to get loud. The knock on the door sounds and my sister shakes her head.

"Look, I'm heading out, so I need to let the babysitter in." She says the last part slowly and with caution.

"Okay, let me say goodbye to the kids." Is Lauren on the other side of the door?

"Mallory, wait for me to open the door." Kelsie rolls her lips in like she does when she's nervous. "I don't want to upset the kids with saying goodbye to you right before I leave. Love you, bye." The screen shuts off.

When the hell has Kelsie ever hired a babysitter? Would Lauren take on the kids alone? I walk past the lounge as Clyde, one of the lounge bar staff, waves me over. If I didn't notice the distress in his normal aloof self, I would continue walking. This lounge is now the epitome of gut wrenching. Instead of the faint perfume and deluxe food hitting my nose, I'm taken back to the cool crisp air as my eyes rest on the back wall.

"You've got to be fucking kidding me," I mutter through gritted teeth. "Not a chance in hell. Take this down." It's my first day on the job and I'm ordering the staff around like an asshole.

"Your father's orders were to keep this front and center with smaller photos around it. You will have to talk this over with him." Yeah, I sure as hell will.

Not only do I have to relive my memorable weekend with Lauren every day as I walk around this hotel, I now know who purchased our star piece photo from Grayson's gallery. The large photo hangs front and center of Lauren and me on the rolling foggy mountain. Another slice goes through me as a reminder of how far I am from the life I want to live.

How did he even know about this photo? With connections to everyone in the city, of course he was tipped off about his son being in an iconic photo. Which, he jumped to purchase for the tacky travel photo wall. If this isn't removed, I'll have to find another bar or drink alone in my room.

I keep my eyes on Clyde, trying to avoid the giant *in your* face reminder of who I've lost. His mop head of hair is styled neatly and his black dress shirt is the opposite look to his off-duty Burton hoodie. Clyde is in his early twenties, with the sole purpose of hitting the slopes every time he's not behind this counter. For the stereotypical ski bum, he cleans up nice. I rest my hands against the smooth counter, debating if a bourbon after my workout will help me fall asleep quicker.

"What's up, Clyde?"

"I was going to call security, but then saw you." He nods to the far corner. "I thought you could talk to her and be more discrete than me bringing in security and making a scene." A smirk rests on his lips. "Or you can take her back to your suite and get rid of your pent-up tension by railing her."

"What the hell are you talking about?" My eyes dart around the room, looking for the problem. "And I don't have pent-up tension," I reply with more aggravation.

"You're always so tense, dude. *Grouchy*. You either need a good joint, a day on the slopes or a good roll in the sheets."

"Whatever," I grunt, confirming what I want to deny.

I hear crude comments from the corner of the booths and do a double take to a middle-aged woman leaning over a couples table. She's inviting them to have a threesome. When they turn her down, looking mortified, she adjusts her breasts and spots me. A dangerous, playful smile appears across her face as she sways her hips my way. *Is this a ritzy desperate housewife?* I peg her around fifty, with a real taste for designer clothing and jewelry. Her boobs, on the other hand, are clearly fake.

"Hey, big bear," she purrs and is close enough for me to catch the wine on her breath. "How about we head to your room, and you can maul this kitten?" She slowly winks as her fingers run down my chest.

Mortified by her public boldness, I brush her hand away and take a step back. Disgust rushes through my veins from her touch. It's clear that she's kinky enough to distract me and relieve my so-called pent-up tension, but she's still not enough to rid my mind of a certain woman. My body remains dormant, indicating zero response to her touch and I can't get past the stale wine on her breath. I don't condone this kind of behavior, especially in my family's hotel.

"Ma'am, you need to leave." I gesture my hand toward the lobby. "Are you a guest here?"

"A guest? Is that how you treat the owner's daughter?" Her hand lifts to her chest in offense.

"Funny, I don't remember having a child who is older than *myself*." I watch her face drop, but her eyes scan me up and down as my post-workout attire isn't believable. "I suggest if you are not a guest, you leave the premises. If you are, please stop harassing the guests or I will make sure you never step foot in any of my hotels again."

With one last scowl, she heads to the elevators. I turn to Clyde and nod, walking past the memory-filled hallways Lauren and I shared here.

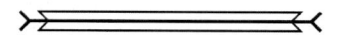

>═══════<

"God, I've missed you," I pant as I lace our hands, driving deeper into her tight wet center.

A breathy moan transmits on my neck as her long legs wrap around my waist, pushing me in farther. "I'm so close." Her erratic breathing continues as she yanks her hands out of my grasp and digs them into my back.

I bend Lauren's knee to the side, exposing her folds to open her farther, granting me better access to grind against her clit. Her breath hitches as her back forms a bigger arch off the bed. My eyes stay transfixed on her mouth as it slightly parts. Her eyes widen, telling me her orgasm is a few strokes away. After my next thrust, I don't ram back in. The tip of my dick remains still, barely poking in her entrance.

"I should stop this right now so you know how aggravating it is to want something you can't have," I grit as her arms and legs wrap around me tightly and she pushes herself up, stealing the pleasure.

I jolt up to the darkness encompassing the room. My body is slick with sweat and my boxers feel moist against my erection. I haven't finished while having a vivid sex dream since I was fourteen. I toss back the covers attempting to relieve some aggression. I didn't want Lauren to have this much of a hold on me, but she damn well does. I scald myself in the shower and try to mentally see through the steam. I'm trying to put myself in Lauren's position. As if understanding her viewpoint will make mine hurt less. She'd rather deal with the bit of pain in losing me now than down the road getting hit with unbearable pain if we can't cut it. But I'm fucking all in. She doesn't realize that I will face any challenge we go through because she is worth it.

I drown myself in the notes of my piano, but my fingers gravitate to the minor chords, adding to my sorrow. What was once an escape for me is now tortured thoughts of the past. I spend the rest of the night going over meetings that I don't want to attend and wondering if Lauren has any similar dreams of me.

Or if she even thinks about us at all. I miss her. I miss my family. Except for Emmett. I've always had to complete his tasks, which is why I'm in this fucking predicament in the first place.

"I haven't been honest with you," I say through the phone immediately after my father's greeting. "I'm thankful for the life you've provided for your children and the family unit, but I don't want the CEO position." I verbally vomit before I can back down like I have so many times before. "I enjoy working with the finances and charts, but I'd rather have a schedule with longer shifts and more days off. I want to enjoy life."

"A shift like a certain nurse we know, perhaps?" he chimes in with smooth contentment and my insides burn with rage, or sadness. I can't tell anymore.

"Dad, she clearly wants nothing to do with me or she would be here by now. Or at least fucking call." I try but fail miserably to hide my aggravation. "Hell, even send a text after I put my fucking heart on the line."

"Did you now?" His voice rises at the end as if he seemed surprised.

"Look, Lauren aside, the past few years, I never wanted to settle down. My job was a void. But even if I can't have *her*, I can aim for the life path I want."

"Thank you, son." The admiration fills his voice, bringing a wave of confusion over me.

"What?"

"For finally telling me what you need. I know this life isn't what you've dreamed of." He pauses with a soft chuckle. "Material things and an extravagant lifestyle aren't something you've taken advantage of, like your brother, or sister for that matter. You would rather drive that cheap shitty street bike than the sports cars. You'd rather the cabin in the woods instead of all the luxury conveniences at your beck and call."

"Then why have you kept giving me more responsibilities?" My ribs squeeze as my frustration grows with how he's been letting Emmett slack and me pile on more than I have wanted.

"Because you have never told me no." He clears his throat. "We're family."

"My father started this company when I was a child. My siblings and I wanted this lifestyle too, and we did everything we could to help him achieve his dream over the years. That being said, your mother and I never expected our children to feel forced to follow our lives, as nice and convenient as it would be."

"But you let us go to school for business and marketing. You have all been grooming us as the next generation of heirs since we were children."

"We never told you that you had to. It was highly influenced, but if you wanted to move out and work as a carpenter or something, I'd respect you following your life path."

The wheels keep turning as everything starts to click into place through my cluttered mind.

"That's why you've never pushed Emmett or Kelsie with her recent three-year maternity leave."

"Exactly. I know Emmett is cut out for this business and if he wants to continue blowing money with his current lifestyle, he's going to need to put in more work for the family business." I can hear his smile through the other line. "He wants this, but your mother and I treated him like the youngest and now realize he needs a push to get shit done."

"Yeah? How will that happen?" I laughed sarcastically.

"One thing I've learned about life, son, is that timing is everything. We will work to get you on your desired life path, Adam. We need to get a few things in place first because I can't let Aspen crumble to hell."

"Thank you for understanding. I'll be here for you until things are figured out."

We hang up the phone and I feel weight ascend in an out-of-body experience. My head feels light as my relief for taking a stand awakens new respect for myself. If I can't have Lauren, I can at least have a bit of my dream life.

Chapter 25

Lauren

The past two months have proven how every day won't heal certain things unless I figure out how to shut them off. It's hard to do when it is about the person who helps heal your wounds. Each task is a constant reminder of him. Every spot of my condo, every bite of ice cream and even my ears hear his damn compliments when I put my scrubs on. I'm haunted by a living being I can no longer see.

I wanted to do nothing more than break down and cling to Adam like a pathetic child and beg him to stay. Beg him to give up everything because he needs me. But it hurts less to accept the fact he is leaving and shut myself down. For once, I wanted someone to have the mirrored fear of losing me. They'd do anything to have me. To feel the real sense of being wanted. But there is no competition when it comes to family.

"Lasagna is getting cold." Lloyd finishes his last bite.

I blink down, phasing back to reality and push the sloppy square around my plate. This frozen lasagna is nowhere near as delectable as Adam's homemade one. *And there he is again.* I knew he'd ruin more than just sex for me.

I've been back in San Diego for two nights, and the first night, I broke down telling Lloyd about everything that's been going on the past few months. Lloyd received more of my truths than my therapist. Our first heart-to-heart was better than I could have imagined.

"I'm not hungry." I shrug.

"Hopefully, Rachel can cheer you up enough to eat tomorrow."

"Don't you have a board game get-together tonight?" I try to change the subject.

"I told Heather I may not show if my daughter didn't want to join." His words flow out so smooth my fork drops, clanking to the cheap plate.

"D-daughter?" My brain freezes, trying to filter through any previous reference of being called that until now. I wasn't adopted, nor ever referenced as his child growing up.

"Yes, I tell people you are my daughter. I know we never talked about it, and we had our basic routine through the years, but Marsha and I weren't able to have children." He folds his hands on the table, looking directly at me. "We decided to start fostering children with hopes of finding the right fit. There was something about you that took over her heart." A tinge of red appears on his cheeks as his smile pushes through. "She knew from the first week you arrived that she wanted to adopt you."

My head feels light. I may faint, or vomit.

"As you know, she got sick shortly after your arrival and then we lost her. I knew with her medical bills that I couldn't afford to adopt you and give up the check from the state." His eyes start to water as his hand brushes over his chin. "I didn't know if you wanted an old, widowed man to even adopt you. I shut down with grief and tried to navigate what raising a teenage girl would be like without a wife."

The pieces click into place as I recall our comfortable routine of sitcom TV and frozen dinners. Our shared love for board games and Lloyd's ability to not press for questions about my past made it easy to go through my motions. If anyone was close to a parental figure, it was Lloyd. I didn't know how to handle what he had been through, like he didn't know how to handle my trauma. Our routine made us self-aware of each other's lack of emotional met needs. He also expected that I'd stay with him during university to save me money. It's not common for kids in the system to get to stay with a foster parent once they age out.

"How come you never told me about Marsha's plan before?"

"I thought it would be a slap in the face that we *would have* adopted you, but then she ended up dying and I needed *your* money to keep Marsha's dying wish; To keep you safe and give you a chance for a bright future."

My lungs deflate with the most foreign emotion I've longed to experience. "Well, Dad." The word rolls off my tongue for the first time in twenty-five years and my stomach sends a wave of butterflies through me. But it feels right. "Let's go win some games."

Lloyd wanted me from the start. I take a moment to relish in this light I feel fluttering through my heart. *Is this what the Grinch felt as his heart grew a few sizes bigger?* Accepting that he cares and wants me is something my therapist will be proud of. I'm proud. My lungs expand with joy, and I exhale with relief, knowing he won't break my heart or choose someone else over me. Finally, I'm someone's daughter.

A silk bag claps against my back as Rachel wraps me in a tight hug. She pulls back, giving me a once-over and I notice she ditched her long braids for a short pixie cut. It's very fairy-like and goes with her fake triangle ears. The glitter on her eyes and winged eyeliner are cute, but the giant purple sweatshirt to her knees and bright-yellow leggings don't add up.

"Dear dildos, my nasty Nordic!" She brushes past me, entering the house. "You look miserably unfucked." I say a silent prayer that Lloyd, I mean *Dad*, had decided to run out to the grocery store.

"I've been too sad to fire up the toys."

A grin appears as the silk bag is shoved into my chest. "You should have come to visit last week. The toy convention was phenomenal. I'm finally a rep for a company and I acquired quite the assortment of toys for you to explore with."

"Oh, boy." I laugh, wondering what took Rachel this long to become a toy rep.

"There's even this growing fairy peen that will have your eyes rolling."

Now the hair and fake ears make sense.

"Are you over the dragon phase then?"

"No, that will always be hard to compete with." She winks.

"Why are we still friends?" I laugh, falling back on the couch and cross my arms against my chest, feeling guarded if she brings up the obvious difficult topic that I desperately want to avoid.

"Because I tell it like it is. So." She softens her face. "Is life a million times better without the man who confessed how much you mean to him?"

"I'm getting by, Rach," I lie, though I know how well she can read me. "Day by day and building wall by wall, it gets easier."

"Wow, bitch." Her eyes widened. "You really had to force that sentence out. Even after sixty-something days apart."

"Shut up." I roll my eyes, but they glass over with tears.

"Oh, honey." Rachel scoots beside me and wraps me in a hug. "I know how much you miss him." She sighs, reading my damn mind.

"No." I shake my head and wipe the single tear I begged not to fall. I hold my breath, fighting the compression building in my chest. "We only shared a few months of getting to know each other." Her touch begins to crumble everything I have spent many sleepless nights trying to repair. "You don't waste tears on something you never truly had."

"Just cry and get it out, baby girl." Rachel tightens her arms around me as I feel my face tighten with heartache. "I promise we will never speak of this moment again. Feel for once."

I almost give in until a flash of my life plays through my mind of all the times I have risen up and pulled through without a tear. My deep breath centers me as I stand. At the drop of a dime, Adam uprooted his life for his family. Their bond is unbreakable, and I should have known that our bond was nothing in comparison. I should have known how dedicated he was from the simple fact he couldn't admit to his father how he really felt about the industry. I am so thankful Lloyd—I mean, my dad and I are not on that sacrificial level and never will be.

"Let's get ready. I promised you that I would give one more club of yours a try."

"Ren." Rachel's voice is full of concern as she gives me a pointed look.

"Don't Ren me." Straightening my spine, I hold out my hand and pull her to my childhood bedroom. "I need to forget."

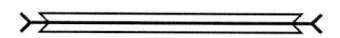

I recline my airplane seat and once again am hit with the fact that I never got to join the mile-high club that Adam mentioned on his jet. Dammit, will I ever do anything without thinking of him? I let my mind wander back to last night. The fairy and dragon themes were not as intimidating as the other mythical creature club Rachel took me to last time. Though, it's still not enough to convert me to the fantasy world or convince me to follow through with the entire night. It didn't matter how attractive the man was, the moment I "flew up" to this dragon guy, my body froze. His lips touched mine, searing them with rejection. They felt nothing like the lips my body craved. Everything felt wrong in every fiber of my skin. My body only ached for Adam's, and I felt disgusted with myself for letting another man put his hands on me.

Where most people in a state of hurt want to run back to their comfort, I refuse to let myself feel it. If swearing off men and resorting to an endless supply of toys the rest of my life helps fill the void of hurt, then so be it. Maybe I'll end up becoming a toy rep like Rachel so I don't break my bank account for orgasms.

My phone dings in flight with an update from Mallory. Her emails have become a regular thing the past two weeks since she was given her own address. I still see Kelsie every other week for marketing and to babysit the kids when she wants to go to a fitness class. Mallory has made it very difficult to shut out of my life. I've had to deal with her questions about Uncle Adam's absence and what I am doing since I *"Obviously miss him so much."* -Her words, not mine.

Mallory's questions face to face have not been easy to avoid. She's aware of our breakup, *is that even what it was?* She just knows her uncle is gone for a while and will be back on occasion. I have learned how amazing the mention of ice cream can mentally distract a child, or me for that matter. Now, if only she'd drop the Aunt Lauren part, my heart wouldn't ache every time I saw her.

I stifle a laugh at her choice of words to describe her nemesis class partner, Julien. She really seems to have beef with this rival classmate. There is something to a name and she sure as hell hates the Beaumont family.

My therapist and I have noticed a slight perception of indifference over the past few sessions, but I'm sure she will be pleased about me opening up to Lloyd and our bond over this trip. I doze off the rest of the flight and drown myself in overtime at work for the next week.

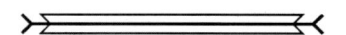

>=====<

"I hate the hot and cold contrast this time of year." Tessa slings her gym bag over her shoulder as we round the corner after yoga class.

"Really? I like the cool air hitting me after a sweaty class." I wiggle my eyebrows at her.

"Maybe because you're always hot and cold, Ms. Katy Perry." We both laugh, walking through the first set of glass doors on the way out.

I push the glass doors open to the entryway. Right as I look up, Max and, who would have flipping thought, Adam both walk through the exterior doors to enter. Silence fills the small entryway, sandwiching us four between the doors. When did he fly back? I don't want to meet the eyes that bear the ability to read every damn thought in my mind, but they lift to his anyway, imprisoning me in place as if he's siphoning my soul. He looks worse than a begging puppy, but I fester up the strength to blink and gain back my power. I track my eyes over Max's body and plaster on my go-to flirty smirk. More to piss Adam off that I have moved on than to actually cause a fight between the friends.

"Enjoy your workout." I mentally hear Max's internal hate speech as I walk past the guys to head outside.

I know Max will give me an earful next time I run into him. I don't blame Max for sticking up for Adam. It's what best friends are supposed to do. I know he doesn't hate me, but he's been short with me every time I've had a run-in with him at Kelsie's. I also know he's stressed with transitioning full-time as a personal trainer and the fact he can't admit he's head over heels for his best friend.

"Wanna go grab a drink?" Tessa suggests.

"I probably shouldn't start because I'll end up hungover at work tomorrow."

"Fair enough."

It's two in the morning and I'm still tossing around my bed. Knowing Adam is only three blocks away from me in his bed makes it even harder. Did he bring someone home? Is he plotting my demise as we speak, and I'll get dog poop outside my door tomorrow? My phone pings and I jump. Rachel has work tomorrow and I don't have other friends.

Charmer: Your new bangs look beautiful.

First, I need to change his name or just delete the number. And second, did he send this hoping I was awake thinking of him too? My fingers hover about the glowing keyboard, debating about responding. Guilt's been crawling around my stomach with how I ended things, even if it was for the better.

Me: Thx.

I don't want to be rude, but I can't bring myself to even type a proper thank you because he may further the conversation. I turn my phone to Airplane Mode and open the silk bag from Rachel.

>=====≺

I am on my fifth work shift this week and exhaustion is starting to get the best of me. The double espresso, which I hate, did nothing except leave a bitter, acidic taste on my tongue and no number of mints can filter out the flavor. An ambulance pulls up as the drivers give us their telltale eyes that it's not an emergency. Given the age of the elderly woman, she may have called from a scare. Our floor doctor nods toward me, and I head over to my new case. The drivers give me a rundown and hand over the chart. She gets wheeled to a quiet part of the hallway before we chat.

The elderly woman winks at the responders before they leave, waving her assorted-stone, ring-covered fingers at them. This woman is bold, and I fight back my smile to remain professional. Eccentric, to say the least, with her flowy silk clothing you'd see someone wear to tell your fortune.

"What brings you here today, Ember?" I look over her chart.

"Those very attractive ambulance drivers. I don't know how you ladies get anything done as they pop in and out of the hospital." She shakes her head and lets out a wicked cough. "I would be all over them like honey on a hot biscuit."

People like her brighten my shift. "You can have them all, men are nothing but disappointment."

"You've clearly been with the wrong men." Her eyes widen as the wrinkles in her forehead grow deeper. "Some men out there know a woman's body better than she knows her own."

"Oh, I didn't mean—" I roll my lips in and feel how true her statement was.

Instantly, there's a gnawing ache in my gut, missing the way Adam's hands feathered over every inch of my skin. The way he knew where to touch to get me melting, succumbing to his spell until he up and left me without a proper fight. Ember's cough rattles through the hall, snapping me back.

"By the look on your face, you just went somewhere. You've experienced a good man."

I clear my throat, hoping it opens enough for me to talk.

"Your cough is concerning." My personal details are not a work topic.

She waves her hand and rolls her eyes. "You're too pretty to not be wearing a diamond. I'm sure you could have your choice of men."

A chord strikes with me any time people associate looks with a relationship. Looks are nothing but an outer shell masking what's inside. Attraction plays a part, but it's never enough to spend your life with fading beauty.

"Commitment isn't my thing," I murmur with a shrug and scan her chart some more.

"Oh, don't bother with that. I'm terminal anyway." Her hands retrieve the chart out of mine, and she places it next to her. "I probably just need some new steroids to get me through the last month of my life." Bold and nonchalant for someone on their deathbed.

"Ember, you had the ambulance bring you in. I should give you a quick checkup."

"The ambulance was to attempt one last bit of fun in the sheets or vehicle before I check out of this world." She coughs again, and I get my stethoscope ready. "They turned me down though."

"Unfortunately for you, it's against their protocol." I attempt to lighten this situation.

"Unfortunate for *them*." She winks and leans in closer. "I've never been one to settle down, my dear. Always a free spirit exploring everything that made me feel good. I would write my own Kama Sutra if I could figure out a damn computer." I nod, knowing most patients who are brought in wanting conversation and attention are difficult to send back home.

"Seems like the best choice. A constant reel of exciting memories and no strings." I pull the buds out of my ears and put my stethoscope around my neck, knowing she will be out of here sooner once she gets things off her chest.

"What's your family like? Are you all close?" I see spots of blood on the tissue she just coughed into.

"It's just me. But that gives me more time to help others at work."

"Ah, you and I are alike on more levels past the commitment issues and stunning good looks."

I stifle my eye roll. "Is there anything I can help you with? What steroids are you on?" I pick the folder back up.

"I was wondering what I can help you with. I'm a goner in no time, but my tea leaf reading today told me to come here." I knew she was into some type of spiritual thing. "My hope was to let the men in uniform have their way with me, like the old days, yet I'm drawn to you."

"It sounds like you've had a lot of deathbed memories." The words pile out before I can stop them.

I feel my face cringe with the regret of my terminology.

"Now that's a good name." Her laugh is airy with a wheeze. "I do indeed have more wild memories than most. I swore I had never needed to settle with one man."

"Exactly. Why put yourself through the possibility of losing them?" Her knowing eyes squint with her wise smile, and I feel like a bunny, hopping toward a sly fox luring me in.

"Your reasoning seems valid until you meet the right man. Until you realize the pain of *what-ifs* is not as important as the happiness that they can give you through the years leading up to a *possible* goodbye." She goes into a coughing fit, and I lean down to listen to her lungs.

"Oh, I only have half a lung left." I move to the other side and things become clearer.

"I'll have the doctor give a listen and write you another prescription." Her coughing subsides, and she clears her throat, taking a long sip of water.

"No need, dear." She takes my hand. "Just remember, all my deathbed memories are still not enough to fill my hand that needs holding as I take my last breath."

Her honesty whooshes the air out of my lungs.

"Don't be me." Her eyes become soft. "Don't collect memories with someone and leave early in hopes that the pain of losing them, in the beginning, is easier than in the end."

"Either way, you could end up alone." I rationalize out loud to myself.

"When has a willing, open heart ever been denied by everyone?" *Dammit, Ember has a point.*

"We accept the love that we are influenced to deserve. Some of us need a reminder of how much we are worth."

"We will run a few tests to help you feel more comfortable." I feel my walls wanting to crumble but hold it together.

A few hours later, while holding my hand, Ember goes into cardiac arrest and checks out of this world.

Chapter 26

Adam

The urge to pick up the phone and demand my office to be gutted and soundproofed pulses through my fingers as they hover over my desk phone. My assistant has been humming every morning this week. From Monday to Friday, she hums as she goes through her damn emails. No matter how much of a grunting grump I can be to her, she still manages to smile and greet me with a cheerful hello. I shut my office door and turn on a random piano playlist while I go through my schedule. Another week of meetings and deadlines that will keep me here all day. I should be happy with this position. Everyone I run into is happy. Our employee satisfaction is ranked high, or at least up until my arrival. Maybe I missed some type of human software download the world sent out. Even Lauren managed to force out a fucking smile the other day.

An overplayed pop piano song filters through my speaker, and I'm whiplashed back to the woman I spend each day trying not to think about. Running into Lauren the other day stole my breath, throwing a whirlwind of punches to my chest. I hadn't known torture until I saw her capability to still smile after our blowup. Sure, it was forced. It wasn't hard to stare straight into her eyes and see *"oh shit, what do I do?"* flash through her layer of heartbreak.

I'm not dumb. I know the flirty smile she flashed Max masked the hurt she'd caused by ending us. I didn't sleep that night, wondering if part of her would come knocking on my door. But now, she has wispy bangs, proving she did that thing women do after a breakup. I don't get why new hair signifies a new you or a statement of moving on. That is one woman ritual I'll never understand.

Clearly, she couldn't sleep that night either, but a simple *thanks* made it clear she wanted to be left alone. I change the music playlist to Spanish guitar because piano and mainstream pop songs are too triggering these days. My heart confirms she may have ruined piano for good. If she was able to fake it or build enough walls to let me go, I should man up and let her go too.

With a mechanical mind, I manage to get through the day. I adjust my schedule in incremental minutes meticulously so that my mind only has time to focus on each task. I'm one thought away from adding bathroom breaks when my assistant pokes her head in and says she's taking off for the day. I glance at the clock and realize I should have been gone an hour ago. If my day is extremely structured for tomorrow, then I'll leave myself no time to think about any unwanted thoughts.

I shower and eat before I sit down at the piano keyboard. Having to wear headphones so I don't disturb the guests has been an adjustment, but at least I can still lay out emotions through music. I have had trouble playing lately, but my fingers relax into the first few chords. Out of the corner of my eye, my phone lights up. No one contacts me at this hour unless it's Mallory. I walk over to my nightstand, huffing in agitation as the unknown number calls a second time.

"Hello?" I clip, not bothering to hide the annoyance in my voice.

"Adam, man." Clyde rings through my ear. "There's a woman at the bar tossing food around."

"What the fuck? Call security or ask her to leave."

"She won't listen to me," he states matter-of-factly. "Security said to contact you."

"What the hell do I pay them for?" What is in this Aspen air and desperate women causing disturbances?

"They like how you quietly don't cause a scene. If they come in with uniforms, people stare."

"Clyde." I give him my best *"are you kidding me"* tone.

"Look, man, this one might spike your interest more than the old hag."

"This is the last damn time you're getting me involved with this." I hang up and take the stairs to blow off steam so I don't blow up.

The lobby is empty as I enter the bar lounge. I keep my gaze low to avoid the statement art piece on the wall of pain. A quick survey shows zero feet are even in the damn booths. I lift my head back to look at Clyde behind the bar, but he is absent. Nothing but a vacant room until my eyes meet the far side of the bar. A woman with long blonde hair tosses shiny red balls over her shoulder.

They're not balls.

They're cherries.

My stomach bottoms out as if I've fallen off the Golden Gate and my breath becomes stuck in my chest. My eyes zone in on the familiar blue dress exposing the long legs that caught my attention months ago. The rapid pulse in my neck sends my heartbeat thumping through my ears. *Am I asleep at my desk?* Everything up to this point feels real, but I have learned how my mind can conjure quite the dreams lately. I take a step forward before someone gets the chance to wake me.

"No." I hear my monotone voice cut through the silence as I shake my head in disbelief.

"I didn't ask a question." She turns and I'm paralyzed.

"You don't have to. You toss cherries around, and men throw their hearts at you." I bounce back into our banter as if no time has passed.

"Adam, I..." She stands and bites her cheek while taking a step closer. "I hope *you* still have a heart to toss my way." Her thumb and middle finger are twisting her pinkie ring.

She is extremely nervous. Good.

"And allow someone else besides family to *own me* too?" My own defense kicks in as the shock of her in front of me slightly dissipates.

"Well warranted." Her head dips down as her forehead creases when she swallows.

She's close to being sick. Her chest expands as she straightens her spine, walking closer without a word. *Please don't puke, Lauren.*

"You're here because?" I keep my tone flat, waiting for her to prove she feels the same as I do.

If she's even fucking here for that. Part of me wonders if she's over me and has gained enough courage to face me for a charity check for her foster bags. I'd be guilted into saying yes, so I don't look like a dick, depriving children of their basic needs. She walks forward until her scent consumes me. Her proximity alone is enough to make me agree to anything. My fists ball so I don't cave and say yes if she suggests a casual hookup.

"Look, Adam, I'm sorry I hurt you." *There is a "but" in her tone.* "I won't apologize for my reaction to your news. There were parts of my past that were brought to light and I still needed to work on them." I open my mouth to respond, but her palm lifts to silence me. "I had only known empty promises and abandonment. That part is textbook. It took time for me to realize that you *leaving* didn't mean you were *leaving* me."

"I told you that," I whisper.

"But at that time, it didn't feel that way to me. It felt like it always had." Her lips roll in as she tries to keep her composure. "It felt like another *'this place will be the last. We can keep in touch.'* Another *'we will take you back if we have room again.'*" Her voice shakes. "All happy promises that were never fulfilled. But you meant yours. You never gave me a reason not to trust you." She shakes her head, takes a four-second breath in and releases it on the same count. "I've been working so hard on myself the past couple of months to be everything I *want*. To be everything you *need*."

Lauren takes a brave step forward, reaching her delicate hands out to grasp mine. The hitch in her breath matches mine, telling me she felt the awaited spark through her body too. Her eyes don't leave mine as she continues.

"In my final days, all my deathbed memories will never be enough to fill the space in my hand the way holding yours does."

If I'm dreaming, this is something I will never recover from. "Are you saying—" I pause, trying to wrap my head around the truth in her words.

"I love you, Adam." Her eyes glass over. "As scared as I am that you no longer feel the same, I still love you. I love you so damn much."

I pause, making sure I'm hearing correctly.

"Adam, I lo—" I can't respond with words, so instinctively, I capture her sweet lips with mine. Wrapping my arms around her waist, I pull her into me, molding her directly to my soul. Too soon, her lips pull from mine with her heart-stopping smile.

"I hope you're not mad that I went to your family for a favor." Lauren's arms lock behind my neck as she leans back, studying my uneasy expression. "It took knowing what I wanted and asking for a favor."

"You asked my family for something?" *Are they now sponsors?*

"In three days, when I fly back home, you're coming with me, Adam. That is, if I'm still what you *need*."

"What?" Disbelief wraps around my brain in circles like the Indy 500.

Through my peripheral, I see someone walking around the corner. I look up and my jaw physically unhinges. There, in a fitted, proper suit and well-groomed hair, stands Emmett.

"I know." He shrugs with a smug grin. "Who knew I clean up so much better than you?" He walks over and gives Lauren a fist pump. "Your girl really cares about you, bro. It is time I man the hell up and stop taking Daddy's money for granted."

"My words," Lauren states with pride.

"I'm sorry as well, son." My father rounds the corner, and I wonder how many people are going to parade out of there. "I knew all three of you needed a push to figure yourselves out. The timing just had to align with all of you." I lean back to check if anyone else is going to pop out. "Your mother stayed back to help Kelsie. There's no one else." My father smiles.

I look back at Lauren, who has her eyes glued to the wall. My heart warms and for the first time since I've arrived here, I smile back at the photo of us on the mountain. This is really happening. There are so many questions to be answered and work to go over, but all I can think about is Lauren in this dress and her sweet smell tempting me in every fucking way. My body hums, coming to life with the need to feel every inch of her delectable body.

"Dad, Emmett, I'm so grateful for everything, but we will have to discuss business at *lunchtime* tomorrow." I grab Lauren's hand and pull her toward the lobby. "You're coming with me."

She squeaks and giggles, sending more love than I ever thought could flow through me.

"Adam, wait!" She stops us beside the front desk in the lobby as guests filter into the bar lounge. "There is one more thing."

I arch an eyebrow and feel eyes on us. "Is there?"

"Yeah." Her gentle hand connects with my cheek as warmth reverberates through my skin. "You're everything I hoped you *would* be."

Epilogue

Adam

Six months later.
"Good morning, beautiful." I kiss Lauren's temple as my wet fingers slide out of her panties.

"Another good morning it is." She rolls on top of me as her arms rest on each side of my head. "I don't think I will ever get tired of you waking me up like that."

"I will wake you up every morning with an orgasm if that is what it takes to keep your past from resurfacing."

Her nightmares had been one thing she couldn't work through until we got back together. Since we flew back from Aspen, we haven't spent a night apart. I was hesitant about my idea but gave it a try, and it has worked ever since. I started to set my wristwatch to vibrate just before five every morning. I was determined to wake her up before her traumatic past kicked in. Each week I'd wake her a few minutes later, and now my girl can finally sleep in until six thirty on her days off.

"Well, let me give you a well-deserved morning pick-me-up." Her lips kiss down my neck as my body fights against itself.

"Lauren, it's obvious how bad I want my dick in you." I push my hips forward over her panties. "But we have to leave our house in twenty minutes."

I glance out the window through the trees, looking out at the ocean. Two months ago, we bought a three-bedroom house on a mountain cliff, just outside of city limits.

"Hmm." She smirks, bringing my hands to the thin lace of her panties. "I don't need twenty minutes to get ready for a hike. Rip off my panties and let me ride you." I can't argue with that.

The mountain air is crisp before the spring sun shines through. Lauren trots behind me, chattering the entire hike about her workweek.

"I explained to the hospital that I'll be switching to part time by the end of this year because I love my time with the foster children and handing out bags." Her donors have grown, and it's been heart melting to see how supportive most companies are.

Lauren still won't take a fucking dime from me even though we now live together. Hopefully after our hike, that will change. My hours at work have changed as well. They allow her and me more time together and a slower-paced life. I want her to follow her dreams, but I also want to help them grow, and my finances can be put to use toward a brilliant foundation. We reach elevation as her hand laces with mine. Together, we head over to the same spot she first witnessed the rolling fog waves.

"I always doubt that hiking this early will be worth it." She laughs. "But *anything* with you is worth it." Her arms wrap around my neck, but I dip down, dropping to my knee. "I love you so much, Adam."

Her head tilts as she eyes my tied shoelaces and her forehead crunches with confusion. Her once haunted green eyes hold nothing but love. I smirk as her lips part with a questioning gasp. Lauren follows my hand as I reach into my pocket and pull out a velvet box.

"Lauren, if anyone had asked us a year ago if we would love someone for the rest of our lives, we would have laughed and said *never.*"

Tears brim her eyes as she nods.

"Till now." My throat constricts as I battle my own emotions. "I want every memory to be with you up until I can no longer make any more. I know you're strong and can handle this world on your own, but I want to be by your side, helping you chase your dreams in every way."

Her palms press together under her nose like a prayer.

"Marry me, Lauren McAllister."

"You're all I want, Adam Wheaton."

I open the velvet box as her shoulders shake with laughter.

"I really never am going to live this down."

I pick up the one-point five-carat oval diamond on a rose gold band and hold it up. Even though I can afford the three carat, I know Lauren well enough that a three carat is too large and flashy for her taste. The fingers on her left hand spread out as she brings her hand forward to me. Before I slip it on her finger, she hits me with a question I knew she'd ask.

"Engraved?" She raises an eyebrow with a smug grin.

My tongue darts out across my lips, and my smile widens. I tilt the ring as she leans forward to read the engraved word: *Yes*.

"You're perfect." Lauren's laugh breaks through the quiet mountains.

I slip the ring on her finger before standing to capture her lips with mine. I can't wait to see the images Grayson, the photographer from before, has captured during this moment. A squeal from a distance echoes to us as Lauren looks around. My family emerges with Rachel and Lloyd. Lauren steps back, dropping her jaw with wide eyes.

"You all knew about this?" Her voice rises with astonishment.

"Adam flew us in last night." Rachel grins and steps forward, wrapping her best friend in a hug. "Congratulations, my nasty Nordic."

"I'm too happy to scold you about that name." Lauren gleams as the sun rises, casting an angelic glow on her blonde hair.

"I guess I get to walk you down the aisle now." Lloyd smiles and gives her a hug.

"That you do, Dad."

After many hugs and tears, I notice one person missing. "Where is Kelsie?"

"At home, puking." Max cringes, lifting James on his shoulder.

"Again?"

"That shouldn't be a surprise to you anymore, bro," Max states as his tone drops.

Right, the one surprise I never fucking saw coming. I can kick Max's ass another day.

"Well, my new *family*." Lauren claps her hands together, cutting off the hostile stare between my best friend and me. "All I have ever wanted was to feel completely wanted and loved." Tears form in her eyes, sliding down her cheeks. "I never thought it would be possible, till now."

THE END

If you loved, Never Till Now, look out for book 2!
Kelsie and Max's story is coming January 2023!

THERE IS MORE!
Want to see where life takes Lauren and Adam two years from now? Do wonder about Ava Rose?
Sign up below for exclusive content delivered straight to your inbox.

https://dl.bookfunnel.com/x4t7x6z3jt

Acknowledgements

First, you the readers. I appreciate every single one of you. I would LOVE to hear your thoughts about my debut. Reading reviews and receiving messages always make my day. Feel free to say hello.

A forever thank you to my best friend Jennifer. Jenn, you have been my sounding board from day one and an endless cheerleader through my mental drainage and applauding every little wordcount increase. For being an extra set of eyes while our kids play at the park, so I could work on this. I'm so thankful to have you in my life.

To my betas- Ananya, Katie, Samantha and Reba. Thank you to Katie G.W. for encouraging me to prove that I could do this. Shout out to my ARC team for taking the time to read my work as a new author. You are the best!

Shoutout to my graphic designer with lilybeardesignco. (Who is also Author Daphne Abbott). Thank you for bringing my cover idea into magical fruition. You're amazing at what you do. You eliminated the stress as a baby indie author trying navigate everything. Thank you for guidance and dedication to help with formatting and graphics. I'm thankful to have you as a friend.

Author Alexandra Hale, thank you. Just thank you for answering my endless questions about site setups and everything in between. You're a gem.

My editor, Ellie, from mybrotherseditor, thank you for editing this book to where it is today. Rosa, thank you for your proofreading eagle eyes.

Jessie, thank you for your book blurb magic expertise!

Katie Lawson- the world needs more cheerleaders and hearts like yours. I'm lucky to have crossed paths with you in this life. Thank you for brightening my days and everyone else's on bookstagram.

Most important, to my better half for giving me every opportunity to get my ideas typed out every chance possible. Thank you for taking the kids on adventures for many weekends while I typed away. You've been nothing but encouraging for me to follow my dreams as an author. You never once have doubted I couldn't finish this book even when I thought I was tapped out. Thank you, my love.

Let's Connect!

Amazon Store

Instagram

Facebook

Goodreads

Website

Link Tree

About Jenna Lockwood

Lover of witty banter, angst and steam! Jenna has a life-long passion for writing poetry and fictional worlds. When Jenna is not consumed in the fictional realm of reading and writing, you'll find her exploring new places with her family, or pretending to be dragon while chasing her two young sons around the playground.

Made in United States
North Haven, CT
07 January 2024